Marlford

Jacqueline Yallop

Atlantic Books
London

First published in Great Britain in 2014 by Atlantic Books,
an imprint of Atlantic Books Ltd.

This paperback edition published in Great Britain in 2015
by Atlantic Books

10 9 8 7 6 5 4 3 2 1

A CIP catalogue record for this book is available from the British Library.

Paperback ISBN: 978 0 85789 106 8
E-book ISBN: 978 1 78239 028 2

Printed in Italy by ⚑ Grafica Veneta S.p.A.

Atlantic Books
An Imprint of Atlantic Books Ltd
Ormond House
26–27 Boswell Street
London
WC1N 3JZ
www.atlantic-books.co.uk

Marlford

Every morning during the bleached summer of 1976, when the drought hard-baked the earth, deep down, so that it held still, Ellie Barton went to the mere. She arrived early, a little after dawn, walking quickly through the new housing estate and dropping down by the chain of yellow pedalos, docked in the hard, brown grass.

The long, sunny days, identical, give the odd impression of time standing still, everything suspended in the heavy heat and the landscape flattening out. The riddle of mine workings below is silent and, for many weeks, nothing seems to happen. But the lake is shrinking, a muddle of tree roots coming clear of the water; rocks standing proud at the edge.

As the weeks go by without rain, change becomes obvious, rapid, the shallows receding further and revealing, each day, more debris, the accumulated litter of unremembered moments. Most mornings some new curiosity rises into the uncertain shimmer of an early mist, like Excalibur thrust aloft by the Lady of the Lake: bicycle handlebars; the rotting timbers of a sunken boat;

a shopping trolley. Ellie walks slowly along the bank, peering at the collection of car tyres and tin cans, bottles and jars and discarded shoes. She wonders how all these things have come to be here.

As the summer wears on, the mere hardly exists. The frogs seem to have gone. Ducks slump disconsolately in the hardening sludge, or squabble over the remaining pools, brown and shallow, already disappearing. When Ellie kneels on the bank and looks closely, she can see fine fractures veining the dried mud, a membrane of tiny fault lines.

She waits for the water to dry up completely, hurrying to the mere earlier and earlier each day, before the dark has even lifted, perching on the bank until the exhausted daylight creeps back and she can make out what it is that lies in the silt.

She wants to be the first to see them. That is important. It does not matter if, after that, police come, or doctors, to take them away, or if it rains, a sudden deluge that quickly fills the cracked basin. Nothing at all matters after that, if she can just see them for herself.

She does not expect the bodies still to be intact; she knows that is not possible. Soft skin would have decayed long ago; discoloured bones, brittle and slight, would have washed apart by now and might look like nothing more than old sticks. There might be little to distinguish the remains from the natural bulges in the mud, the ridges and buried stones. In the end, it might be nothing more than the slightest of clues, an intimation of the past.

But, whatever is left, it will be visible eventually. There is hardly any water at all now, little more than a greenish slime, thick and opaque with a smell of rotten cabbage. It cannot possibly be long until that, too, shrivels in the heat and they emerge. She will see them then, at last, and everything will be substantial; she will understand her place in things, and feel her own corporeal weight again, with relief.

So Ellie Barton comes to the mere every day, waiting for it to vanish.

One

Seven summers previously, the mere had been full, overflowing at one end into a marsh of flag iris and kingcups. The grass grew high and thick; the path was boggy.

Throughout the district, there were rumblings underground and, when Oscar Quersley walked up into the village, he noticed that one side of the Barton Arms had slipped again, the land beneath it slumping: several workmen were busy trying to buttress a tilting wall. A little further on, there was a sharp fissure in the pavement; a section of the cobbled roadway, too, was split, and a wooden barrier had been erected with a notice warning pedestrians of the dangerous ground. He quickened his pace, anxious, but the library was untouched by the subsidence. Everything there was stable.

By the time Ellie arrived, the library looked exactly as it had always done: the front doors were open, the steps swept. Inside, the striplights were buzzing and Oscar was seated at the desk, a book open in front of him and the wooden drawer of catalogue cards pushed to one side.

Ellie put a hand to her head to check the pins in her hair and looked past the desk to the stacks of books beyond, the musk of rotting paper and old leather already drawing her in. The tiny burst of disappointment inside her was almost imperceptible, a soap-sud bubble popping unspectacularly into air.

'I'm sorry… am I… am I late, Mr Quersley? I thought I left on time. I thought I heard the clock strike.'

She could not be sure.

'The stable clock runs forty-three minutes late, Ellie,' Oscar pointed out.

'Does it? Again? But I thought you'd had it fixed.'

'The mechanism is fragile. It's difficult to adjust these days.'

'Yes, well, I suppose so. I suppose it must be running late again – but, you see, I lost track of time. I had to call at the hutments with some clean linen and the men had a complaint and then I dawdled on the avenue because it's such a fine evening.' She let out a long breath. 'I'm sorry.'

'Dawdled?'

'Well, I was going over something…"The Knight's Tale".' She blinked, puzzled by the solidity of the library furniture, floundering still in the shallows of her fantasy.

Oscar closed his book. He looked at Ellie sternly for a moment, and then smiled. 'It's of no matter. You're here now.'

He moved from the stool so that she could sit down. As she made her way behind the desk, she noticed that the rain from the previous night had filled the tin buckets to overflowing; a slop of dusty water ran away along the back wall towards the book stacks.

He caught her glance. 'Now that you're here, I'll empty them and mop round,' he said. 'I heard a forecast on the radio for more showers.'

Ellie picked at the darned fingers of her light gloves, then removed them carefully, folding them to one side on the desk.

'I'll just – sort the tickets then, shall I?'

'If you would.'

The pink readers' tickets were stacked in a thick-sided wooden box, their top edges faded to the colour of sucked candy but the card still vibrant below. Ellie checked their order, arranged alphabetically by surname. There were no aberrations. She placed the box carefully alongside the drawer of catalogue cards and reached underneath the desk, pulling a heavy ledger from the shelf. She opened it at the page marked by a length of blue ribbon.

'There are no loans out, Mr Quersley.'

He was on his knees wiping the floor. When he stood, he was red-faced and flustered, his hair flopping forward over his brow, his shirt-sleeves coming unrolled – emphasising the crook of his spindly wrists – the thick tweed of his trousers stained with damp and sagging. It gave him the appearance of a bow-legged horse trader.

'No,' he replied. 'I imagine not.' He wrung the cloth into the bucket and brushed flecks of peeled paint from his clothes.

Ellie began a new line in the ledger and slowly wrote the date in her looping copperplate hand: *19th July 1969*. She allowed the ink to dry. For several months she had inscribed the paper in the same way without any need to record loans below: line upon line of dates peeled back through the pages, rhythmic, a meditation of days passing without incident. She shut the ledger and returned it to the shelf under the desk. There were no more duties to be done.

'Well, then.' Oscar had smartened his appearance again, as far as he could; he looked like the man Ellie was accustomed to, only slightly shabby and worn, his anxiety little more than the faintest of impressions. 'It's almost eight thirty. We have an hour and a half. Shall we take up the *Enneads* again – or would you prefer Dante? *La Vita Nuova*, perhaps?'

'Oh… I thought perhaps you didn't like…' She hesitated, blushing. 'We've never re-read *La Vita Nuova*. Not after that first time.'

'It's your choice, Ellie.' He could not look at her. He heard the clank of his words, not as he had rehearsed them.

'Dante then. Please,' she said.

Turning to retrieve the book, Oscar grinned. He looked momentarily younger than his forty years, boyish even, mischievous, his eyes sparkling blue, his skin pricked with fleeting colour. If Ellie had seen him in that moment, she might have thought of him differently but, by the time he was seated beside her, with the text between them, he had been overtaken again by the abiding beige and khaki of his tweed, his demeanour studious and his expression drawn in concentration.

Ellie glanced at him then, and wished he was not so stern with her.

No readers came that evening to the library. Once or twice people passed the open doors, their chatter seeming loud; occasionally cars drove by, filling the air with a liquorice syrup of fumes. The click of beetles in the wooden beams became insistent as dusk fell. But that was all; they were alone in a chivalric world where knights roamed on majestic steeds, veils and flags fluttered stiffly in the breeze, fires burned brightly, skies shone an azure blue and everything was intense and jewel-like, uncomplicated by the demands of accurate perspective or three dimensions.

At ten, precisely, Oscar sat back and closed the text. 'We must finish, Ellie.'

'Can't we just read on a little?' She frowned at the surprising proximity of the library, its gloom.

'Ellie, you might not appreciate the lateness of the hour – you know I cannot continue, or I'll be late for the frogs. Next time, perhaps, we can read on.'

Ellie had her hand on the book. 'But could I – I could continue at home; I could take out a loan and read it myself.'

'I'm not sure that's wise. It's just as I always say, Ellie – you might lose it. Or damage it, perhaps.'

'No – I wouldn't. I'd take good care of it.'

'Even so, we've managed perfectly well up until now with the existing arrangement.' He pulled the library keys from his pocket and selected one with care, giving the process enough of his attention to prevent him having to look at her.

'But I wasn't even eight years old when we started reading together – it's been twelve years and, well, I'm... I'm grown up now. It's not the same. I can take care of a book, can't I?'

Oscar picked up the ledger and the box of readers' tickets and locked them in one of the wooden cupboards behind them.

'Quite possibly. That may be so. But, still, a loan seems unnecessary.' He regretted that he had given her the choice of such a text, knew with absolute certainty that she could not be allowed to read the Dante alone. He came back to the desk and took the book from her. 'I believe I'll replace it in the stacks for another time – or another reader.'

'But no one else will ever want to read *La Vita Nuova* – not in Marlford. You know that.'

It sounded like praise. But Oscar just sniffed sharply and shook his head. 'Enough, Ellie. It's not for discussion. I'll be late.'

She conceded defeat. She had read enough already; she felt the bulge of the story in her head, as yet too new to be completely contained, a fresh bruise rising.

'You're probably right,' she said.

When Ellie stepped out onto Victoria Street she felt a momentary queasiness. The dark was not yet steady below the streetlights and, across from the library, the bank appeared to shift within its shadows. Shop windows rippled unreliable reflections. At the top of the village, she could just make out the statue of her grandfather, Braithwaite Barton, rising from the clipped gardens around the Assembly Rooms. In the dusk, his expression was ambiguous.

She turned her back on him and walked with Oscar down towards the almshouses, where the ground was firmer, the road and pavements even. The village was little more than a single street which looped with a final flourish around a circular stone fountain. The nymph at its centre, untroubled by nightfall, poured water with unerring precision into a basin of blue tiles; short terraces splayed away briefly on either side, a few cottages grudgingly suggesting some kind of suburbia. Beyond the houses, wasteland fell away and disappeared into the dark; beyond that, abruptly, was the flare of the chemical works, illuminated with intimidating brilliance, consuming itself in piles of white light, flames spurting from sheer chimneys.

They skirted the unnatural brightness, following a narrow path that edged along the side of the almshouses, leading through a kissing gate that marked the boundary to the estate. They cut across to the drive, a stately avenue of overgrown lime trees, the scents of the day still trapped in the heavy dusk under the canopy. They did not speak. Ellie felt the evening only loosely. She suspected that Oscar might be angry with her: he seemed stiff and preoccupied; there was something demanding about his gaunt profile. He approached the manor steadily, as if it were a trial of some kind, his rigidity either an accusation against her or a defence. She did not know which. She feared that the men had been talking about her again, but she did not dare ask.

She put the thought aside, too old and frayed, conjuring instead the evening's poems, skipping to their rhythm, kicking through leaves, drifted husks and fallen blossom. In the settled quiet, her steps seemed loud, as though echoing back from the polished surface of the mere, which could be seen here and there slicing through the foliage to their side. Her youthful movement was extravagant; it yanked at the dense fabric of summer growth, tugging at the marshy air, dragging the dappled dark, seeds and burrs, the mushroom smell of the soil and centuries of trapped memories, into the uneven rise and fall of her stride.

But if he felt any of this, Oscar showed no sign of it. He paused. 'Well. Good night, Ellie.'

She checked and held out her gloved hand. It hovered, disembodied, the start of a magic trick.

Oscar touched her fingers, bowing over them as he always did, an old-fashioned habit. 'Perhaps we have worked too hard.' He studied her for a moment. 'You should rest.'

But she hardly heard him. She glanced behind, to the familiar, wide façade of the manor house, a mottled backdrop of greying stone, and she felt for a moment that she held all kinds of possibilities poised in the iridescence of her imagination, like a raindrop on a holly leaf.

He did not know what else to say. He bowed again, slightly, and went away.

It was some time before Ellie pulled herself back, feeling her skin thicken, her weight returning to anchor her, a momentary chill. She went quickly then, forcing herself to inhabit the place. But, in the avenue behind her, she knew, another girl remained, not quite out of reach, leading some other life.

Two

Shortly after the death of Ellie's mother, much of the manor had been closed up, the long corridor on the first floor blocked off, the servants' quarters and back kitchens abandoned. The doors on the far side of the magnificent square hallway were locked and, in one case, barricaded with old furniture. The wing that remained open consisted of a breakfast room, a large study and, adjacent, a small, windowless den in which there was nothing except a billiard table, its baize faded. A dining room poked out beyond the breakfast room, an incongruous Victorian extension with fine windows affording views across the gardens and park, towards the mere. There was also a reasonably modern kitchen and scullery, packed with Formica cupboards in an unappealing shade of olive green, reached by a short corridor leading directly from the hallway; two bedrooms perched above.

Despite the closures, there remained a luxurious amount of space: high ceilings, wide passages, generous perspectives. What they were left with felt in no way meagre; in fact, Ellie often had the impression that their rooms were somehow stretching, expanding, their proportions growing even more voluptuous, she and her father shrinking more and more within them. Sitting at breakfast the next morning, she had the momentary sense of the building pitching away from her, bucking and groaning like an enormous old sailing ship in a storm.

Ernest Barton did not seem to notice her unease. He was grumpy. 'I heard the frogs.' He buttered his toast with precision.

Ellie did not look up. She poured her tea very carefully, blowing across the top of the chipped cup to cool it.

Her father tried complaining again. 'After ten thirty, I should not hear the frogs.'

She said nothing.

'And I heard them twice, Ellie, perhaps three times. Like damn banshees wailing in the park. I couldn't sleep, not a wink, not after that.'

It was mournful as much as angry, the unconvincing bluster of a cracked bell. She continued to ignore it, as she always did.

He began on his toast, frowned at the crust and ate around it. Then he looked at her with such solicitousness that the butter dripping from his lips might have been the thick fall of tears.

'Did you sleep? Ellie? Did you hear them? You look pale.'

'No, Papa, I didn't hear them.'

'Are you sure? I can't believe that.' He shook his head, as though it were all incomprehensible. 'It was a racket, all night.'

14

'It seemed perfectly quiet to me. I didn't hear anything. I presumed Mr Quersley was on duty.'

'Well, yes, exactly – he should have been. That's my point. I shouldn't have heard the frogs at all. Not once.'

He dropped his hands to the table. He had a way of looking at her, as though he could not see her properly, as though she were far away from him, too far, slipping into the distance; as though this might be the last glance he ever had of her.

She braced against it. 'Perhaps you were mistaken, Papa.'

Disappointment tightened in his face. 'I was not mistaken. I know the sound of a frog when I hear one. And it cannot be too much to ask, too simple a thing to—'

'It was a warm night.'

'Well, really, Ellie – when it comes to stating the obvious… Of course it was a warm night! Hence, I had all the casements open in my bedroom; hence the importance of Mr Quersley attending to his duties with at least a modicum of diligence.' He stared fiercely at the long breakfast-room window, as though it might have been in some way to blame for the nocturnal disturbance. 'I cannot conceive how it might be too difficult a task. All I'm asking for is a peaceful night. Ellie, really – it's the slightest of courtesies.'

Ellie looked at him steadily. He had been old for as long as she could remember – she supposed he had already been old when she was born – but he seemed gaunt now, haggard even, the bones of his face pushing through where the skin was wearing thin.

His unconcealed age irritated her.

'More tea, Papa? There's more tea, if you would like some.'

Her words grated, stone on stone.

'No, I do not want more tea, Ellie.'

'Very well. Then I'll clear the things.'

She collected their plates with perfect equanimity. Only when she picked up Ernest's knife did she pause in the rhythm of her work. The handle was still warm, her father's grasp retained in the yellowing bone, and she let it drop quickly, drawing back as though she had been stung. Then, without looking at him, she made a neat stack of dishes, balanced it across one arm, and slipped away.

Ernest waited for the men in his study, a room now completely without books, the shelves collapsing. He paced between the door and the narrow windows, the tattered length of his silk *robe de chambre* flapping around him, its jaded colours momentarily unequivocal again, jewel-like in the morning sun.

They appeared as he made a turn at the back of the room, entering without knocking.

'Good morning, Mr Barton,' said the shortest of the three of them, slack in his skin, his expressions curtained. He was stocky, his loose bulk straining the seams of his brown tweeds.

Ernest spun on his heel; the *robe de chambre* swung. 'Ah, Hindy, you're here. Already! Excellent – good morning, gentlemen.'

The men did not respond. Each of them went instead to one of the straight-backed chairs positioned around the walls, dragging it with effort towards the centre of the room.

Ernest unfolded a grubby rectangle of green cloth onto the table, spreading it flat with his large hands. He pressed closed the tears and smoothed out the ingrained ridges. It was a hopeful routine.

'Morning Glories, Ata, if you please.' He nodded in the direction of the sideboard.

The tallest of the men stepped forwards, almost as tall as the stately Barton, very similar in movement, like a younger brother, but his skin darker. He began mixing four drinks in long glasses, a complicated procedure requiring much rattling of tongs and bottles, and a low, intense incantation of what might have been a recipe. He wiped the spillages dry with his sleeve.

The other men waited, seated at the table, the deck of cards shuffled for the first time, piles of coins stacked in front of Ernest, the dealing box aligned carefully with the layout. As Ata came towards them with the glasses balanced on a wooden tray, Ernest looked around at the players, his smile wide and welcoming, the delight in his face so animated that this game might have been something new and special.

'Very well, then, punters. Let's begin.'

They did not respond. They sipped their drinks; Hindy ran his hand slowly over his chin, as though checking the quality of his shave. No one reached for the cards.

'Gentlemen?' Ernest picked up the pack and flicked it, a fresh enticement. 'Are we ready?'

The men looked at each other.

The oldest of them was seated opposite Ernest. He was the smallest of them, too, bent over, his strength taut like wrung leather. 'We have a concern, Mr Barton.' His face was thin and sharp, his voice meagre; the trace of a European accent creased his words.

17

'A concern?' Ernest put the cards down and took a swig of his cocktail. 'I really don't see – oh, what the deuce is the bother now? Well? Luden, spit it out. Let's have it.'

Luden smiled and inclined his head slowly. It was Hindy who spoke. 'It's the bob-a-job.' He pushed his chair back.

'The Cub Scouts,' Ata added.

Ernest grimaced. 'What about them?'

'In recent days, we've happened to come across them from time to time, on the estate – doing jobs.' Hindy was the only one of them who spoke without a burr, the clipped perfection of his English betraying his foreignness.

'Well, of course they were doing jobs. That's what they're supposed to do – that's what they get paid for.'

'You don't understand.' Hindy paused. 'We've never had bob-a-job at Marlford.'

Ernest picked up the cards once more, running them through his hands and flipping them adeptly into a complicated shuffle, his eyes fixed on the quiver of familiar suits. 'I know that,' he said, quietly.

'We thought you must have known.' Luden was abrupt. 'We imagined you were fully aware of the lack of precedent. That's what surprised us.'

'You see, Mr Barton,' Hindy explained, with careful patience, 'we considered it most unlikely that Oscar would have made arrangements of this nature without consulting us. And Miss Barton, of course, would not presume such a thing. So we wondered how they'd come to be here.'

'Perhaps you could offer an explanation,' Ata suggested.

Ernest stared mournfully at the two of spades. 'I thought it would be a jolly good thing, having them clean up here and there. I asked them to pull some of the weeds from the drive and to sweep the paths. Nothing much – they're only boys – but God knows a bit of help from time to time...' Seeing their faces, his bravado failed him; he trailed off. 'It was an experiment, that's all.'

The men seemed to consider this.

'I'm not sure it was a very agreeable one. Nor a very successful one,' Hindy responded, finally. 'It doesn't seem like the way at Marlford.'

'Oh, for goodness' sake – they're Boy Scouts!' Ernest puffed.

Luden shook his head. 'They're an invasion.'

'They didn't come anywhere near the hutments. I made sure of that. They fiddled around with a few weeds on the drive and I gave them a shilling.'

'But it's not just the hutments, is it, Mr Barton?' Ata smiled.

'We would contend that it's something more,' Hindy said. 'We would suggest that it's the principle of intrusion. After all, we share Marlford to everyone's advantage, Mr Barton – for a long time, we've shared Marlford to everyone's advantage – and we know what a place like this should be. All of us.'

'But a few Cub Scouts...'

'A disruption. Unnecessary and unwanted.' Luden offered it as a final judgement.

Ernest regathered the pack of cards and placed it in the middle of the table. 'What do you want me to do, then?'

'It's quite simple,' Ata reassured him.

'We require an undertaking that no such thing will happen again,' Hindy said. 'We would like things to return to normal. Otherwise – well, I believe we would be forced to end our happy years of faro together.'

Ernest flinched. He wanted to rise from the table and walk away. But they had him trapped there between them, in his usual place, and he could not imagine how he might pull apart from them, not now, after all these years.

'But it was nothing.'

He clutched his robe tight to his chest. They heard the slight rip of old fabric. 'I don't understand.'

Luden hissed something in response, too low under his breath to be heard.

'What is it that confuses you, Mr Barton?' Ata asked, with kindness.

'It does seem remarkably simple,' said Hindy.

'No, it's not simple,' Ernest spat back, suddenly irritated. 'Running this place, trying to work out what's best for it – it's a complete bloody riddle. For goodness' sake, when I was a young man…'

'You are no longer a young man,' Luden pointed out.

'I think we're rather losing the point.' Hindy spoke steadily. 'Mr Barton, if you simply undertake to consider more carefully in the future, before you allow such—'

'I'm master here, you know. I'm master of Marlford.'

All three of the men smiled at him, simultaneously, as if their mouths were drawn on a single thread.

'Quite so,' Hindy agreed. 'We would not wish to change that – it's exactly as we would have it, Mr Barton. But if you consult, perhaps…'

'Then you'll agree to play?' Ernest was long ago defeated.

They nodded in unison. 'Then we will play with pleasure,' Ata replied.

Ernest reached for the pack again and riffled the cards, watching the magic-lantern flicker of red and black. 'Very well, then. No more Cub Scouts.'

'Ah!' Luden held up a quick finger.

'Yes, indeed.' Hindy acknowledged his friend's concern. 'Mr Barton, Cub Scouts, as such, are not the issue. We have no objection to Cub Scouts, in principle. Indeed, I think I speak for all of us when I say that we fully endorse the objectives of the Cub Scout movement. You understand that what we require is an undertaking against intruders in general – against the principle of intrusion. Marlford is our home.'

'I know how you want it,' Ernest said.

'So you agree? It's settled?'

'Of course I agree. I always agree, don't I?'

They ignored his pique. They seemed quite happy with the conversation: Ata immediately reached forwards to straighten the layout, Luden began to count his coins, Hindy put a slow hand on Ernest's arm, a reconciliation of sorts.

But the prospect of the game had lost much of its sparkle for Ernest and he did not join in with the bustle. He suspected he had let himself down again; he had the sickening feeling that he had failed. He drank his Morning Glory quietly and wondered, as he often did, how it had come to this.

Three

In the enclosure of the walled kitchen garden, Ellie kept her distance from Oscar Quersley – when he knelt by the untidy clump of lettuce, she stood back by the long weeds, flicking the seed heads with her hand, watching the gossamer float away. The jasmine that climbed up the rusting metal frames between the abandoned peach trees and trailing vines sent out a swirling, opiate perfume, the drone of insects in its flowers closing around her. The rest of the world seemed to have drifted away.

'He heard the frogs last night, Mr Quersley,' she said, at last. 'It disturbed him, you know. He hardly slept.'

Oscar was reaching forwards, his pocket-knife extended, ready to cut one of the largest lettuces through its stalk. He sat back on his heels, but did not look at her.

'It was a warm night, Ellie.'

'That's what I told him. He said it didn't matter. He said he still expected it to be quiet.'

'When the weather's warm, the frogs are more insistent.'

'Yes, I know that. I tried to explain. But, still…'

He bent forward again and sliced the lettuce quickly from its stalk. 'Here.' He shook the leafy head as he stood so that loose soil and insects fell away onto the bare earth. 'I think you'll find that sufficient. There'll be another in a day or two, should you require it.'

'It will be warm tonight as well, won't it, Mr Quersley?'

Ellie stepped towards him to take the lettuce, shaking it again.

'Yes – undoubtedly.'

'But you'll see that the frogs are quiet.'

Her authority was captured for a moment in the statuesque tilt of her head, the ancestral timbre of her voice, the certain statement of her question.

Oscar looked at her, the anxious girl in a brash headscarf. He laughed without taking his eyes from her face. 'Quite the lady of the manor today, I see.'

Ellie met his gaze. 'I just wanted to be sure about the frogs.'

'You're very like your mother when you address me in that way.' He drew his fingers across his face. 'You look like your mother, too. More and more.'

She tried to move away, but he took the lettuce from her again; then held her hand in his. She let it rest there and looked at him. The mass of unruly dark hair, greying at the temples, his thin face, the expression of not-quite-understanding that seemed set there; all this she had known for so long that standing there with him brought her whole life simultaneously upon her. She could not remember how the days had unwound: the seasons seemed to have collided – the autumns in the orchard gathering apples; the long, winter evenings reading together at the library; the radiance of the lime avenue in spring; picking lettuce from the summer garden. It was all there with her in that moment, in the way they stood together on the weedy gravel walk with the warmth from the flaking walls enveloping them; it was all, she saw, so brief, and so unconscionably drawn out.

'I wish I'd known my mother,' she said. 'As you did.'

She spoke simply again, with a childish longing, looking out over the dilapidated garden with new bewilderment, as though she were lost in it.

Oscar nodded, pleased. 'It would have given you a better sense of your situation, it's true.'

'I think about her all the time.'

'You could have learned a great deal, I'm sure.' He spoke firmly, bringing her back to his way of seeing things. 'She was genuinely aristocratic. But the Bartons...' He paused, a pained look crimping his face for a moment. 'The Bartons have been at Marlford for only a very short time, not even a century – not even that – and with no lineage to speak of... commercial success, perhaps, for a while, but nothing of meaning. Your mother's heritage – generations of heritage – the Wilsheres – well, that's entirely different.'

'Yes, I know that very well,' Ellie said. 'You've told me before, Mr Quersley. And the men talk of it a great deal.'

He ignored her interruption. 'It's for that reason that we've always felt it our duty to bring your mother to you, as best as we can.' He went on with the measured inflection of a history lesson. 'For my part, I've endeavoured to keep her in your mind and heart, to bring her alive in some way. So that you can understand Marlford a little better.'

'But I don't think I *do* understand – not always. That's the problem.'

'Ellie, you know that's nonsense.'

'But, you see, it's not.' She looked down at her hands. 'You see, I've been thinking about the babies.'

He flinched, pulling away from her and staring at the resilient whiteness of her face. His words were careful now, slow. 'You know this is not something I usually like us to discuss.'

'No. I know. I'm sorry.' She looked up. 'But, you see, you've hardly ever told me – not really. The men have said things, of course – and you and I have talked about it, but only once or twice, only briefly. Only – I mean, I don't know… I wanted to ask you about it again. I can't ask Papa, can I?'

He gripped his lower lip in his teeth, sucking through squeaky air. 'No, of course not, no. Your father must never know we've had these conversations – never. You promised me that, Ellie, at the beginning.'

'Yes, and I've never said a word. I wouldn't want to. I can't bear even to look at him sometimes, when I think about what he's done. Ever since you told me, ever since the first time, I've kept away from him. Even when he's seemed kind; even then, I've remembered – I've remembered those poor babies.' She put her hand to her chest, as though she could feel the tiny, black nugget of hatred that was lodged there, burning hot under the press of loneliness and betrayal, nurtured over time, crystallising, annealing, becoming hard and bright. 'But, you see, I've got no one else to talk to,' she went on. 'Only you, Mr Quersley.'

He bristled at her softness, shaking the lettuce again fiercely so that the outer leaves broke off and fell away. 'It does not seem an appropriate moment,' he said.

'But I don't know when an appropriate moment would be.'

'But why now? I don't see why you've brought this up now, Ellie. Out of the blue.'

'It was the men, last night, when I was taking the linen—'

Oscar gave a heavy sigh, a moan that interrupted her. For a moment, she thought he was going to walk away but then he thrust the lettuce in her direction. 'Go on, Ellie – what did they say?'

'Well, they had some complaint, about the Cub Scouts that were pulling weeds – and they said that children were never permitted on the estate, that I was the only child that had ever been at Marlford and that was only because...' She was trembling, her words seeming to shrivel, lost in the thick jasmine perfume. 'They were rather unpleasant in their comments,' she went on, quietly. 'And it seems important, Mr Quersley – it really does.'

He looked away, examining something in the straggling vines; then he took a step or two from her, broke a leaf from a branch and rolled it between his fingers, crushing the green fragrance from it before he spoke. 'All right. What is it?'

She began tentatively. 'The babies – my sisters. I was wondering... I never found out how, well, you've never told me how they were—'

'I believe I have told you, Ellie. My father drowned them.' There was a pause. He did not seem to want to go on.

'Yes, but – exactly. Can I ask how, exactly?' The question came oddly, the words buckling.

'He took each of them to the mere and dropped them into the water.' Oscar smiled faintly, as reassurance. 'You must understand, Ellie, that I only actually witnessed him render this service from afar – and not only was I a very young man, a boy indeed, but we never discussed it, he and I. It seemed reasonably efficient. The task was undertaken on each occasion before the child was a day old – they were naturally vulnerable at that age.'

'I see.'

'They made more of a fuss about the journey in the wheelbarrow, I seem to remember. I suppose it jiggled on the rough ground, disturbing or perhaps paining them.' He fixed his gaze on the cut lettuce stump, its white juice already congealing, recalling the ritual like a recurring dream: his father's slow progress through the woods, the unremitting groan of the wheelbarrow pushed to the very edge of the bank. There was a moment – he remembered that – when his father would let go of the metal handles, stand back and steady himself, praying perhaps, the dappled shadows from the oaks dismantling him. Then he would tip the barrow sharply, his head turned aside towards the unblinking gargoyles on the church tower, and there was the unconcerned plop of a weight in the still water, a stone or a baby swaddled tight, drifting awhile, bawling – a heavy sound hardly rising, pulling towards the silt – sinking only slowly, cheap linen soaking through and turning grey, already fraying, threads floating out across the soft ripples like the coarse hair of ducked witches, the mere settling again, the mallard and

28

teal serene, their heads nestled beneath their wings.

'Unfortunately, the barrow was necessary,' he added. 'My father didn't like to hold them.' He waited for her to respond. But she was looking at the ground beyond him, and he could not even be sure whether she realized that he had finished speaking. 'Ellie? There's nothing more for me to tell you. You do understand? There's really very little to say – my father never spoke about it. He preferred not to, I believe. He was following orders, of course, but, nonetheless, I think he found the duty onerous.'

She barely moved. But there was something, a shiver.

Oscar shuffled his feet slightly, as though his shoes were suddenly uncomfortable.

She raised her eyes. 'I don't think I've ever really understood why it happened.'

'Ellie, please.' He touched her on the arm. 'We shouldn't talk so much about such matters. It's inevitably upsetting.'

'But I don't understand. Why would someone do such a thing to such little babies? I don't understand.'

'Do you doubt me, Ellie?'

'No, no, of course not.'

'Because you've never asked such questions before – you've never required further explanation. This curiosity is rather unexpected, you must see that.'

'Yes, I know… but it's as though the questions have been there all the time, and I've only just begun to realize.' She smiled at him ruefully, but she could not explain the tiny, constant goad, the increasing rawness of it; it was embedded too deeply, so that she could hardly grasp it. 'I'm grateful for your help, Mr Quersley, I really am. I don't mean to doubt you. I've never doubted you. But, well… it just doesn't seem quite real. I wonder, sometimes, whether I've simply dreamed the whole story – imagined it, you know. When I look at Papa and I think about it and about what you say happened to the babies – well, I find I want to know why, Mr Quersley. Don't you see?' She blinked at the prick of tears and sniffed, apologetic. 'It's as I get older, I suppose, that's all. As I grow up.'

He remained stern. 'Ellie, it's not a matter with which I wish to become entangled.'

'I know. I'm sorry. But I can't help it. I do try to put it out of my mind, Mr Quersley. I really do, but every day, with Papa…'

'You must not permit yourself such thoughts. It's a simple history and it certainly does not merit this kind of discussion. It seemed right that you should know what happened, that's all, and it was agreed to make the matter known to you – to place you in your family context, as it were.'

He looked away for a moment, taking in the square enclosure of sky above them. She saw the rings of exhaustion around his eyes, the lines cut deep into his face. At this time of year, with the patrol of the mere, all the work at the farm, the gardens and fruit, his days were endless, unbroken, piling age upon him.

It did not seem as though he would say anything else.

'I'm sorry, Mr Quersley, but I need to ask one more thing. Do you think, Mr Quersley… have you ever wondered – what might have happened to me?'

'That's enough, Ellie.' He was sharp. 'I think we've spoken enough of this.'

'But what happened to my sisters might have happened to me, too. I might have been drowned, Mr Quersley, just as they were. Isn't that true? Don't you ever think about that?'

He gathered himself and pressed the lettuce into her hand. 'We can't imagine such things.' He began to walk away from her.

'Please – Mr Quersley…'

'Ellie, I have too much work.'

'You must have thought about it – even then, you must have thought about it, or you wouldn't have taken me to the farm when I was first born. You wouldn't have rescued me.'

He stopped, and turned to face her. 'That's melo-dramatic. I did not rescue you. With your mother's death, there was naturally a great deal of commotion at the manor. I simply removed you to a quieter place, where you could be tended to.'

'But I've been told – the men have told me – how much you did for me.'

'I was very young. I acted instinctively.'

'But, Mr Quersley—'

'Ellie, that's enough. I have my chores.'

'You believed I was in danger, didn't you?'

He could not look at her.

'No, Ellie. You were in no danger.'

And before she could begin again, he had left her, walking quickly through the arched gateway. Ellie remained, the lettuce dripping its thin sap onto her wrist.

Four

Later, from the tangle of the rose garden, Ellie saw the metallic sheen of a strange vehicle making its way slowly along the avenue of limes.

Even at a distance it was resplendent in reds, golds and purples, flashing brilliant beams of chrome through the trees, embraced by two brightly dressed figures, advancing gracefully as though floating on a shimmering sea, like Cleopatra's barge.

She threw down her bunch of roses and ran. 'Mr Quersley!' She pushed through the long weeds on the terrace and around to the front of the manor, but her call hardly reached the stand of oaks at the margin of the old lawns, and she did not receive an answer. She could see the track to Home Farm leading away through high hedges, but the farmhouse was out of sight; she would never reach Oscar before the vehicle arrived. The hutments were closer, the lines of corrugated metal imprinted on the distance, but she knew she could not tell the men about such a thing.

She hesitated. The visitors continued to advance. They were almost upon her, and she could not face them alone.

'Papa… Papa!' Her voice echoed in the ample recesses of the hallway. 'There're people coming. Papa!'

Ernest was asleep in his study. The vague impression of emergency only irritated him; he turned in his chair, pulling a cushion across his face. Ellie tugged at it but he held on hard, breathing loudly through the thick matting of old feathers and bare tapestry.

Finally, he sneezed. 'What? What is it, Ellie, that requires so much commotion?' He wiped his nose on his sleeve.

'There are people coming, Papa, up the lime avenue. I saw them.'

'What kind of people?'

'I don't know. They were… they've got some kind of car, in different colours.'

Ernest was unconvinced. 'Tradesmen?'

'Oh, no, I don't think so.'

'Not those people who turn up demanding lumber and such like?'

'No. Nothing like that. Real people.'

Ernest saw the way his daughter screwed her hands in her work apron, and the tense wrinkle of her brow. He wished he could soothe her many anxieties. He flapped the cushion at them so that they dispersed for a moment, nothing more than a swarm of midges, and he smiled kindly, reaching out a hand that did not quite touch hers.

'Best ask them to supper then, I should think,' he suggested, brightly. 'That should do it.'

'Do what, Papa?'

'Well, I don't know – introduce them to us. At the very least it will do that. Won't it?'

But Ellie was still frowning and, once again, Ernest felt he had failed to solve the insurmountable conundrum of how to be master of this ridiculous house. Perhaps he should set dogs on the intruders, or fire off a round above their heads? Perhaps he should have made Quersley weld the main gates closed to protect them all from trespass? Or maybe that was quite wrong: maybe he should hold court on the portico like a real gentleman, extending a gracious hand and an invitation to dine or shoot pheasants or some such. Perhaps a simple supper was ungenerous.

He did not know what Ellie meant when she looked at him in that way, demanding something impossible; he had no idea any more. It was all too confusing.

He pulled the cushion back against his face and leaned, once more, into the chair.

Ellie was not at all sure how her father's invitation could be offered. She went out to the top of the steps, standing under the shabby stone portico from where she could see the avenue of limes, the pasture stretching away on one side towards Home Farm, the slope on the other sweeping down towards the mere and the village beyond, the hutments between, where the contours of the estate seemed to meet, the ugly scar of buildings only partly obscured by a line of firs. It was all as it had always been, a landscape she could contain quite easily within her thoughts.

The incessant discord of the vehicle's extraordinary bodywork was something else. She wondered if she might have a fever, a sickness; she felt her forehead in case she had a temperature and closed her eyes, as though this might dislodge the fantasy. But when she looked again, the visitors were making good progress, almost at the point at which the trees stopped and the drive swept round in a wide-open curve towards the manor.

She could see them quite clearly now. The first had one arm thrust casually through the open front window of the van, and Ellie could see his hand resting lightly on top of the steering wheel. He was taking in his surroundings with measured glances; once he looked behind and seemed to speak to the other figure, a taller man, his head lowered, leaning his shoulder against the rear doors.

In the end, because it seemed right, she went to meet them. They had come to a stop at the end of the lime avenue and were standing together to one side of the vehicle. She saw the way they stared and she traced with them in her mind the blotted grey dereliction of the façade behind her.

'It's not as it was,' she said, holding herself straight, her arms fixed to her sides.

They did not respond to her apology, continuing to gaze instead at the manor: the central domes, high roofs and tall windows recalling the splendour of mighty French châteaux, the graceful chimneys of the original residence still visible behind, a square brick tower standing guard on the Victorian extensions yet further back, and the Georgian portico thrusting confidently towards them, holding them at bay.

'Papa says you should stay for supper.'

The vibrant colour of their baggy clothing defined them too boldly against the muted histories of the old building.

'If you like, of course… if you're able. There's no obligation.'

She thought for a moment that perhaps they did not understand, and she began to think how she might make the offer in another language. But finally one of the visitors spoke.

'I'm Dan.' He stepped forwards but did not smile.

It was the young man she had seen at the front of the van. His dark hair was pushed back from his high forehead and curled to his shoulders – like some kind of late-Georgian wig, she thought – and he wore spectacles. With his long face and thin lips, it conspired to make him seem bookish and grave. He gestured towards the limes.

'We're travelling around,' he went on.

Ellie frowned. 'Yes. Well, you're welcome, of course. This is Marlford. But I suppose you knew that.'

'Marlford? No, we didn't know.'

'You weren't intending to call on us then, as part of your tour?'

'Here? No way.' He threw a sharp glance at his companion.

'People do come from time to time,' Ellie said. 'Sightseers.'

He looked past her, taking in the impressive scale more than anything – more than the overgrown flowerbeds and sunken paths; the mossy stones and sprouts of weed from odd places, the sag of the roof.

'Yeah, well, our van broke down, you see, back on the main road, by your gates, that's all. We thought you might let us ring.'

It only now occurred to Ellie that the vehicle might be broken in some way. She looked at it mournfully. 'I'm sorry. I didn't realize. But, you see, we don't have a telephone…'

'Don't you?' He squinted at her, as though to make sure of the truth of her statement. 'No means of getting in touch with someone? Even in an emergency?'

The other visitor stepped forward quickly. 'Look – hi, yeah, I'm Gadiel.' He smiled, wiping his palm down the faded cotton of his trousers before reaching towards her. 'We're sorry to have barged in like this. It's like Dan says, it's the van.'

He was tall, with a broad-chested solidity which might have belonged to an older man, but there was something effortlessly, childishly tender in the way his eyes settled on her.

Ellie wondered which of them she should look at. 'Gadiel? How lovely! Hebrew. Um…' She looked at neither of them, in the end, but fixed her gaze instead on a crisp slice of the mere visible between the trees. 'Sent by Moses to reconnoitre the land. Yes, that's right, I'm sure of it. Isn't it? I've never met a Gadiel.'

She stopped, blushing, as though the admission might be shameful. She wished she could have turned, retreated into the house and left them. Already they demanded too much of her.

Ernest stopped at the sight of the flamboyant guests seated at his long table. He brushed energetically at the sleeves of his battered dinner jacket, sank his feet more firmly into the scarlet pumps he habitually wore on fine evenings and balanced himself. Crossing the room to take his seat, he immediately picked up his knife and sat with it clenched vertically in his fist.

'Ah. Yes, ah… I see.' He blinked at them.

'We were invited to come and eat,' Gadiel said, evenly. 'We were invited when we arrived.'

Dan stared at Ernest. 'We are allowed to be in here, aren't we?'

Ernest studied the dining room with some care, as though it might all have changed since he was last there. It was a bright evening; the low sun swept through the long windows, the splits and stains and patches unobtrusive in the generous mid-summer light, but it was as it had always been.

'In here?' he repeated at last, perplexed. 'But where on earth else should we be? Ellie – am I wrong again? We're quite right, aren't we? In the dining room?'

She had just entered, wearing an old-fashioned floral dress and a long necklace of green plastic beads; her hair was elaborately plaited, her bare arms straining with the weight of a huge china tureen.

Ernest took this evidence of imminent supper as a good sign. 'I think we're right.' He looked back at Dan, relieved. 'I think it's perfectly all right.'

Gadiel stood up and went to help, taking the tureen and placing it near Ernest's elbow. 'It's very kind of you, to allow us in like this.' He looked around, as Ernest had done, taking in the faded splendour. 'It's a beautiful room. The whole place – it's beautiful.'

'Yeah, it is.' But Dan's admiration was grudging; as soon as he had spoken, he fixed his eyes determinedly on the old wood of the table, closing off the rest of Marlford from sight, stiffening against its efforts to seduce him.

Ellie put her hands to her hair, pushing at the pins, feeling so insubstantial and grey all of a sudden, such a shadow, that she let them dig into her scalp in the hope that they might prick her back to life.

'But we could have had sandwiches,' Gadiel went on. 'That would have been fine.'

'Sandwiches!' Ernest might not have known the word. He glanced at his daughter but, gathering nothing from her expression, tapped his thumb on the lid of the tureen.

'Ellie, I rather think you should remove the soup to your place and begin serving. We're here to eat, after all. Our guests must be hungry.'

She heaved the tureen to the far end of the table and carefully ladled the thin soup into four bowls, which she passed down the table. They began to eat without speaking, only watching each other intently, as if ready for any strange movement – a jerk, a lunge. The sounds they made seemed loud.

'Have you come a long way? To Marlford?'

Ellie's enquiry was simple, polite, nothing more, so she was confused by the quick exchange of glances between the boys, their hesitancy.

'We're travelling,' Gadiel replied, finally.

'Travelling where?'

He did not quite look at her. 'In the van.'

'Yes, I understand but—'

'We don't have a fixed itinerary,' Dan said quickly, not allowing another question. 'We're exploring.'

'Drifters?' Ernest did not look up; he pushed the word sneeringly through his nose.

'Papa!' Ellie blushed at his rudeness. 'I'm sorry. We don't have many visitors, you see…' She found a drip of soup on the table and rubbed at it determinedly with her thumb. 'And you must have some idea where you're going, don't you?'

'That's not the way we do things.'

Dan seemed to be reprimanding her. She rubbed harder at the stain.

'I just thought… ending up here… at Marlford,' but she could prompt nothing from them, and there was a long silence.

Already Ellie felt that she had failed, and that her failure was important.

'How long have you been here, then?' Gadiel asked, in the end.

She found she was offended by the oddness of the question.

'I've always lived here.'

She was curt; she went back to eating her soup.

Dan watched the slide of her spoon, the unhurried elegance of the action worn smooth by years of lonely repetition. He leaned forward, studying the simple movement, and then with a deliberate flourish scraped his chair back from the table.

Ernest winced at the noise.

'It's your house,' Dan said.

It sounded like an accusation. Ellie did not know how to respond. 'Well, it's Papa's, yes.'

Gadiel stared at Ernest for a moment. 'Oh, I see – but I thought you were servants,' he said. 'Housekeepers or something – you know the kind of thing.'

Dan nodded. 'Retainers.' He glanced at Gadiel. 'We didn't think of it being your house.'

Ernest slurped the dregs of his soup. 'Of course it's my

house,' he muttered. 'Who on earth else would invite you to supper?' He pushed his empty bowl away from him and beckoned to his daughter to collect it. 'This is Marlford,' he declared with ponderous enunciation, as though making a rail announcement over the clatter of a moving train.

'I told them that, Papa, when they arrived.' Ellie came to his side. As she picked up his bowl she looked down the table at the guests. 'But they said they didn't know it.'

The boys exchanged another glance; Dan's raised eyebrows encouraged Gadiel to reply.

'Like we told you, we broke down...' he began.

'Gadiel pushed the van the whole way up from the road.' Dan gestured at his friend. 'Man, we hadn't thought the drive would be so long.' He braced his right arm as a demonstration of strength. 'It's a fair push, all the way – it's a good job he's muscly.'

Ernest seemed pleased by evidence of such virility. 'Good man.' He looked sidelong at Ellie, who was busy stacking the bowls; she must have sensed his attention because she spoke to him quietly, without raising her head.

'They were hoping we would allow them to use a telephone, Papa.'

'A telephone? Here?' Ernest stabbed his knife into the table, where it remained, quivering. 'Whatever would we have a telephone for?'

The boys stared at him.

'Yeah, well, it doesn't matter, man. It's cool the way it is.' For the first time since his arrival, Dan smiled. Ellie felt he was testing them.

'We can direct you to somewhere in the village,' she offered.

42

Dan shrugged. 'Yeah, well, thanks… you know—'

'I'm sure someone will be able to fix it for you. Do you know what the problem is?'

'It's not my thing.' Dan was dismissive. 'I'm not good with mechanics.'

'No, well, if you like…'

Gadiel leaned forwards, interrupting before Ellie could finish.

'Why don't you tell us about the place? About Marlford.'

She started at the sudden request. 'Oh, yes. Yes, I suppose. All right.'

She saw Dan stretch and lean back in his chair, as though he was pleased not to have to go on speaking to her. Gadiel placed his elbows on the table and waited. She shrank from their elaborate awkwardness and looked at her father.

'Would you like to explain it, Papa – would you like to tell them?'

Ernest pulled the knife from the table with a twang and placed it in front of him. It seemed for a moment as though he might simply stand up and leave the room but, instead, he straightened himself in his chair, tugged purposefully at the lapels of his dinner jacket and cleared his throat with a series of small coughs. Then he began. 'The Barton family has lived at Marlford since 1894, when my father acquired the mansion and the estate. I was born here two years later, the third of three sons. Henry and Albert fell together at Passchendaele, so I inherited the place after the war. I am, as you can see, the latest, but hopefully not final, incumbent.' He fixed his attention on a point at the far end of the table, holding his chin high, his expression unwavering in its solemnity. Ellie pulled out the chair alongside him and sat down. 'The original sixteenth-century manor house has, of course, been much altered, improved in particular by my late father, Braithwaite Barton, in the years immediately after he acquired the property. Indeed, the original manor itself, or what we now regard as the original manor, was built over the structure of an existing medieval building. Marlford has been here, you might say, for ever. But you can see...' He could not resist a peek at his visitors at this point but, seeing their disinterest, the smirk they juggled between them, he lost his way. 'Well, the thing is, with a place like this...' He paused, frowning at the heavy quiet, then he thumped the table sharply. 'Damn it, when you think about Marlford, you see—'

But the idea of the place was too knotted. He could not unravel it.

Ellie leaned across him and picked up the knife.

Ernest sighed. 'Yes – thank you, Ellie.' He watched his guests as they passed up their cutlery. He would end with a flourish. That at least.

'At Marlford the ancient and the modern are side by side. The constancy of Marlford, that's what I call it. I – I am the modern.' His voice rang out, quite certain again, his finger wagging at them, driving home the lesson. 'And we have a duty to it – to believe in it, to nurture it through this trying century. Whatever it takes.'

It felt, perhaps, as though there should be applause, but there was just a cheerless silence. Ernest was determined not to break it himself so he braved it out, puffed up and magisterial.

It was Ellie who attempted further conversation. 'Perhaps you stopped at the village on your way through? It's called Marlford, too.'

'Marlford.' Dan repeated the name thoughtfully, as though it was the first time he had heard it, drawing out the sound on his tongue to mean something. 'Yeah. We came through the village.'

'The house was here first, a very long time ago. The village was established much later, by my grandfather, on part of the estate,' Ellie explained. 'It was specially designed for the workers. It has everything they might need, designed in a way to be pretty and yet practical.'

She felt as though she had made too long a speech. She flushed and fiddled with the cutlery.

Dan spoke just loudly, sharply, enough to surprise them. 'Where did he get his money from?' He smiled with tight lips. 'Must cost a bob or two, to build a whole village, mustn't it? I mean, you can't just snap it together from Lego, can you, man.'

Gadiel looked up, sharply. Something passed between them, too quickly for Ellie to fathom, but she sensed the dart of it, aggressive. She, in turn, glanced at her father. Ernest looked down the length of the table as though nothing had been said, and she felt forced to answer.

'Braithwaite Barton was an industrialist. He had a number of interests – shipping and canal building, some banking – but mostly he invested in the salt industry. He opened the mines here, providing rock salt for manufacturing processes.'

'Ah! The mines – yeah, man, of course – the chemical works.' Dan seemed delighted. 'It's all built on the backs

45

of the workers, the sweat of the poor, isn't it? I should have thought of that.'

He sat up and stared at Ernest, quite openly, as though the man were an exhibit behind glass; as though he might estimate the exact extent of the Barton family's culpability from the colour of Ernest's eyes or the rutted pattern of lines around his mouth. It was not immediately clear what such genetic inheritance might have told him, but he leaned back finally in his chair with a long sigh, suggesting that everything had been resolved much as he had expected.

Ernest accepted the scrutiny and then rose from his seat, brushing down his dinner jacket with great care. 'I don't think, Ellie… if you don't mind.' He did not look at the boys but examined his scarlet pumps, flexing his toes so that the soft fabric rippled. 'I have no port to offer. Not today. So, if we're replete…'

'Yes, Papa, I think we've finished.'

'Then I shall retire.'

He made his way to the door. Only when his hand was resting on the doorknob did he turn and look at them.

'Braithwaite Barton was an ingenious and philanthropic man,' he said. 'A gentleman of great principle and foresight. You're wrong if you doubt that – quite wrong.'

After he had left, there was a long pause until Ellie finally stood up and began to gather the dishes; Gadiel sprang from his place, coming round to her and reaching out a hand. 'Look, I'm sorry. Dan's sorry, aren't you, Dan? He doesn't mean to be rude, asking about the money and stuff. He's just… Can't I help you? Let me help you. I'll take something. I'll take the soup thing.'

'Tureen,' she corrected, picking up the bowls alongside, barely glancing at him.

'Tureen,' Gadiel repeated, not laughing at her, not exactly, but trying to make her laugh instead, or trying to force her to look at him, at least. 'I'll take the... tureen.'

She could see that he was attempting to be kind, but he was simply making things worse.

'Thank you.' She steadied her own load and led from the room, walking briskly down the narrow corridor towards the kitchen, hearing him follow.

'Wait – Ellie, please, just a moment.'

Even carrying the tureen, he was quickly upon her. He had balanced it against his chest, leaving a hand free to grab her arm.

She gasped.

'No – please,' he was saying. 'I just wanted to apologize. For Dan. He doesn't mean it. He loves these kinds of places really, but he's into politics at the moment and he gets a bit over-excited sometimes, that's all. We didn't mean to offend you.'

She was taken aback by the concern in his eyes.

'It's perfectly all right,' she said.

The tureen began to slip, and Gadiel had to hoist it further into his grip. Ellie took advantage of the movement to pull back and, the next moment, she had escaped, turning the pinched elbow of the corridor, hurrying on towards the kitchen. By the time Gadiel came through with the tureen she was nowhere to be seen.

When she finally came back to find them, they were loitering in the hallway, Dan sitting at the foot of the stairs and Gadiel crouched near the door, examining the ruts in the old flagstones. She had the momentary impression that they were spectral; not insubstantial or alarming, but simply imagined, completely and accurately, emerging quite naturally from the depths of her mind.

She hesitated. For a moment she thought of Oscar Quersley; she pictured him sweeping the library, waiting for her, the Dante ready on the table, the ledger unmarked. She put the distraction aside.

'Would you like a game of billiards before you leave?'

'Who said we were leaving, man?' Dan sprang up.

Gadiel stood and stretched, smiling at her. 'Don't worry. He's joking.'

'Yeah, well.' Dan glared at his friend. 'I don't play billiards. Who on earth plays billiards these days?'

Ellie tugged at her plastic beads. 'Never mind. It's a very old table, anyway.'

Dan looked at her properly for the first time. She seemed smaller than he had imagined, rounded and plump enough, but with an odd bluish pallor that made her seem fragile, like finely worked porcelain.

'An antique billiards table.' He snorted. 'Well, man, every home should have one, I suppose.' He reddened, turning away and swinging foolishly on the banister, hanging awkwardly for a moment, like an albatross trying to take flight into the massive hallway. Then he spun round to face them again.

Ellie was watching him quite calmly, her expression unchanging. He wondered if his irony had passed her by; she was not quite like any of the other girls he knew, he sensed that already.

'But we could do something else.' He let the idea linger, a plea and an apology. 'Wouldn't you like to come out and see the van? I've had the paintwork done, and the interior. It's cool, man.'

'If he'd had the engine done instead, I wouldn't have had to push it up your drive.'

But Dan ignored Gadiel's jibe.

'Come on,' he urged. 'I'll give you the guided tour.'

Ellie glanced down at her threadbare pumps. 'I suppose so. If I change my shoes.' But before she looked up again, Gadiel had stepped towards her.

'I don't mind playing billiards,' he said, firmly. 'I quite like it.'

She did not see the look the boys parried between them.

'Would you? Yes, all right – that's good. I'll show you.'

Dan trailed behind, pausing at the threshold to the billiard room and leaning against the doorframe. He watched Ellie pull the cord on the low-slung light; its long, bare tube groaned for a moment, clicked, then pulsed out a menacing orange glow that thrust him into uneasy shadow.

They set up the game quickly. Ellie smoothed the baize with slow hands and took two cues, chalking them both and offering one to Gadiel.

'These things need to be aired, you know.' Dan spoke over the click of the balls, his abruptness seeming to stir the dust in the room.

'Come on, Dan, leave it.' Gadiel chalked his cue again.

'I'm just making the point, man – slave labour, all that kind of thing. We see it for what it is now, in the twentieth century. We're clued up.'

It was Ellie's turn at the table. She had never taken on a real opponent; she imagined this was why her hand was shaking.

'Braithwaite Barton was a good man.' She made her shot.

Dan pushed his spectacles into place. He was carefully patient, only raising his eyebrows to signal the extent of his forbearance. 'All I'm saying is – that kind of exploitation... Man, it's no wonder your dad's embarrassed by it all. Who wouldn't be?'

The billiard balls clicked, not quite a friendly sound.

'You're mistaken. Papa's not embarrassed by Braithwaite Barton.'

Dan shook his head and smiled. 'That's even worse, then. That means he doesn't get it.'

The air seemed too dense between them, a barrier.

'Your turn, Ellie.' Gadiel stepped back from the table.

She dipped her cue towards him, a terse acknow-ledgement.

'Ellie – your turn,' he repeated, when she did not come forward to play.

Dan pulled a battered packet of cigarettes from his pocket. 'I'm going outside for a smoke,' he said. 'It's poky in here, man.'

Ellie felt his retreat like a sudden change of light.

Gadiel turned out to be an excellent player. He approached the table with skill and flair; Ellie was captivated by some of his movements: the way he flicked his little finger before settling it on the baize, the stretch of his shoulder. As he played, the faint chink of the balls seemed pregnant with meaning, a series of questions skittering urgently, one upon the other.

'Won't you tell me about you and Dan?' she asked, as boldly as she dared, the frame coming to a close.

'There's not much to tell. We're just travelling, like we said – or would be, if the van was working.'

'Yes, but – apart from that.' She was surprised by her own insistence. 'Not many people come here, you see.'

'We're at university together… we thought it would be cool, for the holidays.'

Ellie felt his careful rejection of her curiosity, his account purposely bland, but she saw how she might begin to measure herself against them, these interlopers, and she was undeterred. 'What do you study, at the university?'

'History. Well, Dan does, and he's into politics as well, like I told you – I'm supposed to be doing history too, but I don't take it very seriously. I'm not sure it's really my thing. I've thought about dropping out.'

'Oh, but, no – surely…' She blanched at such a terrible proposal. 'There must be some aspects of study that interest you. Especially with history. There's so much – there's always something to inspire you.'

Gadiel smiled. 'I think I prefer practical stuff.'

Ellie stared at him and then, realizing her rudeness, blinked and turned her attention to a loose thread of baize.

'Well, anyway, I'd like to hear about your travels,' she said.

'No – it's nothing. We've just driven around a bit, you know. It's just – well, it's the same as everyone does.'

'Everyone?' She was forced to look at him again, astounded, trying to place herself in such an extraordinary statement. But she found that what she came back to was Marlford, and a niggle of resentment.

She drew her thumb round the tip of her cue to clear loose chalk. 'When Dan asked Papa that question – about the money… I'm sorry he didn't answer. But you mustn't think he was embarrassed about my grandfather or about the mines or the industry or anything.'

Gadiel seemed relieved by the abrupt change of subject. 'Look, that was Dan. He's just like that sometimes. He has ideas. He's politically engaged.' He laughed lightly. 'Ignore him.'

'Braithwaite Barton was a genuine philanthropist. The model village at Marlford—'

'It's fine. You don't need to explain.'

'But Papa's rather sensitive…'

'Really. It's fine. Take no notice of Dan – he just gets bees buzzing in his bonnet like crazy. That's all. It's not you. Let's just play.'

'He lost all the money, you see. Everything.'

Gadiel pulled out of his shot and stood up straight. 'Really? You mean—' He waved his arm as though to signal the extent of the Marlford estate and Ernest's losses.

'Yes – Dan rather touched a nerve.' Ellie smiled, sadly. 'Braithwaite Barton made ample provision for the village. And, when he died, he left funds for a great many improvements and expansions – new roads, for example, and an open-air swimming pool for the children to use in the summer.'

She thought she could smell the scent of Dan's tobacco smoke drifting in from the portico but she could not be sure, and she tried to concentrate instead on the tight pattern of angles suggested by the balls.

When Gadiel spoke again, she started.

'Do you mean you don't have any money now? Despite all this?'

Ellie frowned at an obstructed pocket. 'We have very little money,' she replied.

Gadiel smiled. 'Dan'll be pleased to hear that.' But he could not be sure she understood his joke. 'No – look, I didn't mean… it must have been some disaster, though, to lose that much.'

Ellie was scathing. 'It was a remarkable achievement.'

The ferocity of her tone embarrassed him. He pulled uncomfortably at one of the string bags beneath the pockets of the billiard table. The game seemed to have drifted to a halt.

'To lose everything on the turn of the dice… or something.' Gadiel whistled, a kind of admiration.

'No, no – it wasn't that. It wasn't gambling.'

She tried to settle the facts of the old story, always brittle to her, fragments from lives long past, before Marlford was ever conceived, an incongruous prehistory.

'Well, if you want to tell me, then think of it as a history lesson,' he prompted. 'I might learn something.'

The light spat, momentarily throwing them into darkness before flicking on again and settling, its brightness dimmed. Ellie slid her cue onto the table, laying it along the cushion.

She sighed. She saw Gadiel's eagerness, something other than mere curiosity, an irresistible desire to know her.

'Papa was – well, an adventurer, like those old-fashioned explorers that lost themselves in the jungle or were eaten by savages.' She smiled wryly at her father's eccentricity.

'Well, which was it?' Gadiel asked. 'He doesn't look like he got eaten by savages.'

She laughed. 'He got involved with all kinds of strange schemes, and in the end he put up a great deal of money for a British expedition to Canada. He had to take out extra loans to finance it. It was scientific, in its way – it was a genuine expedition. He had support from the British Geological Survey, the War Ministry – all kinds of officials. If it had been a success I believe there might have been a substantial return on the investment. But it was terrible timing: it was 1939, and when war broke out... well – he had to sell everything... almost everything. Except the house.'

Gadiel was struck by the coolness of her manner. 'Couldn't they just have postponed it?'

'It was too late, I think. I don't entirely understand. There's never been many details. Perhaps it was a secret. It was something to do with finding a new supply route, but several of the ships were sunk by German U-boats just south of Rockall – I know that much. My father was on board one of them; he was one of the survivors.'

'But that's terrible.'

'I've never considered it worthy of much sympathy.'

Gadiel stepped back and stared at her. He caught the flicker of something hardly visible behind the steady primness of her face, the tiniest of movements; he could not even say what it might have been, a twitch of the cheek, perhaps, or a fleeting spark in the eye. It was like a stifled cry. He felt he should help her.

'Another game?' It was all he could think of to offer.

*

When he potted the last ball, Ellie was standing by the table, blinking.

'Oh.' The sound crept from her, an involuntary moan.

'Well played.' Gadiel offered her his hand but she did not take it.

She had never considered that she might lose the game. Having her flaws exposed in such a casual, friendly manner seemed perilous.

'Yes, I suppose.'

He grinned. 'You're supposed to say "Well played", too. It's traditional.'

'Yes, of course. You played well. You did. I see that. I didn't mean to be ungracious. It's just—'

'It's just that when you play by yourself, you always win.' He winked at her and offered his hand again, almost touching her. She stepped away and before she could speak, Dan came in to join them again, polishing his spectacles briskly on his T-shirt.

'You know, I think the best thing is if we just push the van somewhere out of the way and I get someone to come for it.' He was newly purposeful after slipping through the histories of the house in the scented dark. 'That'd be OK, wouldn't it?'

Ellie anchored the base of her cue into the forgiving old wood of the floorboards. 'Oh, yes, of course. Yes, I don't see why not. I don't see that Papa will mind. Why don't you... you can put it in the stable yard, if you like – there're no horses any more.'

'What, no string of thoroughbreds?'

Ellie shook her head. 'No, just rats. And some birds. A few old saddles, I think.'

She wanted to laugh at her assessment of Marlford's livery, to show she understood how ridiculous it all was, but the boys were already hurrying out of the house, pushing at each other, jostling, Dan making a fuss of looking for his keys in his pockets, their quick footsteps crunching on the front gravel. She was left behind.

She did not join them again until they had heaved the vehicle under the archway and stowed it safely in the yard.

Dan brushed his palms together, creating a brisk series of claps. 'That should do it, man.' He appraised the van's garaging arrangements as the echoes of his gesture subsided, then looked hard at Gadiel.

'We'll be off, then,' Gadiel said.

Ellie sensed his wariness, but did not understand it. 'It's been very kind of you to visit.' She held out her hand.

This time Gadiel touched her, but she hardly noticed.

'It was most pleasant,' she said. 'I'm so glad you could come. I'm sure Papa enjoyed your company a great deal.' She looked off to one side, impolite in the speed of her farewells. Her head was full of something painful: their faces there in front of her — coarse, she thought, gloating in the dusk — seemed too close and intrusive. It was such a terrible confusion.

She scurried away, leaving them.

The boys stood together, watching her go.

The dark was settling quickly, blurring the lines of the old stone. The stable clock struck ten. Dan looked at his watch. 'This place is mad. Even the clock's set to a different age. It's nearly eleven.'

Gadiel tapped the side of the van. 'What are we going to do, then? Are we sleeping here?'

Dan ignored him. There was something set in the wall at the far end of the yard that seemed to attract his attention, but Gadiel could see only the uneven texture of the old bricks, a couple of metal fixings and a half-closed window.

'What about heading into the village? We could find somewhere – there'll be a pub, I bet, and there'll be the Apollo stuff – if we can find a television.'

Dan was still.

'Come on, Dan,' – Gadiel shoved at him – 'astronauts, you know… men on the moon? Hanging around here all evening, we've missed the best of it.'

Dan stepped out of reach.

'She should have come to see the van.'

'You're not going to hold that against her, are you? It's just a van. Girls don't get that kind of thing.'

'She can't shake old habits, can she? Playing billiards after dinner – all that stuff.'

'The billiards was good. You'd have liked it. You shouldn't have lied about not being able to play.' Gadiel shook his head. 'Come on, let's get going. It'll be more fun in the village. And Ellie let me in on some family secrets – I'll tell you as we go. Come on, Dan.'

Dan turned to him, finally. He was solemn, excited. 'I've got an idea,' he said.

Five

Ellie cleared the kitchen, stacking the washed dishes on the shelves and tying up the sack of peelings for the farm. She worked quickly, with something like anger in the abruptness of her movements, then she changed into her wellington boots, tied a scarf over her hair, took her raincoat from the pegs by the back door and slipped outside.

The van was shunted against the wall; there was no sign of the visitors. Bats criss-crossed above her head, looping and diving; something moved in the old stalls, disturbing the rancid hay. She walked up to the van, her booted footsteps slopping loudly against the cobbles in the stable yard, and she touched the side of it, rubbing her hand along one of the sweeps of colour. In the rustling twilight, it seemed as though the vehicle should be magical, a genie's lantern perhaps, but when she repeated the movement and looked around, there were still just the old walls on all sides, a heavy sky above, disappointment sinking within her.

She started at a dull sound and turned quickly. By the narrow back entrance the men were standing, watching her.

'Oh. Good evening. Have you been here all the time? I didn't see you.'

In reply, Ata pointed to the stable roof. Hindy nodded. 'A tile has slipped,' he said.

Ellie followed their gaze. There were tiles missing all over, holes gaping open to show the rotting wood beneath; some had fallen at unsettling angles into the clutch of the sloping gutter.

'I don't see how you can know.'

But they did not respond. For a while longer they scrutinized the roof, then Luden broke from their ranks and came towards her, his bent figure cracking the shadows. He, too, touched the side of the van, gingerly, as though it might burn him.

'It's – it's awaiting repair,' Ellie explained. 'It's temporary.' She watched as Luden poked at the paintwork. 'It's only just arrived. Just this afternoon.'

He looked along the length of the vehicle, bending down stiffly to examine something beneath. Whatever the result of his investigations, it seemed to satisfy him. He returned slowly to Hindy and Ata.

'Really – there's no need to worry about it. It's being towed away, for repair.'

They did not seem in the least interested in her explanations. Hindy put a consoling hand on Luden's shoulder; Ata shook his head slowly, with great sadness.

She waited, knowing they would speak in the end.

'You should go to apologize to Mr Quersley,' Hindy said. 'He'll be on patrol at the mere.'

She sighed. 'I'm very tired.'

'I'm not sure that makes a difference.' He looked to

Luden and Ata, who both shook their heads. 'No, as I thought, you see – unfortunately, that makes no difference. Apologies need to be made. And in good time. You have a commitment to join Mr Quersley in your duties at your grandfather's library – and that commitment was broken this evening.'

'But I wasn't to know they would come. They simply arrived – their van broke down on the road and they pushed it up here, all the way. I had every intention of going to the library but... well, it just happened. Unexpectedly.'

It felt like throwing pebbles at a wall, her words dinking back at her without making the slightest impact.

'Miss Barton.' Luden was stern. 'You know what we expect – of you, of the mistress of Marlford.'

'We had hoped to make that clear, over the years,' Ata added, smiling.

Ellie looked again at the van, its looping rainbow faint now in the distorted dark.

'Can't it wait until tomorrow? I am really very tired.'

'It has to be done now,' Hindy pressed. 'So that we can be sure there's no further disruption.'

Ellie placed her hand very slowly on the vehicle's side.

'Miss Barton,' – Hindy's tone was a warning – 'we never offer our advice without consideration.'

'And yet, if I may, we've recently sensed some resistance,' Ata added. 'Would that be accurate to say? Some opposition on your part?' He smiled again. 'Despite our good intentions.'

'I don't oppose you.' She was surprised at the sudden anger that sparked in her as she spoke. She pressed her hand harder against the cold flank of the van.

'Resentment, perhaps,' Ata continued, reasonably. 'At the menial work to be done at the hutments.'

'I've always done that. I don't think of it.'

'At the way we monopolize Mr Barton's time, then?'

'You shouldn't take Papa's money.' She spoke quite calmly. 'You take too much. When there's nothing to begin with.'

Ata smiled again. 'A run of luck, I'm afraid. The turn of the cards.'

'But there's three of you and only one of him. You're bound to win. At least three times as often, you're bound to win.'

Ata opened his hands and shrugged, his smile steady.

'There's no good reason for her wilfulness.' Hindy shook his head. 'It's just a phase, I imagine. We should just press on. You'll come round, won't you, Miss Barton?'

'Her mother was just the same. You remember? The trouble we had? At first?' Lunden clenched his lips, something of a smile.

'I remember,' Hindy replied.

'But she was a bright woman, and sensible,' Luden continued. 'She understood.'

They looked at each other, the warmth of nostalgia holding them apart from Ellie for a moment.

'I have to go.' Her anger was still sharp. She pulled away from the van and smoothed the folds of her raincoat.

'Ah, good – yes.' Hindy broke from his reminiscences. 'You'll rectify matters with Mr Quersley, then.'

'No,' she replied. 'I'm going in to bed.'

She sensed the way they stiffened.

'I've had enough. Enough of all your – foolishness.'

The word seemed visible for a moment, glowing faintly between them. 'I don't see that there's any urgency. There's no reason why Mr Quersley should object to my absence. It was perfectly justified. I'll explain that to him, the next time I see him.' She found her breath was coming noisily, too fast.

'Ah now, wait, Miss Barton—' Ata began, smoothly.

'No. I'll not wait. I'm perfectly able to decide these things. For myself.'

There was a long moment of quiet. Something scuffled again in the stables. Ellie glanced towards the sound, as though it mattered.

'You see, Miss Barton? You see how these visitors have disrupted us?' Hindy finally asked.

'Corrupted, I would say,' Luden added.

'No. No. It's nothing to do with them.' She clutched her hand to her stomach as if she could calm the uneasy sensation there, the slow growl which had come on with the arrival of the van earlier that day, like an odd hunger, insistent now and gnawing. 'I've not been in the least disrupted.' Her voice was rising high. 'There's just no reason why I should do as you say.'

They smiled, all three of them, at her resistance. Ata scratched thoughtfully at his head.

'But you see, of course, there is,' Hindy said. 'I believe we've explained this before, Miss Barton, several times. I believe we've been clear. You do understand, do you not?'

There was an instant, perhaps, when Ellie might have continued to resist, but it was too fleeting.

'We know what is best for Marlford,' Hindy went on. 'You'll understand that we've given it a great deal of consideration. On the whole, we don't like to bother you with our deliberations, of course, but this evening we clearly need to ensure your relationship with Mr Quersley remains on a good footing. On an excellent footing, indeed. So, as we suggested at the beginning, an apology will be quite the right thing.'

She could hear the frogs, their song quiet, a distant consonance, the mechanical repetition indistinct. The sound seemed to lure her residual anger from her and all she felt was the weight of an old weariness, unshiftable.

'It would only take a few minutes, I suppose,' she said.

'Time well spent,' Ata agreed.

'It's just this evening, with everything…' She sighed. 'But I suppose I could go.'

'If you would, Miss Barton. Straight away,' Hindy urged. 'It's for your own good, you know that.'

'That's what you always say.'

'And isn't it always true?'

Ellie slumped into the deep grooves of an old conversation. 'Perhaps.' She shook her head.

The men watched her closely for a moment without speaking. When they were satisfied her resolution would hold, Hindy smiled. 'Excellent. Our exchanges are ever a pleasure, Miss Barton. We will leave you to your task and bid you good night. It's rather late.'

And the men left her, going back one by one through the narrow entrance and disappearing silently, only the faint echo of their words lingering.

There was no sign of Oscar Quersley. Ellie followed the bank around to the ruined boathouse, disturbing a pair of ducks that flapped away, panicked and raucous. Beyond it, the trees and thickets of bushes were too dense, the weeds too overgrown; she was forced to retrace her steps.

When she finally found him, he was sitting on the damp ground under an ancient yew, his back against the buried wall of the old ice house, swishing his stick uselessly in wide arcs through the air in front of him.

'Good evening.'

He jumped to his feet, brandishing the stick stiffly like a weapon. 'Ellie – my God, Ellie, it's pitch dark. What on earth are you doing?'

'It's not quite dark.' She gestured to the dip of the mere: a moon was rising low over the water, making it ripple silver. 'It just seems darker under here.'

'Nonetheless.' He tucked his stick under his arm. 'I didn't think you ever came here. I didn't think you liked the mere.' Stepping past her, he resumed his slow patrol, marshalling the historic quiet with the arrhythmic swish of his stick. He was angular in the chill gloom.

Ellie hesitated. 'I wanted to apologize for not coming this evening for library duty.'

'It was a quiet evening. There were no readers.'

'That's as I thought. But the men suggested I come to explain. To apologize.'

'Think nothing of it, Ellie. You weren't required.'

'They thought you might be... I don't know – offended, I suppose.'

'I was not offended.'

She could not say anything after that; she could not reply to his brusqueness, so she just walked alongside him, listening to the beat of his stick.

'They're quiet tonight, aren't they?' she asked, after a while. 'The frogs.'

He did not answer.

'They're probably waiting for the rain. It feels like it's going to rain, doesn't it, Mr Quersley?'

He might have nodded, she could not be sure; it might simply have been his movement through the clumps of long grass. Somehow it mattered.

'Don't you think so? Don't you think it might rain, Mr Quersley?'

He stopped, cocking his head. A frog very close to them began with the lightest of groans. In response, a chorus started up all around, strident, undeniable, filling the night with urgent desire.

Oscar held his stick aloft, not quite still. Ellie could see the shiver of the brutal metal tip. For a moment he was poised, then he took one long, quick step sideways, turning, bringing the stick down in a graceful arc, driving the point of it hard into the ground. Ellie saw something flailing.

He straightened himself, pulling the stick out of the earth with a sharp tug and holding an impaled frog towards her. Its legs waved at her frantically, swimming through the damp air; a dark slime squeezed over the bulge of its stomach.

'Aha! You see?'

It was a slight trophy, but he stood squarely behind it, proud. She put her hand up to keep it away. The frog became still.

With a deft flick of his wrist, Oscar loosened it from the stick and let it drop to the ground. He put his heel on it, twisting his foot several times. Then he looked up at her. 'That doesn't happen very often. A clean strike.'

He wiped the sole of his boot on the long grass and Ellie moved away, avoiding the crushed body of the frog. The rain started, slow, heavy drops, intermittent. She pulled the edge of her light scarf over her fringe.

'You'd better go home, Ellie. It's going to rain hard. After this hot weather, too, there may even be a storm.'

The drops fell harder.

'But I just wanted to tell you, Mr Quersley...' In a sudden burst, the rain descended furiously, rumbling against the ground and the deep water of the mere. She raised her voice. 'I wanted to explain. In case you thought I'd simply forgotten to come, or that I couldn't be bothered—'

He, too, was shouting against the noise. 'Really, I told you, Ellie – it's of no matter. I... in fact, I hardly noticed your absence.'

His words were squandered by the gusting breeze and he strode away, purposeful.

Ellie stood in the rain, hanging her head, seeing nothing, her scarf clinging now to her hair.

It was several minutes before she began to trudge back through the trees, her pace slowed, perhaps, by the uncomfortable flap of her wellingtons. By the time she reached the manor, she was soaked.

It felt like she had been punished for something.

Six

There was so much: pictures peeling from heavy frames, the skeletal remnants of dark furniture, cupboards stuffed with broken trinkets, lurching statues pale in the gloom, doors everywhere, unlit passages and narrow stairs, collapsed plaster and crumbling stone, the smell of rotting carpets and doomed wood, the irrepressible majesty of the confident spaces.

In the end, they chose a room that was empty apart from a four-poster bed with mouldering curtains, a greening mustard-gold, their edges frayed and their seams splitting.

Dan stepped warily towards the window, testing each of the floorboards in turn. 'Turn on the light. Let's see properly.'

Gadiel searched both sides of the doorframe for a switch. 'I don't think there is one.' He went back out to the corridor; when he returned he was puzzled. 'There aren't lights anywhere. I don't think there's any electricity.'

'Nothing at all? Don't be stupid. There must be, man. Even stately homes have electricity. Even the rich need toasters.' Dan scrubbed angrily at the glass of the window with his wrist, working a circle into the grime and peering through it, as if to find the cause of such a complicated deception. All he saw was his own reflection, flat against the dark.

He pushed at his hair, turning away and flinging himself full length, backwards, onto the bed. They heard the squelch of the springs and, moments later, smelt a stale must. 'We can't let it put us off, man. Not now, when we've got a good thing going. And I bet there'll be electricity downstairs. We should go downstairs again. We can set up the wireless.'

'I don't know.' Gadiel went over to the bed and fingered the curtains gently. The fabric flaked, disintegrating under his touch. 'I quite like it up here. There's something about it… it's as if they've lent us their bedroom, as if we've been invited to stay.'

'Oh, come on, we're not house guests, man. This is a squat. It's a radical act of subversion.'

'Still, I think it's a cool room. I think we should stay here.'

Dan sat up, brightening at a sudden thought. 'OK – yeah, I see. It'll be ironic. A statement. The modern politics of equality and opportunity in the boudoir of the ancien regime.'

Gadiel rubbed away the greasy dust between his thumb and forefinger. He laughed. 'You talk rubbish,' he said.

When they had first forced their way into the rear of the house, they had left their bags by the door. Now, they could not find their way back. The bedroom corridor was longer than they remembered; there were several flights of stairs.

Only the faintest glow squeezed through the scarred and dirty windows and the darkness disorientated them. They had not thought to mark their route and neither of them had noted any features by which to navigate. They had to feel their way, keeping close together.

'We should have left a trail of string, like that Greek guy,' Gadiel said.

'Theseus.'

'Yeah, that's it – Theseus.'

'And the Minotaur,' Dan reminded him. 'It's just the kind of place for Minotaurs.' He pounced on Gadiel, gripping him by the shoulders. *'Rargh!'*

Even such a stupid joke disconcerted them.

They found themselves on the ground floor in the most ancient part of the manor, the rooms smaller and low-ceilinged, panelled in thick wood and flagged in stone, the air cool, trapped from winters long past. They came to a dead end where the passage was blocked by a wall and had to retrace their steps. They chose another door. The internal configuration of the house was baffling: different periods were overlaid one on top of the other, each wrestling with the next, grappling to overcome structures that had gone before: there were doors at odd angles; windows packed with stone or sulkily offering abbreviated views; cupboards and closets knocked through into airy chambers; elegant reception rooms eroded into cupboards and closets. The fabric of the manor seemed uneasily held, the aggression of its reconfigurations barely contained.

'We could be here for ever at this rate, man, going round and round,' Dan complained. 'I can't believe they could live like this. Why would they want to live like this?'

It seemed too insubstantial, their hunt for an untidy pile of carrier bags, tiny evidence of the present in the vastness of the past.

'I suppose they knew their way around,' Gadiel answered, reasonably.

Dan opened another door to a dead end. 'Look, man, in my house you open a door and it goes somewhere. There's a reason to open it. There're no tricks. It's honest. Here – well, it's… it's pointless.'

'It's cool, though, too, don't you think?' Gadiel answered. 'Isn't there a part of you that thinks it's really cool?'

'I'm not taken in like that, man.'

'I bet you are, really. I bet you love it.'

Dan gave a short, bitter laugh and walked on.

At last, and all of a sudden, they found themselves in another set of rooms, defiantly simple. Somewhere a tap dripped.

'I remember that! I remember the tap!' Gadiel was triumphant. He rushed ahead. 'Look, Dan, that's the window we broke to get in.'

They were back at the bags. Everything was as they had left it: shards of glass kicked into a corner, a window wedged open. They stared at the evidence, baffled by it, in the end, as much as relieved; it drew them back from the illusions of the manor's interior, unexpectedly confirming the ordinariness of their arrival.

'And look – there're lights here and everything. Look!' Gadiel pointed above his head to a single bulb, brown with filth, stuck with flies, the most marvellous of discoveries.

He found the switch and flicked it on; the bulb buzzed

and gave out a dim glow, enough to grasp the extent of the kitchens, stores and pantries, small workrooms at the back of the manor, which led one from the other, looking out on to an internal courtyard through a row of wide windows. Pale blue paint peeled from the plaster; cupboards hunkered against practical brown tiles.

Gadiel extracted a cobwebbed bundle of wax candles from the shelves and examined it solemnly. 'We should borrow some of this stuff,' he said, but there was little left to scavenge and they were steadfastly practical, looting nothing more than some string, a dish of clothes pegs and a bar of green soap, nibbled at the corners by mice.

As they collected their things, Dan pulled a portable radio from one of the carrier bags, holding it up solemnly, a trophy. 'We have to listen. They'll be nearly there won't they, already?'

Gadiel flattened his hand over his mouth, making his voice crackly, distant. 'Apollo 11, this is Houston...'

They laughed together.

They argued about the route back to the bedroom corridor, and, in the end, it may have been only by chance that they came upon the narrow, turning staircase that took them up. They paused at the barricade that marked the end of their part of the manor: the corridor was properly truncated here, bricked up with roughly cemented breeze blocks that prevented access to the wing in which the Bartons were still living.

'It's not much, this.' Gadiel tapped lightly on the barrier. 'They'll hear us. It might frighten her.'

Dan held his candle high. 'Who?'

'Ellie. I don't want her to… you know, she might not like it.' Gadiel leaned forwards, putting an ear against the breeze blocks.

'But that doesn't matter.' Dan spoke more loudly than he needed to. 'What she thinks doesn't matter – this is a political act, man.'

'Sssh.' Gadiel flapped a hand to try to quieten him, and the candle flame leapt. He drew back from the barricade. 'Of course it matters. She's been nice to us. They gave us supper; we just turned up at the house and they gave us supper.'

'You make it sound biblical.' Dan smirked. 'Come on, Gadiel – we're squatting. It's a recognized form of protest. It's a movement.' He pressed his spectacles hard against his nose. '"*In place of the old bourgeois society, with its classes and class antagonisms, we shall have an association, in which the free development of each is the condition for the free development of all.*"' He shrugged. 'You see?'

'But it's not as simple as that,' Gadiel insisted. 'Not here.'

'Come on, that's Marx. Karl Marx. Don't you believe in a new social order?'

'Yeah, I suppose.'

'Of course you do. That's why we went travelling, isn't it? To see something of the world, to make a difference.'

'I thought you just wanted to try out the van.'

'Oh, come on. I had bigger ideas than that.'

'Not till the van broke down and we turned up here, you didn't.' Gadiel grinned.

'Yeah, I did. But I knew you wouldn't come if… Man, you see? I knew you'd be like this if I'd proposed a radical agenda.'

Gadiel was unmoved. 'How had you planned to change the world, then?'

'*See* the world, I said. *See* the world.' Dan poked at his spectacles. 'Which is what we're doing.'

'Well, we've not seen much of it. It's not been a week since we left.'

'Yeah, and already we've started a squat. Come on, Gadiel – you're being negative, man.'

'But there's only two of us,' Gadiel pointed out. 'And no one even knows we're here. How's that going to make a difference? It doesn't make sense if there's only two of us.'

Dan slapped his hand against the breeze blocks. 'Others will come, won't they, in time? They'll come and join us. Other people will hear about it and come.'

'What other people?'

'I don't know. But that's how squats work, man – they grow.'

'Yeah, and what will happen then? To Ellie? We'll have to go back to university at the end of the summer and – well, then what?'

Dan shrugged, setting off for the bedroom, his candle light bobbing. 'It'll be out of our hands, man,' he answered, talking as much to the fickle shadows as to Gadiel. 'The squat'll have a life of its own by then.'

Seven

Ellie turned away from the lime avenue and the mere, on to the rutted tarmac lane that led to the hutments, walking unhurriedly to the two lines of oblong shacks, patchworked in corrugated metal and wooden panels, greening in the damp shade of a row of fir trees. The buildings were featureless. The hutment closest to the manor, still in use by the men, was in reasonable repair – it had been mended in places; the ground around the doorway trodden smooth – but the rest were overgrown with brambles and spiked through with twisted saplings; they created an ugly scar of ruined shacks, their roofs collapsing and rusting, their walls splayed. The barbed wire that had once coiled around them was denuded, like the coarse hair of a very aged man. It sprang in odd directions, forced into crude and unexpected sculptures, finally slinking away towards the end of the lane and disappearing into a shallow sinkhole. The field beyond, bounded by a black-and-white metal fence, was neatly planted with barley, pale and dense, almost ripe.

Ellie collected water from the standpipe so that she

could wash dishes in the wide, flat sink which was secured to a wobbling trestle of sorts at the side of the hutment. From the lane and the strip of cleared land alongside, she picked up empty beer cans and a number of dog-ends, then went behind to the toilet, which she sluiced with water from the hose, jamming the wooden door open with its wedge to air the cramped and foetid space within.

Inside, the dormitory was laid out with two parallel rows of metal bedsteads, twenty in all, most of them empty; a single, large table was the only other piece of furniture. She made the three beds nearest the door and collected the washing piled on the floor.

As she cleaned, she recited Shakespeare, the complaints of injured Caliban accompanying the brisk scratch of the broom. But the verse flustered her; she found the conversations of the previous evening cramming back into her head, the words stripped and prickly, meaning nothing now. She grabbed one of the metal bedsteads, letting the broom drop, breathing hard, sickened with the dizzying sense that she was falling. It took her a while to compose herself. When she set to work again, she took care to sweep more slowly, beginning a leisurely dramatization of *The Lady of Shalott*, transporting herself to a springtime of lilies; a blossoming island where she drifted on the dark river of Tennyson's long poem, beautiful and bewitched, half-sick of shadows. Standing on her toes, she looked out of the high window, expecting to see the approach of an armoured knight through the narrow slot of brilliant light, his figure massive on the jewelled saddle of his heavy horse. She heard the thunder of hooves from the fields beyond, the rattle of armour, her sigh.

She could not quite believe it when he did not appear.

She pushed the trailing washing into a sack, smelling the men's familiar scent of stale cigarette smoke and damp cloth.

'We've been considering the matter of the van,' Hindy said.

Ellie started. They were standing by the table at the end of the hutment, watching. Alongside them, the door was still closed. She wondered if she had somehow summoned them by flapping out their smell from the grubby linen.

'And the young men who came to supper last night,' Hindy continued.

She hoisted the sack over her shoulder. 'I thought I explained. The van is broken. It's awaiting repair.'

'We've been to Home Farm to suggest Oscar makes a visit to the stable yard. And we've decided to have a word with you.'

Hindy and Luden looked at Ata steadily; he stepped forward.

'Miss Barton, when we first came here, it was a real country estate,' he began. They must have allowed for the kindness of his tone, his natural sympathy. Something about his slenderness, too, and his dark skin, gave his words a delicacy. 'It was in many ways, for us, the apotheosis of England. Of civilisation, if you like. It's what we'd been told about, as boys – it's what we'd imagined when we came to this country. But we found ourselves trapped in the cities, jaded and disillusioned, unable to find a place for ourselves, overlooked on account of our way of speaking, our manners and our clothes. It was coming here, to

Marlford, that changed everything. It was what we'd been searching for.'

There were no interruptions. The other two men stood expressionless, their eyes cast down, while Ata represented them.

'There is no doubt,' he went on, 'that Marlford was where we wanted to be. But, over time, Miss Barton, we've found we've had to work with increasing determination to preserve our place here. And now, with the van in the stable yard and unknown young men invited to dine – well, we're concerned. You might say we're anxious.'

Ellie wished she could think more clearly, but there was still the rhythmic gallop of her knight's steed clacking in her head and beneath it, like the rumble of distant thunder, voices, glances, the unanchored words of the boys' arrival.

'Look, I know how you like it, of course I do. But I don't really see that anything has changed. Marlford is fine. It's just a van.'

Ata began again. 'If Lady Wilshere had remained, we would have been confident of—'

'Please don't! My mother has nothing to do with this.'

He put up a hand in apology and smiled. 'We don't wish to cause hurt, Miss Barton, of course. But it's clear to us that if Lady Wilshere had remained at Marlford, then this conversation would never have been necessary. She was such a young woman when she came, hardly older than you are now, I suppose—'

'The same age.'

He inclined his head very slightly in acknowledgement. 'But her influence was immense.' He glanced for the first time at his friends, for validation of his assessment. They both nodded. 'We grew to trust her extraordinarily quickly. And she grew to trust us. To rely on us, I would say.'

'I don't quite see what you want,' Ellie said. 'I've heard these stories before.'

'We're simply making known our concern, Miss Barton.' Ata paused. 'We're beginning to find your father – well, unreliable.' He wiped his hand across his mouth. 'He's very much the youngest son, I'm afraid, and ever since we first had the pleasure of his acquaintance, well… of course, he was thrown after the war – coming back a hero, and finding there was no one to come back to.'

'We've advised him as best we can, given the circumstances,' Hindy muttered.

They looked at her, expecting something she did not understand. She glared back in return; they had never before called him a hero, she was sure of that, and she found the idea irritated her.

'I have a great deal to do.' She took a step towards the door but it was clear they would not let her pass; they shimmied very slightly sideways, blocking her exit.

'We simply want to speak to you, Miss Barton,' Hindy said.

'But what about? Not about the van again, surely? I really don't see what I can do.'

'You're the future of Marlford, Miss Barton.' Hindy made it a simple fact. 'We have to speak to you. We're old men. When we're gone—'

'Oh, wait – no.' Ellie felt a stab of fear. 'I don't see how I'm the future of Marlford. Not at all. With all the debts and Papa and… you're mistaken.' She tried again to escape, pushing forwards towards the door.

Luden hooked his arm through Hindy's to brace their line. 'We hoped for sons, of course – everyone did,' he said. 'We spoke to your mother a great deal about it. But, in the end, circumstances being as they are, there's just you. It's an outcome we all have to accept, however painful.'

Ellie felt her cheeks burn. 'How dare you? How dare you say things like that?' It was not as angry as she had intended. She heard her own distress too clearly.

'Miss Barton, we just want to help,' said Ata. 'We regard it as our duty…'

But she could not listen to any more. She threw the sack down and pushed past them, flinging her arm hard against Luden's bony shoulder. She might have called out, she was not sure; all she knew was that she was running from them, ripping through the long, damp grass, her tears choking her.

Turning into the woods, following a line of old trees, Ellie pulled through the brambles and trailing ivy, the hawthorn that snatched at her arms. She ignored the pricks and grazes; she went on too fast, her dress tearing, pushing on, deeper into the wood. She did not know where she was; she had no sense of Marlford, only of the clasp of foliage around her and the men somewhere behind, tilting space, so that no matter how fast or how far she ran, she was always tumbling back towards them.

Bursting out at the far limit of the woods, she was brought up sharply by the sudden cleanness of the sky, and the boundary fence at the edge of the estate, with a crop of barley sparkling beyond. A figure was sitting on the metal railings, precariously balanced, his back to her approach.

He was so out of place, such a breach in the confusion of her thoughts, that she did not recognize him, but there was something in the curve of his silhouette that drew her, and she went on watching him.

She stood quietly, knowing only gradually that it was Gadiel. Even then, it was several minutes before she spoke. 'Did you find a garage, to fix the van?'

He continued to be still; she thought he had not heard her. When he finally turned to her, he seemed grave. 'No. Not yet.'

She went up to the fence and followed his gaze across the field. 'It's a nice day.'

He resisted her pleasantries and slid down from the railing. 'I felt we might be out of line,' he said. 'Last night. Turning up like that.'

'Oh, no – not at all. Hardly anyone comes. No one comes. But that doesn't mean...' She pulled at the fabric of her dress in an attempt to conceal the rips, then worked with quick fingers, gathering up her disordered hair and pinning it tightly. 'It was a pleasure to meet you. I'm just sorry that supper wasn't more elegant.'

'I enjoyed it.'

'Did you? Good. That's good.' She dabbed at a graze on her arm and, for a while, nothing more was said. She wondered at his silence but she liked the way it settled between them, and did not disturb it.

When he finally spoke, it was with reverence. 'This is such a beautiful place.'

'Oh, I don't know...' She was taken aback by his solemnity. 'It's not what it was.'

'That's what makes it beautiful, don't you think?'

This seemed a remarkable statement.

'I could show you around one day, if you have time. There are some lovely corners left, even now. And you might be here for a few days if you're waiting for the van to be mended.'

'I'd like that.' Gadiel smiled at her. 'But I've explored a fair amount already.'

'Oh, no, not just around the village—'

'I wasn't at the village.'

'Weren't you? But you found somewhere to sleep?'

He brushed something from his arm. 'Yeah, fine, and well... I came back and had a look round. That was all right, wasn't it?' He spoke quickly, not allowing her time to answer. 'And so I've seen quite a lot. I was up all night. You can see quite a lot in a night.'

She could not believe this was true. 'I was up early, too.'

He shook his head. 'No – all night. I never went to bed.' He laughed at the look of dismay on her face. 'Don't worry. It's not a crime. We tried to get the radio going so we could listen but there was hardly any reception, so I thought I'd come out and watch the moon instead. But there wasn't much to see.' Patchy clouds had quilted the dark; there had been few stars, the sky flat and homely. 'It was a shame, though, about the radio. Did you hear it?'

Ellie fiddled with a crusted spot of rust on the fence. She had no idea how to reply. So she shook her head.

'You missed it, too?' he went on. 'It's miserable, isn't it? It feels like we've missed out on something massive.'

He offered her a sad smile; she did not understand the sympathy in it.

'But I hung around outside, anyway. I needed the air.'

He reached out and took her by the hand, peeling her fingers gently from the fence. 'And I found something. Something amazing. Come on, I'll show you.'

He ducked under the lower railing and led her over the uneven ground that skirted the field. After a while, they turned back towards the manor, looping right with the mere at their backs, dipping down into a kind of dell, shaded by overhanging trees; huge slabs of coloured quartz, stabbed through with grass, rose in tortured walls high above their heads, closing them in, so that Marlford was out of sight, leaving just a rough sky and an uneasy sense of isolation.

'It's the rockery,' Ellie said.

'Just wait.'

'It's not natural. It was a fashion. They wanted to create a kind of magic landscape. It was a romantic construction – it's not real.'

Gadiel did not seem to be listening. He pulled her on, sinking slightly into the moss which banked up under an old silver birch but when a fern grazed softly against his leg he stopped, glancing down, and was suddenly aware of her hand in his. 'Oh, sorry. I didn't mean…' He let go and stepped to one side. 'Look.'

She knew what it would be. In an almost perfect circle of flat ground, enclosed by the largest of the rocks, there was a fantastical stone zoo: a host of small dogs with wings; angelic cats sprawled side by side; horses almost in flight; a petrified piglet with a slumping belly; a rabbit; two owls and a peacock; a mongoose; a kangaroo and some kind of monkey, all draped with stone veils and shrouds, wings stretched, magnificent. The muddle of growth was trimmed here, the statues brushed free of lichen and grime. The animals sat proud of the grass, glaring at the intrusion.

'It's the pet cemetery.' Ellie hardly moved.

Gadiel walked forward into the circle and bent to caress one of the dogs. 'Really? That's what it is? All this?'

'It was my mother's. She was very fond of animals. She kept all kinds at the house – a sort of menagerie, really. When they died, she had these memorials commissioned. They're all buried here, around and about.'

'But they're fab. A bit weird, obviously – but really fine workmanship.'

'I believe one or two of them cost a great deal. They were the work of quite well-known sculptors.' Ellie paused. 'But most of the originals have been sold to museums – these are just concrete, just replicas.'

Gadiel came back towards her. 'Your mother must have loved her pets a lot. To do all this for them.'

'She did. She doted on them. That's what I've been told. The dogs especially – she was never without a little dog. I suppose they were company for her. She was sad, I think. She came here when she was very young. It must have been very hard for her.'

'You never knew her, then?'

'No. She died when I was born. There were complications at the birth and she just... faded. But I've been told all about her. And I think about her all the time. So it's as if I knew her, I suppose.'

There was only the slightest of pauses, and when Gadiel spoke again his tone was bright.

'Last night, when I found all this – well, it was dark and I was lost – I'd been walking for ages, thinking about things – and I thought I'd slipped into some kind of enchanted wood.' He laughed uneasily. He did not tell her how long he had stared at the animals, paler then in the half-light of dawn, more distant, more celestial. 'It was scary.'

Ellie laughed, too. 'I'm sure you could have fought them off if they'd turned savage.'

'What, a herd of magical stone animals? How strong do you think I am?'

It made her glance at him, his broadness. She frowned and looked away, fixing her gaze on the false angels. 'It's nice that you've shown me.'

'But you knew it was here, anyway.'

'Yes, of course. But, even so. I don't come here on my own.'

'I thought I'd discovered something amazing.' He walked a few steps away.

Ellie felt fixed to the spot. 'Oh, but you have. It's quite rare, these days, this kind of thing. My mother was old-fashioned; not many people of her age… well, it is quite amazing, in its way.'

He looked at her. 'But you don't like it, do you?'

She was quiet for a moment. 'I've never liked it. I think it's grotesque.' She seemed forlorn. 'But I've never told anybody that.'

He wanted to hold her. Even if he could take her hand again, that would be something. But he did not dare.

'It gave me a shock, in the night, I can tell you,' he said, too brightly again, making it too much a joke.

'Yes, I imagine it would,' she replied.

*

They walked on, emerging from the dip of the rockery, awkward together. The morning felt oddly indefinite. Ellie did not know what to make of this boy alongside her; she found she was puzzled by the sway of his T-shirt, and his scent, like fresh vegetables.

Gadiel spoke again as they made their way across open ground. 'Look, Ellie – about us coming to the house, and the van, and Dan—'

'Oh, it doesn't matter.' She was quick to answer.

'You see, when we left you last night—'

'There's no harm in the van staying at the stables for a day or two; no harm at all.'

'No – it's not that.' He fell silent again.

'Really,' she said. 'If you want to leave it...'

He stopped and turned to her. His hair was shaggy from the long night outside, his face pale and stubbly, his lips dry. Even the colour of his T-shirt seemed to have been drained by the demands of the morning. Framed by the tree trunks of the old woods, he seemed part of the land, his physical strength offering some kind of protection; Ellie could not help but think of fairytales.

'Look, I'm not making much sense, I know.' He tried to settle his voice. 'But, you see, I can't tell you everything, not yet, even if I wanted to, but... but, Ellie, listen...' He paused, closing his eyes momentarily before beginning again in a new tone. 'Anyway, me and Dan'll be around for a few days. You might see us. And if you need anything – well, we can talk again.'

'I rarely spend much time in the village,' she replied. 'There's no need.'

'No, no. I suppose not. But, well, you never know.'

Just then, the stable clock struck, the tinny notes seeming to shimmer on the mere, a faltering memory of many days.

'Oh.' Ellie was flustered. 'I'd no idea it was so late. I have to go.'

He shrugged. 'Fair enough.'

'The clock runs late anyway, and I have to go to the library.'

'Really – it's fine. It was nice.'

'Thank you,' she said, as if he were releasing her, and she hurried away.

Eight

A thin mist hovered low, a breath of damp air creeping across from the mere, silvering the grass, but above it the day was becoming bright and clear, solidifying. Ellie slipped quickly through the haze, the dew soaking her legs, chilling her.

Oscar called to her from a distance. 'What's that, Ellie, at the stables?'

She stopped, not quite sure what she might have heard.

'Ellie!'

He swiped his stick ahead of him in the long grass, sending water spraying into the air; there was, just for a moment, a fluorescence around him, sparkling bands of colour. She reached for the stone balustrade that marked the edge of the old lawns and attempted to anchor herself there; if she went towards him, she knew, her perspective would shift and the rainbow would vanish.

'Ellie? There's a van – in the stable yard.'

He was ordinary by the time he reached her, his coat sagging and wet.

'Yes, I know,' she said. 'It's broken. They're sending someone to repair it.'

'Who? Who's sending for someone? Whose vehicle is it? The men came first thing this morning to tell me… and I had no idea – I could not imagine… there's a vehicle there, Ellie.'

The impact of such an alarming idea slapped him to a halt.

'Didn't they tell you about the visitors?' she asked.

'No. They simply directed me towards the stable yard, at which point I discovered the vehicle.' He looked over her head in the direction of the manor as though the van might at any moment come hurtling towards them through the neglected gardens.

'Well, never mind… it's all right, Mr Quersley. I know. I know about the van.'

'I supposed you must. I supposed somebody must. But I wasn't prepared for such a thing.'

'It's just being parked there until they come to mend it. I agreed it would be all right. It's not in the way. Some people came to the house with it. I tried to tell you.'

He hardly seemed to have heard her, and she did not know where to begin or what she might say. It was like remembering a windy day: there was only an impression of billowing voices, insubstantial colour, a buffeting sense of something extraordinary. But she could not have said exactly how it had been, nor could she have adequately described it.

'It's rather an eyesore, Ellie. It should be removed.'
She held quite still. 'I like it.'
'Don't be ridiculous. How on earth can you like such

a thing? It doesn't belong here.' He looked about him, reassuring himself that everything else was as it should be: the line of oaks that marked the furthest extent of the old gardens; the thickening trees towards the mere; the balance of earth and sky in this particular horizon, so perfectly known. 'It was a shock to see it there, and I'd prefer it was removed. It's not my place, of course, to take charge of things beyond the farm, but if you need my assistance with it – I can make arrangements, Ellie.'

She shook her head. 'I think it's all right. I'm sorry – I should have said something sooner, I suppose.'

'Yes, well – now that we're clear. We are clear, aren't we, Ellie? It cannot remain.'

'They promised to have it towed,' she assured him.

There was nothing else to be said, and they began to walk, leaving the park and taking the narrow path to the village.

Scaffolding had been erected on the side wall of the Hepworth Barton Bank, securing it against the sinking land, its accurate angles and solemn pediments giving way to the clasp of the metal poles. A little further up the street, they noticed a new crack in the road; further still, a dribble of muddy water on the library steps caused Oscar to crouch and shake his head. But, inside, everything was as it should have been. Until their routine was interrupted by the unexpected appearance of two boys.

'It's about transport, miss,' the boys explained to Ellie. 'It's our holiday homework. Modes of transport.'

They sat side by side at the table by the desk. She brought them books about ships and trains, old maps of canal routes and several technical pamphlets tracing the development of the motor engine.

'The information might be a little dated, I'm afraid. You see, we haven't acquired any new books in rather a long time.' She glimpsed Oscar out of the corner of her eye, stern, flapping his hands hard at her in an effort to prevent such gossip. 'But there's something about bicycles somewhere, I'm sure,' she added, trying to ignore him.

'What about aeroplanes, miss?'

'Oh, no, I don't think so.'

'There's that Concorde plane – the new one. We've heard about that. Have you got anything about that? That's so cool.'

'No – really. I don't think so. I'm sorry.'

She did not entirely understand the request, but she saw the boys' disappointment.

'I'll have a look though, to make sure. Why don't you get started on those for now?'

When she went along to search the stacks, Oscar followed her. 'You'll put people off coming, Ellie, if you make out the library is somehow – lacking.' His whisper was sharp; he tidied a row of books so that he would not have to look at her.

'It's true, though, isn't it? In all my life I don't remember us acquiring any new books.'

'Sssh! They'll hear you.'

'They're just boys. They're ten years old.'

'Such rumours are insidious.'

She was suddenly, inexplicably, tired of it all. She moved on down the narrow stack and pulled out two books on bicycles. She held up the first to him: its blue card cover featured a drawing of a penny-farthing being ridden by a very upright gentleman in a top hat. 'You see, Mr Quersley?'

He snatched the book from her and opened it, holding it up in turn so that she could see the frontispiece: the Barton family crest, magnificent in green and gold; a bookplate inked in blue in an elaborate hand. 'This, Ellie, is one of the original books with which your grandfather founded the library in 1895. It's a very significant piece of history, and tangible evidence – for future generations – of his philanthropy and foresight.'

'But what good is it, now, to those boys?'

She had never asked such questions before. He stared at her.

'What on earth do you mean?'

She wished she could explain, but he looked at her with such uncomprehending anxiety that it confused her all the more.

'I don't know. I just thought… I'm sorry, Mr Quersley, I've got a lot on my mind.'

'Take the books to the readers, Ellie. And then perhaps we can do something ourselves, something to settle us – Shakespeare, perhaps? That would be nice.' He blushed, smiling at her with sudden warmth, but she had already walked away, carrying the books to the table and showing them to the boys.

She knew immediately there was nothing to interest them and although, for a while, politely, they bent forward over the illustrations of old bicycles, they wrote nothing.

Soon enough, they forgot even to turn the pages.

Tired of the pretence, one of the boys suddenly leaned

back, swinging the chair onto its back legs. 'What did you think of Neil Armstrong, miss? Wasn't it fab? We watched it at Mrs Turton's – it was just fab.'

It was the most mysterious of questions. Ellie came across and, looking over their shoulders, studied a page of dense text that appeared to discuss the geological requirements for laying level rail track.

'I'm sorry,' she said, at last. 'I don't know what you mean.'

The boys laughed and nudged each other, liking her the more for her joke.

'You haven't got anything about that, miss, have you? Nothing about Neil Armstrong? No books about that, not yet? It wouldn't be out yet, would it, miss?'

Ellie could not find a way through their gibberish, but she smiled at them anyway, because their exhilaration was so startling.

'No. I'm sorry. I don't remember anything by Neil Armstrong. I would know the name, I'm sure.'

They did not mind. 'It'll be on telly again, I bet. All the time. We'll see it again. We'll ask Mrs Turton.'

'Ah.' She was beginning to grasp something at last. 'It was on television. I see.' She laughed at being taken in by their enthusiasm and shook her head, flicking the world back into place. 'You should be reading books, not watching television. You'll learn a great deal more from books – a great deal more. Let me find you something on shipping. My grandfather was involved with several shipping lines; there'll be some excellent books, I'm sure. Just wait here a moment.'

She hurried again to the stacks, smiling still at the boys'

odd excitement. She spent several minutes browsing the shelves on the back wall, edging slowly along, running her hands over the familiar spines and ignoring the archive boxes of deeds and papers, the lines of periodicals and tracts. It seemed important to make the right choice, and she was methodical and intense in her search.

She picked out two volumes, wiped their covers with her sleeve, and lodged one of her fingers at the page with the most impressive illustrations of steam ships. But, as she turned to retrace her steps, she noticed that there was another reader in the library, crouching by one of the shelves, his back to her.

'Oh, my goodness – I'm sorry – can I help you?' She stared at the loose fall of his shirt, unable to think quite what to do with such a visitor. 'If you're looking for something in particular…'

The reader did not answer her. He kept on scanning the books.

'Hello again,' he said at last, still crouching, looking at her askance. It did not seem a very clever greeting after such an expectant pause.

'Dan – I didn't expect to see you here. I never thought…' She could not go on; she found she could not be entirely sure, for a moment, that it was him; it seemed already as though she might simply have imagined him, a wish.

'No. I suppose not.'

Ellie gripped the books close to her body. 'Are they coming to fix the van?'

'No, no – not immediately. It's nothing like that. I just came in to the market, to stock up. I'm… shopping.' He stood up. 'I noticed the library and came to investigate.

I find books irresistible.' He pushed at his spectacles, his mouth set hard.

'Oh, yes.' Ellie was breathless. 'So do I. I remember the lines and say them back to myself, when I'm on my own. It's a whole world to me, the world of books. Sometimes I think it's saved my life.'

He took a step away from her. 'It's more study, for me. Textbooks, you know, and political commentaries.'

Ellie dropped her gaze. 'Oh, yes. Of course. Yes, I see.'

'Do you work here then?' He nodded towards the stacks.

'Well, I suppose so.' She was surprised by the idea. 'I assist Mr Quersley – he's the librarian.'

'You didn't say you had a job.'

'Well, it's not a job, as such.'

'What is it then?'

'I'm not altogether sure.' Her smile faded. 'Look – I have to take these books to the boys. I promised them.'

But he followed her, and, after she had delivered the books, they went out onto the front steps, as though they had agreed it, standing by the open doors, watching the drift of the street.

When Oscar emerged from the stacks he saw them standing together, on the threshold. He stood quite still for a moment, trying to take in such an unexpected sight, and then he rubbed his palms with sudden ferocity on the sides of his trousers to clean the dust from them.

Ellie caught a glimpse of the movement out of the corner of her eye.

'Oh, Mr Quersley. This is one of the people...' But she had not told him about their visit to the house, and knew she could not say anything now. 'I met him yesterday,' she said instead. 'And already he's come in – to the library. As a reader.'

'A reader?'

Ellie supposed this must be why he had come. 'I think so.'

Oscar was unprepared for such an unlikely claim. The visitor seemed very young, rather shabby. There was confidence, arrogance even, in the way he leaned towards Ellie. Perhaps there had been a mistake.

'Ah – I see. Yes, very well. So you'd like to join the library, sir?' His doubts leached through, unwelcoming.

Dan bristled. 'Actually, I was just looking.'

'It doesn't cost anything to join.' Ellie was encouraging.

'That was one of Braithwaite Barton's express conditions. All this' – Oscar gestured briefly at the dingy rows of books nearest to them – 'all this, for the people, for free, for ever.'

'It's fine. Thanks, man.'

'We're available four evenings and two mornings a week, and by appointment, if necessary.'

'Yeah, I was just looking.'

'So – you don't have a particular interest, sir, which drew you here, with which we could assist, perhaps?'

Dan looked away from him, back to the street, where a woman wheeled a pram cautiously around one of the fractures in the ground. The uneven slump of the roof-lines opposite seemed somehow ignominious.

'I'm into political economy, actually.' He faced up to Oscar now, a challenge. 'Well, political science in general, I suppose.'

Oscar was surprised. 'Machiavelli?'

99

Dan shrugged. 'Only as history.'

'You're a scholar?'

'Kind of, I suppose. I'm at university, and I read stuff. All kinds of stuff.'

Oscar rubbed his hands again, more fiercely. 'But you don't study Machiavelli?'

'Not much. Why would I?'

'Why?' Oscar seemed astounded by the question. 'If I may say so, I would have considered a grounding in Machiavelli essential to a proper understanding of political science – indeed, to an understanding of how politics works anywhere, of how the world works anywhere – even here, in Marlford. We have several copies of *The Prince* in the library collection, one of which I have annotated with some care. I can direct you to the entry in the catalogue, if it is of interest.'

'Yeah, well… thanks, but I think I'll give Machiavelli a miss, man.' Dan smiled tightly. 'It's a bit – out of date.'

Oscar reeled at the slight. 'I think you're mistaken. I consider it timeless. I find it unerringly apposite – I refer to it without hesitation.' His eyes settled on Ellie for a moment, narrowing, as if he was making a calculation.

When he spoke again, his voice had lost its enthusiasm. 'May I ask who it is, then, that you read? Perhaps John Stuart Mill?'

'You want to know?' Dan sniffed while he considered his answer. 'Well then, Marx. And Guy Debord – and Lukács, of course.' He uttered the names carelessly. 'They're modern, you know. Modern thinkers, man. Have you heard of them?'

Oscar did not answer. He had found a loose thread

on his sleeve and pulled it out between his thumb and forefinger, twisting it hard before pulling it sharply to sever it from the tweed.

When the emergency tailoring was complete, he spoke abruptly. 'I'm not sure this is quite your thing, Ellie. I think perhaps I should deal with this request myself.'

'I don't think we can help him at all, can we, Mr Quersley?' she replied. 'I've never seen any of those names in the catalogues. I would remember.'

He glared at her, a warning. 'Perhaps if you could continue your research with these two little boys. They seem to have finished with the volume on automobiles.'

The children were comparing the length of their middle fingers by measuring them with a wooden ruler, the books pushed to one side of them.

Dan gestured loosely at the packed shelves. 'I take it you haven't got anything, then? No Debord hidden away amongst the knitting patterns or Mrs Beeton, or whatever it is.'

Ellie collected the books from the boys' table. 'It's a very good library,' she said, firmly.

'Yeah, man, I suppose. If you need to read up on etiquette – or the rules of billiards.' He snorted a quick laugh but did not quite meet her eyes. 'Looks like the place is falling down, anyway. Perhaps that's for the best.'

Ellie was stiff. 'If you need me, Mr Quersley, I'll be with the boys.'

'Yes, yes. That's quite right.' Oscar offered her a slight bow and then moved thoughtfully towards Dan, addressing him in a strained undertone, anxious that Ellie should not hear him. 'Young man... the names you mentioned

– there's nothing quite like that in the collection, I admit, although as regards historical material—'

'The world moves on, man.'

'Well, yes, indeed – quite so. And the philosophy of political economy is one that interests me a great deal. Perhaps if we were to talk—' He felt the buzz of possibility in his head.

'No, I don't think so. If there's nothing to read, I'd probably rather help Ellie with her work.' Dan shrugged. 'Thanks, man.'

'Miss Barton does not work.' Oscar was suddenly too loud. Everyone looked at him, surprised; even the two boys glanced at him fearfully, in case they were in trouble.

'No?' Dan was confused. He frowned at Ellie. 'I thought you said—'

She tried to explain. 'No – I meant... you see, the Bartons – I'm a Barton...' But it all seemed too embarrassing suddenly, too complicated. 'Well, it's a hobby, I suppose. A kind of a hobby.' She placed the books down very carefully on the table, brushed the front of her skirt and felt each of the pins in her hair. They watched, her distress mesmerizing.

'Here – miss?' One of the boys leaned towards her kindly, holding out a page torn from his notebook. 'We've drawn you a picture of Neil Armstrong on the moon. Look, you see? In his spacesuit and everything. You can have it if you like.'

She took the gift and stared at the bulbous figure, crudely done, smudged, but somehow astounding.

'I listened,' Dan said. 'Well, sort of. It crackled on and off, so I didn't get much – it was only on the radio at the squa—' He stopped himself just in time, glancing quickly at Ellie. 'Yeah, well, it was a shame, man, with the radio, but even the bits I caught… it was amazing.'

Ellie's interruption snapped between them. 'Do you know what this is, Mr Quersley?' She held the drawing towards him.

'It's Neil Armstrong.' Dan winked at the boys.

She ignored him. 'I can't make head or tail of it.'

Dan stared at her. 'Don't you know?' He paused, looked hard at her. 'Man, you really don't know, do you?'

She stiffened. 'No,' she said. 'I really don't know. There are many things I do know, but this is not one of them.'

'But that's the moon landing. Neil Armstrong is one of the astronauts on the Apollo 11 mission. You must have heard of it? Even here – surely you've heard of it? Don't you have a radio, even? Newspapers?'

She still held the paper out. 'Mr Quersley?'

Oscar cleared his throat. 'We haven't talked about it, Ellie.' He took the drawing from her at last and glanced at it. 'It's very good, boys, very good.'

'But I don't understand.'

Dan's eyes were wide open. 'My God – you really haven't heard—'

'This is… something has happened? This man, this Mr Armstrong, has landed on the moon?' She tried to piece it together, but Ellie had nothing more than the boys' drawing and the bizarre expression worn by Oscar Quersley. 'Is that right?'

She looked at Oscar, unbelieving. He nodded.

'Surely you must have—?' Dan began again, but she cut him off, her anger crisp, translucent.

'A man has walked on the moon. And you've kept this from me? Something of this – magnitude?'

The boys were giggling.

'No, no, Ellie – no.' Oscar shook his head, a series of quick apologies. 'I haven't kept it from you. You misunderstand – I've done nothing on purpose. It's simply that we haven't discussed it. Remiss, on my part, perhaps, but not purposefully obstructive. I just didn't consider that it might be – important.'

'Important?'

'Relevant, then. Not relevant. There didn't seem the right moment, when it would have been relevant.'

She snatched the drawing back from him. 'This is mine.' Her voice was rasping, like dried leaves on old stone. 'I'll leave you to finish here, Mr Quersley. If you could.' She gestured towards the boys, who stifled their giggles and cowered, afraid that Ellie might come at them and shake them in her anger, but she simply walked out, crossing the street and disappearing from view as a lorry passed.

'Blimey!' Dan whistled through his teeth.

'She can sometimes be imperious,' Oscar said. 'It's her breeding. It comes naturally.'

'No, not that, man – I mean, not knowing about the moon landings. Not even knowing that.'

Oscar did not quite answer. 'I've known Miss Barton all her life. I have a great respect for her, a great admiration,' he said, instead.

Dan shook his head. 'Well – that's like… that's evidence, isn't it, man? Right there – of just how isolated these kinds of people are. How obsolete.' He pressed his spectacles against his nose and pushed the curl of his hair behind his ears. He looked out after her, following the line she had taken down Victoria Street.

Oscar noticed the stiffness of his stance, his anxious lean forwards as though, perhaps, he wanted to go after Ellie, or haul her back. He busied himself by helping the boys to pack away their homework.

'But, you know, even though she's such a dinosaur – there's something about her, man, isn't there?' Dan added.

Oscar accompanied the young readers to the front steps, wiped down the table and piled their books away neatly. Only then did he speak again.

'Perhaps I should have made sure she was better informed.'

'But it's not your job, man. It's what I said – it's the decadent elite. You can't be held responsible for all that.'

Oscar finished tidying laboriously, as though Dan was not there, then he took up his position behind the desk, standing very straight, with his hands on the open day-book of loans.

'She probably should have known about it,' he admitted, quietly. 'I could have told her.' He slid his palms over the ledger, pressing into its solidity, and then, with a sudden, brisk gesture, he said, 'But, young man, allow me to tell you about the Braithwaite Barton Memorial Library…'

Nine

Gadiel sat in the sun on the stone rim of the fountain. A breeze skimmed across the flat land and the flashes of waste brine by the chemical works, squeezing up the terraced streets and blowing spray now and again onto his skin. The hours that crept so slowly at the squat, demanding and accusative, lay more gently here. Cars came occasionally, circling the nymph; women walked up from the cottages and headed towards the centre of the village; a tractor started up on the playing fields behind, making growling passes up and down the cricket pitch. This slight activity added to the sense that nothing was happening.

He did not want to think of Ellie again, or the unsettling intimacy of the odd arrangements at the manor, so, while he smoked, Gadiel tinkered with perspective, trying to hook smoke rings over the top of the works' chimney. The task was more difficult than it looked: when he blew out a ring, he found that the chimney was not quite where he had expected it to be after all. Getting to his feet, he hauled himself up onto a higher ledge and perched alongside the water nymph, wrapping his arms across her bare shoulders, steadying himself by gripping the loose folds of her stone gown in his fist. She pushed her tipping urn against his chest, as though he might help her with the weight. He dangled one leg over the trickle of water and puckered hard, leaning, so that he could puff his smoke ring high and true. Still it squirted away.

He shuffled around the fountain, the reflections from the tiles slapping blue squares onto his skin. Facing Braithwaite Barton, looking towards the pull and plunge of the roofs at the centre of the village – the confident strata of brickwork thrown into confusion by the sag of the land – he saw Ellie, coming quickly towards him.

Gadiel started. He pulled away from the nymph, breaking the steady trickle of water as he jumped down, brushing his hands over his clothes and flicking away his cigarette; it fell into the shallow basin with a hiss. He started across the cobbles that flared from the fountain, his legs oddly unstable.

She was wearing an odd kind of shawl: a poncho knitted in two shades of faded pink, fringed with knotted wool in a selection of pastel colours. It hung limply over her shoulders, longer at the back than at the front. She had not seen him yet.

He took a long breath and stepped forwards. 'Hello, Ellie.'

She looked at him, her eyes wide. 'I had no idea – that there'd been a man on the moon.'

He was going to laugh, but then he recognized the same expression that he had seen on her face when they were in the billiard room – anguish only barely concealed, closer to the surface now, about to break through. He was worried that she might crumple there in front of him.

'Look – why don't we have a walk?' he offered. 'I've been hanging around here for ages. I could do with stretching my legs.'

'No, no. I have to go.' She went to pull away. He knew that she hardly saw him.

'Look, Ellie. I don't know what the matter is, but I'll help. Whatever it is – honestly, I'll help you.'

He brushed his hand playfully against the fringe of the poncho, and Ellie watched the tassels dance between them.

All he saw was the way she looked down.

'Ellie, really – I didn't mean to say anything wrong. Don't be angry.'

'Oh, no – no, it's just – I don't know what's happening. At the library, they told me about a man called Neil Armstrong. Some little boys told me – young boys, hardly more than ten years old.' But it was Oscar Quersley's crumpled expression she remembered, and Dan's astonishment. 'I don't know anything about it.'

Gadiel only partly understood. 'Is that all it is? But, look, there's stuff about it everywhere. If we go to the newsagents we can probably pick up one of those special editions. They'll have all the facts in there – if there're things you want to know.'

'I want to know all of it.'

He laughed. 'Come on, then.'

But her eyes were hard and dark. 'That's what you meant, when we were talking in the woods – when you were talking about listening on the radio. I didn't understand.'

'I thought you were a bit vague.' He tried to preserve

his smile in the face of her anger. 'That's why I went out to look at the moon, you see – I mean, I didn't expect to see space rockets or anything, but you know…' His voice trailed away.

'I didn't understand,' she said again. 'I had no idea what you were talking about.' She looked at him, pleadingly. 'Why didn't you tell me? Why didn't you tell me about Neil Armstrong?'

'I thought you knew. I thought everyone knew.' But he saw that he had let her down. 'Look, Ellie, let's go and buy some papers or something. You can read about it – everything about it.'

He offered her a hand, but she swept by him, her poncho tassles swaying as she went on ahead.

'It'll be too late, though, won't it?'

Gadiel waited under the striped awning outside the newsagents, leaning back against the wall, one foot propped against the brickwork. He watched the customers across the street at the sunken fishmonger's: only the top section of the shop door was visible, the rest of it was buried beneath the pavement. Alongside, the wide window, too, was mostly hidden below street level; what remained was jammed open with a cut-off broom handle, creating a narrow aperture through which the fishmonger passed out a paper packet. His head barely reached the knees of his customer, who stooped low to take his fish and pay.

Gadiel only slowly took in what he was seeing – the unlikely angles of the skewed window and door, a child's drawing of a shop front – and, before long, he was distracted by the far-off chime of an ice-cream van.

By the time Ellie emerged from the shop, he was bouncing impatiently from foot to foot, blushing violently with the prospect of pleasing her. 'Do you want an ice cream?' He beamed at the magnificence of the proposal.

Ellie gripped her magazines hard to her chest, as though he might threaten to steal them from her. 'An ice cream?'

'Yeah, from the van. It's not here yet, not quite, but I can hear it. Can't you hear it?' The tune was coming louder, the notes more shrill. 'We'll go up to the top of town. Meet it up there.'

'Wait – Gadiel – I can't…'

'It'll only take a minute. Come on, have a treat. Have a treat on me. I can hear it getting closer.'

They pushed back up towards Braithwaite Barton just as the van trundled into view from the edge of the salt pits, orange and crimson trumpets on its roof spewing an elongated nursery rhyme.

As Gadiel set off towards it, waving, Ellie gave in to the sense that the day was beyond her, distorted and strange. The chimes played one more loop then stopped, making everything oddly hushed.

She sat on the bench at her grandfather's feet, placing her magazines neatly beside her. Gadiel brought two ice creams, the thick, bright red sauce dripping onto the pavement leaving a trail that might have been blood – his hands were already scarlet.

He held one of the cornets out to her and settled against the wide base of the statue, licking the gloop from his fingers.

Ellie held the treat at arm's length and studied it. But

she was too slow: her scoop of soft ice cream, inadequately sculpted, slunk from its cornet and landed with a soft *splat* on the pavement.

She could not bring herself to look at the mess, grubby pink, already watery. It felt like a desecration.

'Never mind – share mine.' Gadiel held his cone towards her.

She shook her head. 'Thank you. There's no need.' Her voice was grainy, threatening tears, but haughty, nonetheless. She rose from the bench and stepped away from her grandfather's protection, turning her back so that all she could see were neat flowerbeds, inscribing perfect parallels either side of a raked gravel path.

The sun was in Gadiel's eyes. He squinted at her while he licked ridges in the dome of his ice cream. He thought there was something new in her bearing but perhaps it was just a trick of the light, the smudge of rough shadows.

He watched a while longer. She was still, half-turned from him, her chin lifted to the sky. He saw how much she looked like the statue above them.

'All done then?' He felt he ought to speak, otherwise his quiet scrutiny was too much of an intrusion. 'Shall we head back?'

'Yes, thank you. Thank you for waiting.' She glanced at the magazines on the bench and said then, with desperate intensity, childlike: 'I want to go home.'

She led him from the gardens. They skirted the repair works in the street and walked briskly down the slope. Ellie did not glance at the library. She continued purposefully beyond the nymph and up an alleyway by the almshouses, quickening her pace as she drew near the kissing gate.

Gadiel offered his arm. She took it without looking at him but also without hesitation; he drew her close. She gripped the magazines in her free hand with new determination.

She tried to picture them walking together. She auditioned a variety of scenarios, flicking through them like picture postcards stacked in a tray, but none of the images would hold steady; they would not quite come clear: her imagination failed her. She was thrown back to their unremarkable tread, the broken surface of the old driveway, the unkempt limes, the soft green light webbing around her, the strength of his arm beneath her hand, and something she could not determine, a thrill of some kind, an ache.

They were in sight of the manor. It had never looked so beautiful, the façade shadowed, the windows dark, the domes imposing in the slanting sunlight. The brick tower had somehow sloughed off its utilitarian ugliness; it seemed solid and reassuring, its plainness confident. The scattered weeds of the gravel drive, the sinking roof of the portico, the shabby flowerbeds: all this seemed as it should.

Ellie saw the men sitting together on one of the stone benches on the terrace. They had a long, wide view from there, the whole of Marlford laid out before them. They would have seen her approach with Gadiel, she knew that.

Then she heard the stable clock strike, a long succession of unsteady notes. She broke from Gadiel's arm and hurried on more quickly, alone. 'I need to read this,' she called over her shoulder, gesturing towards him with the magazines.

He caught up with her. They had not finished; there was so much more to say. 'But, Ellie, we were having a good time.'

'Yes – exactly – you made me forget.'

'Forget what?'

She glanced towards the men, but from this distance she could only guess at their expressions.

'About Neil Armstrong. About the boys. About everything.'

Gadiel was halted by the ferocity of her accusation. He stood still.

She pushed on more quickly, the green and yellow sense of summer, the swirl of heat and colour adding to her muddle, everything unexplained, nameless and formless.

After a moment, Gadiel began to follow her, wary. 'Ellie, don't run off. Just stay and talk for a moment.' Before she could reply, he had slipped his arm under the drape of her poncho, the pink wool flowing over him like molten marshmallow. 'There's nothing to worry about, I promise you,' he said, simply. 'We'll sort out everything. Even the man on the moon.'

She gasped at the feel of his hand around her waist; she had no idea what to make of it. She was so intent on its weight, its warmth against her, that she could not keep hold of her bucking thoughts.

'No – please. You should go back to the village now. Please – go. Go away.'

She glanced again at the men, and pushed at him. They were both surprised by the force of it.

Ten

Their pace was dictated by Luden's shuffle: a slow, stately progress, filing along the side of the Victorian extension, briefly passing a blocked door and two windows in the Georgian style, turning the corner under a round, pinnacled tower, working their way inexorably towards the low roofs of the medieval buildings. They might simply have been taking a walk back in time.

Luden stopped on several occasions to catch his breath; as the expedition continued, he reached for Hindy's arm, leaning heavily. Once they paused to examine a crack in one of the flagstones, shaking their heads at it sadly and poking round about to determine the cause, but they negotiated the turbulent contours of the pitted courtyard with steady determination and went directly to a wooden door, its grey paint peeling. They stood in front of it, in a line, crenellated, their differing heights a makeshift comedy.

Ata took a small, square tin of 3-in-1 from his pocket and put the nozzle into the keyhole, squirting until oil spilled down the door like hair tumbling from a clasp, then he fitted the key and turned it smoothly. The door gave inwards with a creak.

They were immaculately prepared: Hindy had two torches, one in each of his jacket pockets, their batteries new, their beams bright; Ata had a further selection of keys, each on its own length of string, tied together at the top in a heavy, impenetrable knot. He hung them over his wrist and arm; they jingled as the men went on into the house. Luden sniffed noisily. It did not seem impossible that he could smell out their route.

They could see Dan with his back to them, boiling a kettle on the hob in the cavernous kitchen. The scuff of their steps was inaudible over the breathy almost-whistle of the rising steam and they watched for a while, Luden stabbing an angry finger at the pile of broken glass kicked into the corner behind the door.

They took in the signs of haphazard habitation: empty tins, dirty plates at one end of the long deal table, a carrier bag spilling groceries onto the floor by one of the dressers, stubbed-out cigarette ends in a blue saucer.

'Young man?'

Hindy spoke up, but Dan only cocked his head, not sure what he had heard.

'Young man – you, at the range.'

Dan gasped and spun round. 'Blimey, man... what? I thought I heard something. You crept up on me, man.'

'Might we ask what you are doing here?'

Dan found that his hands were trembling. He stuffed them into his pockets. 'Who are you, anyway?'

116

Hindy repeated his question, not varying his intonation. 'Might we ask what you are doing here?'

'What are we doing?' Dan began to gather himself. He moved from the range, placing himself squarely in front of them so that they could fully appreciate his defiance. 'We're squatting.' He pushed at his spectacles slowly, taking time to settle them on his nose, folding his arms across his chest.

'Squatting?' Ata squeezed the question, rattling keys.

Dan caught the lilt of his accent and noticed the bronze lustre in Ata's thin face, the almond curve of his eyes.

'Yes – do you understand?' He spoke slowly for the benefit of the gangly foreigner. 'Squatting. It's a word meaning… meaning… well, you see we—'

Hindy interrupted, in his perfectly honed English. 'Young man, of course we understand the notion of squatting. We just don't understand why you're squatting here, amongst us. In this house. At Marlford. Perhaps you would care to explain?'

Dan raised his eyebrows at a patch on Hindy's tweeds, then turned back to the range.

'Miserable vermin.' Luden was still breathless.

Dan lifted the kettle and set it aside. He watched the steam rise for a moment before turning back.

'It's an official squat.' He took in Luden's expression of withered disgust, the thrust of his sharp chin. 'By installing it here amongst the waning influence of the privileged few, we're proposing a reversal of ingrained social and financial hierarchies. We're proposing a new social order. A revolution, man.'

The men kept their eyes steadily on his face.

'You'll have to leave,' Hindy said.

'Oh, no, you can't force us to leave. That's the thing about a squat, an official squat. And there're more of us on the way. It'll grow, man. It'll draw together a community of like-minded people. It'll become a genuine movement for change.'

Luden stepped forward with a slight, compact movement. 'What you are doing is illegal. If you do not leave the property immediately, we will call the police.'

'That won't do any good.' Dan smiled. 'Squatting's a civil offence, not a criminal one.' He was certain of this, smug.

'A matter of splitting hairs,' spat Luden. 'You are trespassing.'

'No, we're not. We're in the unoccupied part of the house. You see, that's why we're squatting. We'd only be trespassing if we were in Mr Barton's part of the house.'

'It all belongs to him, though. It's all his house, isn't it?' Ata asked. 'Couldn't he be said to be occupying it, but simply not using it all at any given time?'

The question seemed reasonable.

Dan glared at him. 'No, man, only a section of the house is inhabited. The remainder is abandoned – derelict – a common resource.' He took a deep breath, clearing his head after the confusion of Ata's sophistry. 'The question of ownership is irrelevant.'

Hindy sighed. 'Young man, take our advice and leave. This is not your house; you have no rights here. When Mr Barton discovers your presence, he will be sure to take action.'

'He can't evict us by force, man. He has to get a possession order.' Dan was on confident ground again, delivering the rubric with authority. 'There are protocols, you see.'

'Not if he has a gun,' Ata pointed out, amiably.

Luden chuckled at the idea, but Dan had recovered himself and was scathing.

'Flushing pheasants? Hunting to hounds? Oh, come on, man. He's not going to shoot us,' he snapped at them irritably. 'I don't see what you've got to do with it, anyway. You've not told me who you are, or anything. What's it to you if we're squatting?'

Hindy raised his eyebrows at his colleagues. 'It has a great deal to do with us, young man. A great deal.'

'You want to join us, man, is that it? You want to be part of the new generation?'

'We simply cannot allow this kind of intrusion,' Hindy replied, steadily.

'They've changed the cupboard,' Ata said. He held quite still, the keys quiet. 'There.' He stared at a point on the old unit next to the stove.

Dan started to laugh. 'Home improvements, you see – part of the bargain.' But he felt the men stiffen. 'Oh, come on – all we did was make a handle, man, so we could store our stuff in there. We just twisted a bit of string.'

Hindy glanced at Luden. 'It appears rather a singular situation, requiring careful consideration.'

'Get rid of them.' Luden shrugged.

'Yes, indeed. But an affair of this nature… if we're not careful… Perhaps – young man, could you summon your colleague?'

Dan shook his head. 'I'm not "summoning" anyone. It doesn't work like that, man. There's no one in charge here;

it's a democracy.' He waited for them to respond, but they went on looking at him in silence. He shifted his weight and pushed at the bridge of his spectacles again. 'What about a compromise? I could take you up if you like, to the squat.'

'Stairs.' Luden thrust his head sharply towards the ceiling. 'I'm not climbing stairs.'

'I know, old chap, I know.' Hindy put an arm on Luden's shoulder. 'But it might be for the best you know.'

Ata added encouragement. 'We'll be rid of them all the quicker.'

Something about the performance was suddenly intimidating. Dan broke from them and went to the door. 'Do what you like,' he said. 'I'm going up anyway.'

Hindy coughed loudly. 'Haven't you forgotten something?'

Dan paused. 'What? No. What on earth—'

'Your kettle, young man.'

'I don't want that, man. Not now.'

'But it's fully boiled,' Ata pointed out. 'You can't waste it.'

Dan looked across to the kettle as though it might be the most remarkable of objects. 'Look, leave the flipping kettle, man. If you want to come up, then come up. Otherwise...' He rolled his eyes and ran his hand through his hair. 'It's no big deal.'

He did not meet their gaze. Instead, he flung a final glance at the kettle and left the kitchen, his steps slapping on the tiles.

After a moment, the men followed, Luden's breath coming in short, loud puffs. They did not keep pace with

Dan but pushed slowly through the echoes he left behind, climbing the stairs with difficulty, finally squeezing three abreast into the confines of the bedroom corridor. The bunch of keys jangled on Ata's arm like the rusting chains of tortured phantoms.

Dan and Gadiel sat on the bed; the three men brought in chairs and positioned them at intervals around the room.

'You've made some changes,' Hindy began. 'Aside from the obvious removal of furniture and the matter of general detritus, there's a cracked floorboard, I believe, and an improvised repair to the windowframe.'

'One of the doorknobs in the corridor has been reattached,' Ata added, sharply.

The men looked at each other. They did not smile; Ata closed his eyes, resting his head against the thick flock of the wallpaper and tucking his legs tightly together, trapping the keys between his knees.

'You live here, don't you?' Gadiel was pleasant. 'On the estate. I've seen you coming to the house. I've seen… Ellie, she…' It sounded too much as though he might have been spying. 'It's nice to meet you.'

'Yes, we live here,' Hindy replied. 'We're prisoners of war.'

Dan laughed and rolled into the slump of the bed.

'I don't understand,' Gadiel said.

Hindy began wearily, as though the old story was worthless. 'We were incarcerated here at Marlford in 1914. We arrived within weeks of each other and, being considered a threat to British interests, we were placed here securely as aliens. I am German, of Russian decent;

121

my friend here, Luden, is Austrian; and Ata is a Turk. At the beginning, during the war, there were many more of us and we were kept quite separate from the house but, after Armistice, everyone went away, quite suddenly, and those of us who remained made a home here. When Mr Barton returned, he chose a few of us as companions. We continue to live in the hutments of the old prisoner-of-war camp, on the southern flank of the estate towards the main road; we consider ourselves residents of Marlford.'

Luden and Ata appeared content with the summary.

For a moment, no one spoke; it seemed too fantastic a thing to begin on.

Dan broke the quiet first. 'I don't understand, man. Do you mean – really… do you mean prisoners?' He seemed to be accusing them of something.

Hindy was unperturbed. 'Yes. I believe I've given a full explanation.'

'But you just stayed?' Gadiel added, more gently. 'Why on earth didn't you go home? Why did you stay at Marlford?'

'We became fond of the place,' Hindy replied. 'We had established ourselves here and had very little reason to leave. And Mr Barton took an interest in us.'

'We took an interest in him,' Luden said.

Hindy smiled. 'Indeed.'

'On Mr Barton's recommendation, we adopted new names.' Hindy made the introduction, indicating each of them in turn. 'I became Hindenburg, my friend here became Ludendorff, and that gentleman became Atatürk.' He looked at Dan, taking in his blank expression. 'You're probably too young to understand the significance of the names, but in 1918, during the war, these were the names of important men, military strategists. Powerful men.'

'I've heard of Hindenburg – wasn't there a line or something?' Gadiel asked. 'Or a wall?'

The men were silent.

'Yeah, well, I know the names,' Dan said, his confidence unconvincing. 'It's just I don't see the point.'

'It helped him remember us, I think,' Ata explained.

Luden sniffed a dry laugh. 'He believed he had the enemy under his nose, where he could keep an eye on it.'

'But you don't still use those names... after all this time?' Gadiel asked.

'Of course we do. It's part of being here, for us. Marlford has made us who we are,' Hindy replied. 'I'm not sure I can remember what I was called before.'

'I am the same,' Ata agreed.

'That's impossible.' Dan knelt up on the bed, shoving a curl of hair angrily from his forehead. 'Everyone remembers their own name. I don't believe you.'

The men's gaze was steady.

'It's not impossible, young man.' Hindy sat up straighter, a challenge. 'It's as we've told you it is.'

'No way, man. Listen—'

Gadiel intervened. 'And there's just you three; there's no one else... no other prisoners?'

Hindy kept his eyes on Dan, but answered pleasantly enough. 'There are three of us remaining. The majority of prisoners were rehoused or deported, or just went away. There were four of us originally who stayed: one of our number died eleven years ago, from an aggressive form of cancer.'

123

'I think you're lying,' Dan said. 'I think you're having us on, man. It can't be right. It doesn't make sense. No one would stay so long.'

'Indeed. It is a long time. A lifetime,' Hindy agreed. 'We're old men now.'

'You do mean the First World War?' Gadiel asked.

'I do. During the Second World War, they established a small military unit here at Marlford, but that was different, quite different. And by then we were established as Mr Barton's companions. We arrived, as I have outlined, at the beginning of the conflict in 1914. We've been here for fifty-five years.' Hindy sat stiffly, upright and smart, his tweed jacket neat. The shabbiness of the room seemed suddenly significant, the stains and cracks, the tears and blots and chips betraying the illusion of permanence.

'But all this time?' Dan narrowed his eyes, pushing at the rim of his spectacles, still doubtful.

'We regard it as time well spent. We couldn't have done better,' Ata replied. 'What could we have done that would have been better?'

'You could have gone somewhere. Got jobs. Lived lives – man, I don't know. Surely there was something you wanted to do?'

The men sat back in their chairs. There was a moment of quiet.

'There is nothing we have ever wanted more than this,' Hindy said.

Gadiel spoke quietly, with reverence. 'I can't imagine what it'd be like. To be here all that time.'

Hindy smiled. 'We've rather enjoyed it.'

'Oh, come on!' Dan slapped his palm against the

bedpost, affronted by their games. Tiny flakes of rotting fabric floated around him. 'How could you enjoy it? You said you were prisoners.'

'Indeed. We were.' Hindy stretched, preparing to rise, a signal. The other men shifted in their seats. 'But that was a long time ago. I was simply recounting our history for you. As a matter of interest. But you should know that we really are quite happy with arrangements as they stand. Quite happy. Our freedom is in no way curtailed.' He looked at his watch. 'Now, we should report your presence to Mr Barton.'

Dan slid from the bed with a thud. 'Wait! When I brought you up, you said you wanted to talk.'

'We've decided the best thing is to tell Mr Barton,' Hindy continued.

'What do you mean? You can't have decided! There's not been any kind of discussion, man.'

'We've seen enough,' Luden said.

'If we told you about ourselves, perhaps...' Gadiel began. 'Would that help? If we explained our intentions?'

'I don't think that interests us,' Ata answered.

'Your intentions are clear,' added Luden.

'How? How can they be? If you won't talk – if you won't listen...' Dan flapped a frustrated hand at them. 'Why did you bother coming up if you're just going to sit there?'

'We wanted to see what was going on. We wanted to consider. And we've considered,' Hindy explained, evenly. 'And now we shall inform Mr Barton of your presence here, and recommend action.'

'No way! You've no right to do that, man.'

'Isn't the purpose of a squat to confront ingrained social customs? To publicly advocate an alternative means of domestic organisation?' Hindy smiled. 'And isn't the effectiveness of such a gesture rather diminished if the existence of the squat remains a secret?'

'More like a camping holiday,' Ata said.

'It's not a gesture, it's more than that and' – Dan tugged at the bridge of his spectacles – 'we're just starting. We're the advance guard, that's all, man. There are others coming.'

'We hadn't decided how to tell them – Ellie and Mr Barton,' Gadiel explained. 'You see, it's not a personal attack on them in any way…'

Luden stretched out the stiffness in his hands. 'I don't want to waste time. I want to get this finished; it's dragged on long enough.' He glared at Dan. 'You're intruding.'

Ata stood now, too. His keys clinked.

'But you don't have the right to do this,' Dan protested. 'It's a betrayal – of our efforts, of our common situation.'

'We have very little in common with your situation,' Hindy replied.

'But you do! Don't you see? You're the oppressed, man, like us. You explained – you're prisoners here.'

'You don't appear very oppressed,' said Ata.

Dan was loud. 'You don't know what you're doing. Come on, think about it. You haven't thought it through.'

'You'll find we've thought it through entirely,' Luden replied.

The men smiled at Dan's anger, a ripple of shared satisfaction.

Dan scowled. He looked at Gadiel, but Gadiel was

standing quietly by the window, his arms folded and his feet planted, watching the men quite calmly.

'We will wish you a good day.' Ata moved away, his keys rattling quietly. His companions followed him from the room. They did not wait for a reply.

Dan kicked at the bed frame. 'Man, why didn't you say something, Gadiel? Why did you let them get away with it?'

Gadiel looked at him steadily. 'They're probably right, don't you think? Don't you think Ellie and her father should know?'

'But they're holding us to ransom, man. It's not fair. It's not… it's iniquitous, that's what it is.'

'It won't be so bad.' Gadiel sat down wearily on the bed, waiting for the creak of the springs to subside before speaking again. 'It'll just mean everyone's straight with what's going on, that's all. Anyway, what could I have done?'

Dan snorted. 'You're the strong one, aren't you?'

'And what do you want? Do you want me to beat up three old men?'

'Don't be stupid, man. But we're supposed to be in charge here. We're squatters, man – we've got the power of the people.'

Gadiel lay back, his sigh swallowed by the puff of the old mattress. 'Perhaps they're bluffing. Perhaps they won't go through with it. They seemed weird enough.'

'We need a plan of campaign,' Dan said. 'I'll come up with something. I need time to think, that's all.'

Ellie was surprised to find the men in the study at this hour. She paused at the door. 'Is something wrong?'

'It seems we have interlopers, my dear,' Ernest replied, turning slightly to acknowledge her arrival. 'Those blighters with the van.'

'They're squatting,' Hindy said. 'Occupying the house. Apparently it's a political statement. They've taken root in the kitchen and disordered the bedroom corridor. They have established some kind of headquarters in the room with the gold four-poster.'

Ellie tried to keep her voice calm. 'Well, they could stay for a while, couldn't they? Since we know them.'

'They have to go, Miss Barton.' Luden narrowed his eyes at her. 'Immediately.'

Ernest could not stay still. His hands ran over chair backs, the table; he pulled at his trousers. 'It does seem rather absurd,' he offered, gingerly.

'Absurd?' Hindy was scathing. 'Mr Barton, it's insupportable.'

'They deserve to be flogged,' Ata added, amiably.

'Oh, now wait—' Ellie began.

But her father was already taking his cue from the men. 'It's true.' His tone was hardening. 'I don't want yobs traipsing round my house. It's my bloody house. It's Marlford, after all.'

'After all,' Hindy agreed.

'But, Papa, you know they're not yobs. You met them yesterday. They're perfectly nice.'

Ernest glanced across at Luden. 'They're trespassing. They shouldn't be here. Should they?'

The old man shook his head slowly, with mechanical regularity.

'Exactly.' Ernest spoke too quickly. 'Exactly.'

'They might find out what happened here,' Hindy said. 'They might begin to ask awkward questions, Mr Barton.'

Hindy's suggestion seemed to unleash sudden energy in Ernest. He began to dart from side to side, in case the squatters were hidden perhaps, tucked away in dark corners, or cowering behind the sideboard. 'I'll get the police.' He slammed his fist against a section of empty shelving; the split wood moaned. 'I'll get the bloody army.'

The three men shuffled more closely together, closing ranks. Ellie stepped forwards from the doorway, but they turned their faces towards her. She took it as a warning and stopped.

'Better to deal with the affair yourself,' Hindy suggested, calmly, directing his attention back to Ellie's father.

'Indeed,' Luden agreed. 'Better get rid of them our own way.'

Ernest bit his nails.

'Haven't you always kept Marlford safe?' Hindy went on.

Luden fixed Ernest with a steady gaze. 'More or less.'

'And you could secure it – everything,' said Ata.

Luden snorted. 'Or you could stand there and let them rampage, and lose it all.'

Ernest looked hard at the men, his resolve stiffening.

'Mr Barton, out of respect for the family legacy, and as master of such a place…' Hindy did not need to finish.

'I'll shoot the lot of them.'

He announced his intention quietly. There was no reply. He raised his voice. 'Ellie – get me my gun.'

She did not move. She was pale and fixed, insubstantial

129

against the stones of the long wall.

'Ellie! Gun! I will not have strangers in my house.'

With a sudden lunge, Ernest pushed past Ata, grabbed the poker from the set of irons at the fireplace and strode towards the door, brushing his daughter aside.

'Papa! Wait!'

Hindy restrained her. 'I should be careful, Miss Barton. We shouldn't get involved.'

By then Ernest was out of the study and in the hall, the poker fixed at a defiant angle, an old soldier.

Ellie groaned. 'You've made him do something terrible,' she snapped. 'How can you just stand there? You've set him off again and now—'

'We simply made him aware of his duty,' Hindy replied, amicably.

'No. No, you know that's not it – you know.' She felt them moving towards her, in a line, impregnable. She backed away. 'If something terrible happens, it will be your fault… if he does something terrible…' But her accusations deflected back, like water running against a dam, and the men were still advancing. 'Please – don't…' she pleaded. 'You know what I've said is true.'

'Miss Barton—' Hindy began.

'No.' Her ferocity silenced him. 'I'm going for Mr Quersley,' she said. 'I'm going to the farm.' And she slipped away from them, hurrying across the hall as her father had done.

But Oscar was not to be found. She searched the yard and the barns, completed the perimeter of the farmhouse, scrambled over the gate that led to the wood store, and ran to the hay meadows through the flat moan of small insects.

Standing on top of an old stile, balancing herself with one hand against a tree, she willed the slight, black slice of him to appear against the mottled summer foliage. But there was no sign of him: just a glimpse of the mere, and the church beyond. Only the idea of him remained, a tiny kink in the familiar panoramas, as though he were just passing through.

All she could do was return to the house alone and wait.

Her father came home a long time later, after dark. She heard the air sigh as the front door was pushed open; a few moments later, her candle flame convulsed. She left her bedroom, stood in the corridor and listened. There was just the blunt sound of Ernest's unhurried footsteps on the stairs.

Her bedroom was at the very end of the corridor, no more than ten yards from the squat. As the flame from her candle leapt and flickered, her shadow cavorted against the barricade. Even though she was motionless – stretched taut by the sounds of Ernest's arrival – the spectral girl behind her danced, unstable, frolicking against the newer bricks, edging into the cracks and joints, beckoning. Ellie felt the movement like the flit of a bat or a bird. She tried not to look at it. As soon as she returned to her room, she closed the door and extinguished the candle, preferring to undress in the dark.

The room was as it had been since she was a child: clean and plain, more or less empty; the single bed, pushed into the corner by the window, a heavy wardrobe occupying the wall opposite. A photograph of her mother stood in front of the mirror on her dressing table, her hairbrush to one side and a small sheaf of banknotes tucked behind. Her shoes were at the foot of the bed, where a rag rug pulled up towards the faded green counterpane; on the wall was a sampler worked at Marlford many years before, in tiny confident stitches, knots of faith in the future.

Ellie sat at the dressing table to pull the pins from her hair, her features barely visible in the dark mirror, a breath across the glass. She touched the photograph, imagining Elizabeth Barton, the warmth of her mother's face against her fingers.

The manor creaked. She undressed and slid into bed. But the night seemed strange; everything had changed. There were people in the house now, not far away. She thought of them playing cards, or dominoes, or dice, perhaps reading by the poor light from their candles. She thought she began to catch the faint, alluring smell of them, a warmth, the tingle of their breath.

She sat up, unable to sleep, the dark congealing about her. She felt her heart pumping hard; she could hear its rhythm in the empty spaces of the house. She was consumed with a sudden loneliness that was entirely new.

When Ellie finally lay down, she pushed her face into the mattress, forcing the pillow over her head. But even with the familiar smells of old linen and the comforting grumble of the oak beams, she had the queasy feeling of being thrust far away in a tin rocket, piercing the fabric of space, hurtling along at enormous speed, the stars and the moons shivering in her wake, her velocity so great that she was conscious only of a thick, buoyant slowness, an elongation of time, glutinous and distorted.

Eleven

Gadiel came to the edge of the portico and leaned on a column, sheltering from the steady rain, waiting. Beyond, at the bend in the drive, where the soaked grass hung long over the gravel, he saw the three men. They seemed unperturbed by the weather. They did not move and made no attempt to signal to him. They simply watched.

He tried to ignore them. As Ellie came round from the stable yard, her face hardly visible under the droop of her mackintosh hood, he jumped forwards, springing towards her.

'I'm not supposed to make friends with you,' he announced.

She pushed her hood from her face and looked at him coldly. He had not expected this, and for a moment he hesitated.

'Apparently people like you have privatized the country for your own benefit.' His enthusiasm sounded too strained now, rehearsed, but he pressed on. 'For generations, you've taken food from the mouths of the disenfranchised poor by monopolizing the best land for your own use and luxury.' He shook his head in mock disappointment. 'So now we're not allowed to be friends.'

'You didn't tell me,' she replied. 'You didn't tell me that you'd come to Marlford. You didn't tell me about the squat.'

Gadiel's smile finally drained away. 'You know? They told you?' He nodded towards the men.

'They've told Papa to get rid of you.' Rain dripped from the bottom of Ellie's mackintosh, darkening the fabric of her skirt.

'Oh, no, he can't do that. You see, squatting's a right—' He caught sight of her expression and stopped. 'I'm sorry,' he went on, weakly. 'I did want to tell you.'

Now that he was in front of her, she found that her disappointment at his betrayal stung more than she had imagined: it was physical, engrossing, like bees beneath her skin.

'You didn't tell me about Neil Armstrong and Apollo 11, did you? Even when we went to the pet cemetery together and... and now this, about the squat, when you could have told me.'

'It had to be a secret, Ellie. Dan wanted it kept a secret. I'm sorry.'

She did not acknowledge the apology. She was determined to maintain her composure, her distance. She had expected too much of him, she knew that now.

Gadiel saw the way her hands were clasped in front of her, curled tight, her nails digging into her palms. 'Look, Ellie – it doesn't matter. You know now, that's the main thing, and it needn't make any difference. We can—'

'Of course it matters. Don't you see? I invited you to Marlford, as guests. I accommodated your needs with regards to the van. And that implies a certain amount of trust, and you have thoroughly betrayed that trust.' She glared at him through the rain.

He wondered, for a moment, if she was beginning to weep; it was not clear with the drops falling so steadily on her face.

When she spoke again, her voice had lost its tone of reprimand. 'I thought you were taking account of me,' she said, softly.

He scuffed the gravel with his boots.

She was suddenly frightened that he might try to touch her, perhaps hold her. The idea came unbidden, unwanted, settling timorously like a mayfly over water. She stepped away.

He started, as though her retreat had pricked him. 'Come on, Ellie. Cheer up! Let's make the best of it. I'm bored to bits being stuck indoors. Let me do something to help you. You're always trudging past going to work. Let me help you.'

'Thank you, I'm fine.'

'Surely there's something?'

'No. Thank you. I greatly appreciate your offer of assistance, but there's nothing to be done.'

Her hauteur was unassailable again; Gadiel could not find a way to answer it. 'Come on, Ellie. Don't be like this. Don't hold it against me. It was Dan's idea. It wasn't up to me. And, besides, we're not doing any harm up there. We've not damaged a thing. You can come and see for yourself, if you like.'

'Thank you. I'd rather not.'

135

'Oh, Ellie, come on. This is stupid, being like this. Let's be friends.'

The rain still fell heavily between them. Ellie pulled up her hood again, over her hair, allowing it to fall low on her forehead so that her expression was obscured. 'I'm mistress here at Marlford,' she said. 'I have a right, I have a duty, to know what happens.'

'Ellie, I've known him a long time. We've always been mates. I couldn't just blurt it out – I had to stand up for him. I've always done that.' He paused and smiled an apology. She did not say anything. 'I've never let him down, Ellie.'

'Very noble.' Uttered so scathingly, the word unsettled her, drawing her eyes somehow towards the broad sweep of his shoulders. She looked away quickly. 'But you've put me in a very difficult position,' she continued, sharply. 'With the van in the stable yard – and the invitation to supper. I could be seen to be complicit. They'll think I had something to do with it.'

'What? Who will?'

Ellie inclined her head very slightly towards the three men. Her hood slipped.

'Oh, come on, Ellie. No one will think it's your fault. How can it be your fault?' Gadiel stepped towards her.

They were close now. She could see the flecks of colour in his stubble; she knew how softly his eyes had settled on her, how hopefully.

She concentrated on the patchy gravel between them.

'You didn't think about me at all, did you, when you intruded into Marlford like that – unfairly?'

'Yes, Ellie, I did, I honestly did. Dan will tell you…' Gadiel reached out and drew her to him for the slightest of

136

moments; so short a time that she was never sure whether she had actually lain there against the damp cotton of his T-shirt, or whether she had pulled away at his first touch.

She shook herself hard, her hood falling down and raindrops scattering from her. 'I'm afraid I can't overlook what's happened. You should have told me about the squat. I should have known.'

When Gadiel looked at her, his face had taken on an odd, aged sternness. 'Yeah, well, I've said I'm sorry. There was nothing I could do.' He kicked at the gravel again. 'Look, never mind. Forget it. I've tried to explain, but you won't have it. I'll go and see if Dan wants anything in town.'

She heard his footsteps, too brisk. She slapped her wet fringe from her face and stuffed her fists into the pockets of her mackintosh. One of the seams tore. With a quick movement, she ripped the rest of the pocket from its stitches and flung it away from her. It settled in a clump of dandelions, a false yellow.

When Gadiel had gone, and Ellie had walked on towards the hutments, the men held a conference of some length. Luden threw several stiff gestures at the front of the manor, although there was nothing obvious to prompt his anger; just broken panes here and there, and an accumulation of moss, pigeons nesting on the wide sills, feathering the grainy stone and staining the wall below. There might have been a moment of disagreement, Ata turning his back on his companions and walking away to the edge of the drive, but if that was the case, it was quickly resolved, and, at the end of it all, the men took the track towards Home Farm with new determination, their age no hindrance despite the ruts underfoot. They linked arms as they walked, celebrating, as though they had settled a conundrum, or won a wager.

Twelve

Penned in the stable yard, the shadows moved slowly. The day hardly seemed to progress at all, the morning trapped between the high walls and fallen roofs, the clock tolling out a unique interpretation of time.

Oscar examined the van undisturbed, tracing connections and wires, inspecting plugs, caps and cables, beginning to understand. He found the oil reserve, identified the radiator, the battery and the spark plugs; he became absorbed by deposits of grease around the carburettor, spending a long time wiping them away, layer by layer, with a clean rag. As he worked, the rain poured down his face, soaking his collar and shoulders, chilling his back.

'What on earth is this thing?'

Oscar yelped, pulling up sharply and cutting the back of his hand against a rough edge in the engine. He rubbed angrily at the scrape. 'I didn't see you, Mr Barton.'

Ernest was staring at the van. 'What *are* you doing, Quersley?' It dawned on him that the vehicle must be connected in some way with the squatters. 'Are you in league with them?'

Oscar pressed the cloth against the seep of blood from his hand. 'With whom do you suggest I might be in league, Mr Barton?'

'The bloody kids rampaging all over the house.' Ernest was fully dressed, a maroon tie knotted neatly at his collar, his dark suit more or less clean, a brushed overcoat slung across his shoulders. He carried a huge black umbrella, like bats' wings, held so high above him that the rain continued to splash in beneath. 'I've been looking for you, Quersley – don't know where the dickens you've been hiding. I need your help with them. Though, of course, if you've already defected to their side—'

'Mr Barton, I have not defected to anyone's side. I am not in league with anyone.' Oscar dabbed with care at the cut on his hand. 'I presume you refer to the squatters. The men came to the farm and informed me of the situation. They suggested you might be requiring my help.'

'Squatters! That's what they call themselves, but they're just kids, trespassing. Getting in the way. I want them out, Quersley.' Ernest slapped his hand against the side of the van, making it ring, almost musically. 'I want them out of Marlford.'

Oscar considered Ernest's palm, flat against the rainbow paintwork. 'One of the young men – a Marxist, I understand – came to the library. We discussed one or two matters of some interest, actually.'

'There're two of them, that's all.' Ernest was not listening. 'A bolshie one with specs and another long-haired one, solid though, built like a proper man. Better have a shot at them before they start multiplying, that's what I say.'

He stood straight. In his suit, with his hair combed, he looked younger, stronger, the athletic bearing of his past rekindled.

Oscar slowly peeled the cloth from his hand and inspected the wound, bending to suck at the broken skin, tasting the worn-coin dustiness of his blood.

Ernest stepped forwards. 'Come on, man – what are you waiting for?'

Oscar did not reply.

'Quersley!' For a moment it looked as though Ernest might hit him; he lashed out, as if to gouge at Oscar's face, but in the same movement let his arm drop.

'Well, I suppose we should evict them,' Oscar said at last.

'Evict them?' Ernest snarled. 'We're not bloody tiptoeing around – we're going to mobilize. I've already spoken to the men. We're going to mobilize, Quersley, that's what we're going to do. That's why I need you.'

Oscar wiped his hand slowly across his face, leaving a smear of engine grease.

Now Ernest lunged for him, pulling him into the open yard by the baggy rim of his overall pocket. 'Stand up straight. Get your wits about you.' He brandished the umbrella towards the rainbow paintwork as though it might be a campaign map, bold lines of attack in bright colours. 'I've given it a lot of thought. Tactically, they're naïve, that's clear. But they're younger than we are, stronger too, probably, at that age. So we've got to be nifty – you know, a bit...' He did a quick-footed jig, shuffling his shoes on the rounded cobbles of the yard, pumping his arms. The umbrella lurched. 'We need something daring. I did a quick recce last night, and I've got it all in my head.

There was an incident at Suez in '15 – a great rollicking risk of a thing. I had four men with me, hand-picked, the best. We'd had information that the Germans were linking up with the Turks—'

He looked past Oscar to the lines of men, the tents and horses, the knot of officers, the sand blowing across from an unknowable desert, the small troop of daredevils waiting for him. The glint of light on his face was from a distant sun.

'Mr Barton…'

Ernest seemed surprised to see Quersley so close. He huffed.

'Look, Quersley, the men point out – and they're quite right – well, we don't want a fuss here, Quersley, with outsiders. No police. No interference. No surprises. That's the way with these old places – you have to be prepared to stand up for them, at all costs. You're born to it, I was born to it – I'm master here at Marlford, and I know what's best. Quersley, the men will back me up on this.'

'I'm sure they will, Mr Barton, but I don't see—'

'The kids have got some claptrap about their rights. They want to make a thing of it.' He grimaced. 'To cut a long story short, we'll need guns.'

Oscar was unmoved. 'Which is why you require my assistance.'

'I've got the rifle, and you've got two shotguns at the farm, haven't you?'

'Yes. Two shotguns in good order.'

'Exactly. That's what I thought. And if I marshal the men, even at their age…'

'But I'm not prepared to hand them over, Mr Barton.'

Ernest blinked, taking a moment to understand what Oscar had said.

'Oh, don't be bloody wet, Quersley. Besides, it might not even come down to shooting them.'

'Nonetheless, I won't let you have the shotguns.'

'Rubbish! Of course you will. And muster a good supply of cartridges, will you?'

Oscar bent down and began to collect his tools, replacing each one carefully in the toolbox. Then he reached up to unhook the release for the bonnet.

'Quersley? Quersley, what are you doing?'

'I'm going back to the farm, Mr Barton. To give some thought to the situation in which we find ourselves, and to milk the cows.'

'Don't be such a fool. We need to get on quickly with this, before they hunker in. I told you, I've been thinking about it – I've worked it all out. Just fetch the damned guns.'

Oscar let go of the bonnet; it slammed shut. At the same time, as though prompted or woken, the stable clock struck the hour. 'I have discussed this with the men, Mr Barton, and we are perfectly agreed: I'm not your servant. You don't pay me any wages; you have no hold over me. I simply live near you – we're neighbours, if you like.' He shifted. 'There was, once, I grant you, a more formal arrangement between our families. But any agreement, written or verbal, has long since expired; you know that. Now I simply help you when I can.'

'Rubbish, you have Home Farm—'

'Yes, my farm. I work it and I take what little profit comes from it. It's nothing to do with you.'

'It's on my land.'

'I've never paid you any rent.'

Ernst glared. 'An oversight. My generosity, that's all – taking pity on you. You're downright splitting hairs, Quersley.'

'Mr Barton—'

'And what about the frogs, eh? What about that?' Ernest jigged again, pleased with the sharpness of his interrogation. 'Why do you go on with that if you're not on the Marlford staff?'

Oscar hoisted the toolbox into his uninjured hand. 'Over time, by custom, my family has helped yours,' he replied, calmly. 'There is history between us – I recognize that, Mr Barton. I can't fail to recognize it. My father, in particular, was diligent in his duties.' His face was pale and fixed, weariness sinking his features; his grip on the toolbox was so tight that his arm shook. But his voice came surely enough. 'Those days have passed. Our obligation was settled, more than settled. You should not now count on me or my loyalty.'

He crossed the puddled yard, shrinking into the gloom of the arched entrance, a workman weighted with tools.

'Oh, poppycock. What are you doing? You're not going?' Ernest flapped the umbrella, making the rain dance around him, unbalancing himself. 'What on earth…? Quersley, be fair.'

Oscar halted. He let the heavy box fall from his grasp and it thudded onto the cobbles. But he did not turn for a long while, holding Ernest at bay with the stiff set of his shoulders. When he finally spun on his heel, he came quickly back, his eyes narrowed.

'Would you make a deal?'

Ernest wrinkled his nose. 'What kind of a deal?'

'The men suggested you might make a deal. In this situation.'

Ernest shook his head sharply. 'It goes against the grain to bargain with you, Quersley. You know that. I should just let you go; should have had rid of you years ago. There's plenty more odd-job men to chase frogs and milk a few cows.'

'Very well.' Oscar glanced purposefully towards the arch. 'Then there's nothing more to say.'

'Wait – wait, man.' Ernest put up a hand. 'For God's sake—'

'I really have to see to the animals, Mr Barton.'

'But I need your help with this. I can't have these people at Marlford.'

'Then you'll need to bargain.'

Ernest sighed, letting the umbrella drop and the rain fall unhindered. 'Quersley, I've given up everything for this place, everything. And I've never quite got it right. I've never worked it out. It's been too much for me – you must have seen that. But now… this is my last chance. I have to save it.'

'I'm not sure such anxiety is entirely justified, Mr Barton. You said yourself – they are just kids. It doesn't sound like much of a threat to Marlford – nor, indeed, much of an opportunity for you to redeem yourself.'

'I need the guns.'

'If so, then you should listen to my offer.'

'An offer? Something you've concocted with the men? I doubt there's much for me in it.' Ernest closed his eyes. 'Well, then, spit it out, man.'

Oscar worked his lips as though rehearsing the words.

His voice would not come at first; then it was squeaky, less impressive than he had intended.

'If I help you with this, will you give me Ellie?'

The question seemed to stop time, leaving the two men suspended there.

'Ellie?' Ernest's voice was small, almost lost in the noise of the rain.

Oscar nodded, slowly. 'In return for my assistance.'

Ernest stabbed at the cobbles with his toe. 'What do you mean, will I give you Ellie? Quersley, it's balderdash. What do you mean? For goodness' sake, I just need the guns and someone who knows how to use them.' He took a long time to fold his umbrella, fidgeting even then with the fastening. 'Explain yourself, Quersley.'

'I think you understand perfectly what I propose, Mr Barton. I'm asking you to consent to a marriage.'

'Against the girl's wishes?'

'Not necessarily. I'm sure you could persuade her.'

Ernest poked the umbrella towards him. 'She has more sense than to fall for you – I'll give her that, at least.'

Oscar caught the tip neatly, thrusting it back towards Ernest with new force, the handle driving into Ernest's stomach. Ernest gave a winded grunt, stumbling backwards.

'You're not helping your case, Mr Barton,' Oscar said, calmly. 'It's a simple transaction. My assistance – my final act of duty – in return for Ellie's hand.'

Ernest steadied himself. 'You won't sneak any advantage by wedding her, you know – she has nothing now and she'll have nothing in the future. She has no prospects, you know that?'

'It would be in the order of things, though, wouldn't it? You would save Marlford. You say you want to save it, and this way you would. I suppose I would be the son you never had.'

'Never.' Ernest was trembling.

'After all these years you can resolve it, Mr Barton. You can be sure of the future.'

'No, Quersley. You ask too much.'

'But think about it. Everything would go on as it should.'

Ernest looked at the man in front of him, wet about the head and shoulders, his threadbare overalls soaked through, his eyes too hard and bright. He saw Quersley's lithe, fretful strength.

'And what if she's not in agreement? What if she doesn't go along with it?'

Oscar did not reply. He seemed to hear Barton's words from a distance, spoken elsewhere, his fatigue, his longing, making everything ethereal. He stood stock still, as though the slightest of movements might split the moment, spilling the flaccid guts of his dreams.

'I think she'll accept it,' he answered, finally. 'She has no birth certificate, she's never been to school, she's hardly ever left Marlford except for the work at the library – she's never existed. Why would she refuse? And there's not a soul on God's earth who would bother to intervene.' The placid light in the yard seemed suddenly dazzling. 'It will be the right thing. She'll see that. She'll do as she's told.'

Ernest frowned. 'I want to get on, Quersley,' he said, weakly. 'I need to get shot of these damned squatters. Otherwise we'll all be stymied, Ellie as much as the rest of us.'

Oscar smiled slowly and offered Ernest his hand.

Ernest hesitated. 'And you say the men have discussed this proposal? It makes sense to them?'

Oscar took a moment to reply. 'Imagine Ellie outside here. If something were to happen to Marlford, if she were pushed out – by circumstances, by the squatters, perhaps. Imagine how she'd be, Mr Barton, how poor and how lonely. She'd crumble like a handful of dry clay.'

Ernest looked up into the ashen sky. 'But if she marries you…'

'Then Marlford will be secure. You'll be protecting it – keeping all the secrets. You'll have worked it out at last, the whole thing.'

Ernest's face hardened.

'You're blackmailing me, Quersley.'

'It's a simple matter of reputation, Mr Barton.'

'This is ungentlemanly.' But he stuck out his hand nonetheless, touching Oscar's briefly.

Oscar blinked, raising his eyebrows in mockery of his own manoeuvring. That such a thing could be achieved so simply seemed a joke of some kind. He could not think of anything to say.

Ernest let his hand drop quickly. 'The guns then, Quersley? You'll fetch the guns?' His questions came uncertainly; his voice had taken on the tremble of age.

Oscar shook himself. 'They need stripping and oiling.' He was matter of fact. 'I'll bring them up as soon as I can.'

'It'll be for the best, Quersley, won't it?'

But Oscar did not seem inclined to discuss the squat any further. He returned to his toolbox, picking it up and swinging it once or twice, his arm straining. Then he walked away.

Ernest watched him disappear into the mouldy gloom beneath the stable arch. He looked around, lost for a moment. The rain drummed on the roof slates, ironic applause. In the polished leather of his shoes and on the soaked stones of the yard he saw his reflection many times: skewed and stretched, fractional, foreshortened, fairground illusions of a man who could not recognize himself or what he had done.

Oscar returned to the farm. He placed the toolbox in an old stone trough sheltered by the barn, slipped off his overalls, folded them neatly on top and rinsed his hands and face in a spray of cold water from the outside tap. The yard swilled with mud, the animals sulked in their stalls. Only the pigs ran to him, squealing their hunger; he pushed them away, glanced at the sodden cows in the near meadow, shook his head sadly at the slung weight of their full udders and moved on quickly along the edge of the field where the hay was flattened and grey, ruined.

His breath came in short, shallow bursts. He could feel the bounce of his pulse in his swollen fingers and aching brow; around him the familiar landscape of the old farm flickered, his vision blurring, his thoughts mired. He walked quickly, hearing only the occasional croak of the frogs. Something had happened – something marvellous and unconscionable. He could not quite grasp what it might be, only a joy and a regret, a kaleidoscopic longing. It was like rolling down a shorn bank on a hot day, tumbling over and over, faster and faster, glimpses of colour one upon the other, a brief scent of grass, a shard of sky, laughter and shrieks, tears, a pain somewhere hard and unwieldy, losing the sound of everything, knowing only the unstoppable motion itself.

It was the distant creak of the frogs, coming to him faintly from the mere, that finally brought him round. He stopped and listened, letting the noise draw him, a comforting burr recalling him to duty and simplifying everything.

Thirteen

As night fell, a rumbling began, deep in the belly of the exhausted mines, rising slowly into the village. The cobbles began to skew, then to sink, the pavements cracking. After that, events moved quickly. As if anticipating disaster, the streetlights went out; a moment later, the road caved in with a sudden crash. Two buildings opposite the library slumped into the crater, tearing themselves from their neighbours on either side. Roof tiles scattered and window glass smashed; stone and timber gave way with an unpleasant groan; a parked car slid backwards into the hole, disappearing; the half-repaired fissure alongside the Hepworth Barton Bank burst open again, spitting rubble and swallowing the scaffolding posts. A number of dogs began to bark.

Braithwaite Barton, unscathed, oversaw proceedings with an avuncular smile. At the other end of Marlford, the nymph continued to pour clean water with careful precision into the blue basin at her feet.

The following morning, when Dan and Gadiel arrived on an expedition to the general stores, they gawped at the crumbling hole, wary of coming too close: there was still the occasional noise of collapse, the groan of rock deep below.

'Do you think… do you think it's safe?' Dan edged forwards, clinging to one of the makeshift barriers. 'It smells disgusting – swampy.' He lifted his boot, gazed forlornly at the smeared leather and wrinkled his nose. A slime of brackish mud oozed around them.

Gadiel looked towards a group of men standing on the library steps. The building seemed to have sunk at one side, its doors were wedged open and a trickle of brine dribbled out, back down the slope of the depression into the worked-out pits that skulked below. 'Do you think Ellie knows? We should tell her. She'd want to know,' he said.

'It's like the whole world is hollow.' Dan tapped gingerly with his foot as if to test the theory. 'As though we could just fall in. It could be a metaphor, couldn't it, man… about how the world's been eaten away by the forces of capitalism? Destroyed from within. Yeah, that's it – eviscerated.'

'We should help.'

'Man, this is such a cool place to have the squat. When the others come and they see the village and everything…'

'No one's coming, Dan. I mean, you haven't done anything; you haven't told anyone—'

'Yeah, but I will, won't I?'

'But why would they come?'

'Why? I've just told you, man – we can make such a cool statement. Even the ground beneath our feet is a statement. The past consuming the present, just like Marx says. Look at it.' He flung his hand towards the hole.

'I'm not sure people will want to come,' Gadiel said. 'I'm not sure they'll understand.'

'Of course they'll understand.' Dan pushed his hair from his face and adjusted the balance of his spectacles with some care. 'Gadiel, I can't believe you sometimes. You don't see things, do you? You don't see the wider picture – the history and the future.'

Gadiel did not answer. He ducked under the barrier and walked slowly around the crater. At the far side, he paused to speak to some of the men. They made slow, wide sweeps with their arms, marking the magnitude of something. The conversation went on, then one of the men laughed and shook Gadiel's hand.

He came back to Dan and offered him a cigarette. Gadiel smoked in long drags, stubbing the butt on the barrier. Only then did he speak. 'They're moving it.'

'What do you mean – moving it?'

'The library, the whole thing. They're pushing it down to the end of the street.' Gadiel glanced towards the nymph, a distance of a hundred yards or more. 'The land there's safer, more stable – not so much over the mine, that's what they told me. And the buildings were put up that way, apparently, so they could be shifted around.'

Dan frowned. 'Don't be stupid.'

'I'm not being stupid. That's the plan. They're moving it. I agreed that we'd help them – well, I said I'd help, anyway. It's something to do with pushing it onto rollers.'

'You've been taken in, Gadiel, you know that?'

'I have not been taken in.' Nonetheless, Gadiel glanced anxiously towards the men still lounging on the library steps. 'It's true, apparently.'

Dan laughed briefly, little more than a smirk. 'Well, then you stay and help them. I'm going back to the squat. It's only a squat as long as it's occupied. And this place' – he gestured towards the hole, the evidences of instability, crevices here and there, lopsided shops – 'this place isn't worth any effort, man. It's not worth saving. Its time has come. They should let it rot and run coach tours here, that's what they should do, to show the decay of, well, of everything.' He grimaced and kicked at the deceptive ground.

'Come on, Dan. It'll be way better than sitting around. And it won't take for ever. We'll just slide the library down.'

'Gadiel – it's a distraction, man. We have a purpose here. A new world order.' Dan turned away. 'You still don't see that, do you?'

Fourteen

Dan saw Ellie at a distance, coming into the village along the narrow path by the almshouses. He waited.

'I've got something to show you.' He took a step or two towards her.

She looked puzzled.

Dan smiled. 'You know you told us, when we came, about the village and your grandfather constructing it on the broken backs of the poor?'

'I didn't say that.'

'You said it. You just didn't admit to it.'

Ellie kept on walking. 'I have a few essentials to collect from the chemist. I'm afraid I can't dawdle.'

'I'll go that way with you.' He trotted casually alongside her. 'That's what I want to show you, anyway.'

'The chemists? It's very kind but—'

He took her arm. 'Come on, Ellie. Don't be stuffy, man. Let me show you.'

The creaks and groans of the village were subsiding. No new fissures had opened, and the wet mud in the streets was already hardening in places, holding footprints.

A plume of steam rose almost vertically from the chemical works; behind, a drift of ochre smoke cast a faint tint of sepia on the flayed land.

Ellie only slowly realized what had happened. 'Oh, my goodness.' She squinted at the gaunt form of the old library. 'Someone should tell Mr Quersley. He'll want to see to the books. He'll want to check everything's all right.'

'There's no point, man. Apparently they're moving it.'

She stared at the building, seeing it already off balance. Dan was surprised to see tears falling steadily down her cheeks, her eyes wide and soft with sympathy, as though she was contemplating an injured animal. She could not speak.

'Ellie, come on, man – this kind of thing was bound to happen sooner or later.' He spoke kindly enough but with an odd desperation, as though she had talked at some length, challenging him, and he had been forced to take up the argument. 'It's a legacy of destruction, from the old mines.' He rested his fingers on the bridge of his spectacles so that his face was partly obscured. 'You see – it's the carelessness of the past catching up with us. Dominant material relationships – that's what Marx called it – the way the ideas and actions of the ruling class affect everything – in the past, in the present and in the future.'

The sight of the library still held Ellie's attention.

'Did all this happen – just with the rain?' she asked at last.

Her mournful glance irritated him. 'Oh, come on, man – haven't you been listening? You knew about the mines.'

She was suddenly fierce in return. 'Of course I knew about the mines. I'm talking about everything.' She gestured at the pit. 'All this.'

156

'Yeah, and the mines are only the symptom... Ellie, the disease is something deeper, more... more – what's the word? – pernicious. That's it, man, pernicious.'

Ellie rounded on him. 'I hardly think this is the time for political generalisations. Your, your philosophy, if that's what it is – it's completely irrelevant. You don't understand, do you?'

'Me? You're accusing me of not understanding? Man, that's rich. When I was trying to explain it all.' But he felt himself draw back from her. 'Yeah, well, quite a shock, I s'pose...' He heard the spite in his tone but could not stop it, not with her looking at him in that way, as though he did not matter. 'Quite a shock for the land-owning classes to discover the land they own has disappeared – zap – down a big, salty hole.'

He saw the little crease of dismay that flickered across her brow at his words and he was ready to defy her hurt, if that was what it took; he held his ground.

But Ellie's face cleared, her anger had already faded. She simply shook her head, sadly. 'But, still... to have happened so suddenly.' She did, finally, look at him then, so gravely and openly that he could not face her. 'And did you say they were moving the library? Is that what you said?'

Dan shuffled. 'Yeah, man, that's what I heard. That's what Gadiel told me. I don't think it can be right, but—'

'Oh, yes, it will be right. It was always planned that way. It's quite possible to slip it out and roll it down to a new location. Rather like moving the furniture.' She smiled at the idea, sliding her hand smoothly in front of him to demonstrate the elegant glide of a make-believe library.

157

Dan took off his spectacles and spent a long time cleaning them on his T-shirt. Ellie watched the rub of cotton between his thumb and forefinger, the occasional glint of the lenses; she felt as though she was balanced on the quicksand of the old mines, everything sinking, disintegrating, the structures of her world twisting, their shapes unfamiliar now, grotesque.

Finally, he lifted his eyes to her face with an expression she did not recognize and took her by the arm, so that they could turn their backs on the library, looking instead towards the unperturbed nymph.

'Why don't we go for a walk?' He was quiet now, purposeful. 'There's nothing going on, not for now – nothing to see. I can explain about the squat.'

The cottages here were undisturbed. Swifts swooped and screeched around the eaves, repeating time; the neat gardens were bright with geraniums and busy lizzies, draped washing and children's plastic toys. There was the sound of radios playing. In all her life, Ellie had rarely walked this part of the village – there had been no need – and she regarded it now with a detached, intense curiosity, as though it was important to record the smallest of details. She recognized the same thrill she felt when she was reading a new book: the prickling urge to take it all in; the lament, even at the very beginning, that too soon it would be finished, and she would know it.

Dan came closer alongside her; she felt the swing of his arm against her own as they walked down another street. It was short, no more than three or four cottages in a truncated terrace, the village ending abruptly, Braithwaite

Barton's vision unfulfilled. Beyond was just scrubland, shabby and flattened, sloping away to a small, stagnant lake of muddy water. Dried salt crusted at the edge of the shallows; another deposit – a tainted pink – seeped through an old pipe and dripped inexorably into the pool. The bulk of the works loomed close, its intricacy suddenly apparent: the grid of pipes laid out tightly ahead of them at ground level, steam hissing from the seams; loops of hawsers, heavy rivets, unmarked sheds, metal ladders; everywhere the ploughed ridges of corrugated iron; light deflected, decomposed, disordered.

They followed one of the worn paths, knocking dandelion heads, dislodging seeds which floated languidly around them, nothing more than thickened air. A brown cat slunk away and disappeared into the scorched grass. Dropping down a slope, they stopped short of the pool, sitting on a segment of ruined wall, its bricks crumbling; the ground was scuffed and trampled, littered with cigarette ends, sweet papers and lurid bottle tops.

From here, the view was of the rear of the works and the wasteland behind, hardening again into short streets. It was a workers' slum, a knot of makeshift houses, split and weary. The roofs and walls were coated in a fine, white dust, as though a perfect snow shower had gently settled, consecrating them, drawing the eye to the bruised brown and grey streets that sliced between.

Ellie only glanced across; she did not really see any of it. She fussed instead with her skirt as she sat down, trying to steady herself on the uneven brickwork, pushing her feet hard against the wall, jamming her legs tightly together, bowing her head.

'It's not actually anything against you and your father as people – just what you represent, in the larger picture,' Dan was saying. He had been talking for a little while, looking at her intently, as though this might drive the lesson home. She found she did not mind it. 'So when the others come to join us—'

'Others? You've invited more people?'

'Yeah, man – it's an open invitation. That's how these things work. Word gets around, man. We expect them soon. The place will gather momentum, you'll see.'

Ellie thought about this for a moment. 'But why would they want to come to Marlford?'

'Don't be dense. Marlford is an excellent example of the way in which power and wealth has been siphoned off for the benefit of the few. By locating the squat at the heart of it—'

'But aren't you very cold up there in the old rooms? Isn't it rather damp?'

He pushed himself off from the wall. 'No, look' – he screwed his face up, drawing his mouth tight – 'it's not… you've got it wrong. It's not like that.' He flapped at a thistle in frustration, kicking at something in the grass and throwing such a pained glance at her that Ellie thought, for a moment, that he might just walk on and leave. But he just cuffed his hair roughly from his face and resettled his spectacles. He stood still then, and set his gaze hard on the cluster of unsteady houses behind the works. It was only after a long silence that she realized his pose was somehow a question, or even an accusation.

'Look,' he said, finally. 'Look at that. You see?'

When he turned to her it was a plea. If she failed to

understand, he would consider it his inadequacy more than hers; she saw that at least.

'I... I'm not sure—' She tried to work out what the revelation might be. 'If you mean the houses... we don't have anything to do with that – we don't own the works or the salt mines, not any more, not for years.'

'You don't have to own them, man. Questions of power and necessity are not always as direct as that.'

'Most of those houses have sprung up since our time. It doesn't look it, I know, but even the chemical works is quite new. It's nothing to do with Marlford – the old Marlford.'

'And you don't ever ask why there's that, over there, falling apart – sinking – people living in rubbish houses, working in the factory, and you, back at the manor, swanning around?'

She giggled. 'Is that what you think we do... swan around? When we're so poor...'

Dan came around in front of her. 'Ellie, you are not poor.'

'Oh, but we are. It's why Marlford is closed up, and why there're no servants, or gardeners even – no one to keep the place. Just Mr Quersley. All the money that my grandfather had, that all went long ago. Long before I was born.'

'I know. Gadiel told me. But it makes no difference.'

'Of course it does. Now... well, we're poor – really poor. It's just – if you don't pay attention – it might not look that way.'

He growled. 'It's not just a question of money in your pocket, Ellie.'

'No, but we don't own the village any more. We don't receive rents. We have no say in anything, no influence.'

She waved at the view he was obscuring. 'You can't blame me for any of this. And, really, I don't mind at all about the squat,' she added, as kindly as she could.

'But you don't see, do you? The squat's part of it, man. You just don't see the iniquities, do you – the inequalities? You're quite happy to let it all pass you by, to go on as you always have, to live in the past like some lady of the manor. Ellie, Marlford itself is… it's a temple to greed and exploitation.' He caught her arm. His desperation seemed odd, unnecessary, wasted on her.

She slid off the wall and pulled away, stroking the place where his touch had been. 'Well, that's a new vision for the place, I suppose.' She smiled. She was tempted to argue with him again, but his frantic reasoning had an innocent charm to it, like the spring twitter of birds, and she let him speak.

'Look at me, Ellie. Listen to me, man – I'll explain.'

She wondered at the unsteadiness of his voice.

'Your grandfather's village – it's about reinforcing the hierarchies that keep the poor in their place. Don't you see?' He did not wait for her to answer. He went on, his hands and eyes in perpetual movement, as though he were performing a trick of some kind, a sword exercise that sliced through the damp air, dazzling. 'It's part of a system of production where workers are just instruments, just things – they're estranged from their humanity, cut off from themselves – their real selves, their thoughts and their imagination – by the system and by the demands of other people.'

Ellie stared at him.

'But at the time – surely,' she began, 'surely what was

162

important was a basic standard of living. I think you're…
I think your approach is anachronistic…'

He was mistaken and obtuse, outlandish too, poised in
this way with outstretched arms, his feet apart in the dry
grass. A glossy, red crisp packet had blown up against his
boot, his hair was curling into his eyes, his spectacles sliding
from the bridge of his nose, the wasteland stretching away
behind, bleak and unpeopled. She should have laughed
him out of sight, disdainful, but she found her erudite
ideas skidding away like sprats in the shallows, nothing
more than a glimmer, disappearing.

And she could not take her eyes from him.

Dan wondered if he had said too much, too quickly,
confounding her with the quicksilver flash of his oratory.
He searched for something simpler that might reassure her.

'Wait.' He reached forward gently. 'Cool, man – look.
You've got a ladybird – just…'

He put his finger against her neck so that the insect
could crawl onto it; the ladybird hesitated for a moment,
moving sideways, trying to avoid the sudden barrier,
before eventually creeping onto his nail. He bent down
and tapped it onto a dock leaf. It crawled away and then, a
moment later, took flight.

He seemed so grave, and so pleased with what he had
done, that she smiled and did not shake him off when he
touched her neck again, very gently.

'I can help you understand. I really can,' he said.
'You'll see in no time. You'll break free of the old ways, the
outdated modes of living that bind you.'

She did laugh now; she could not help it. But she tried
to be kind. 'I'd like that.'

And he pulled her to him, kissing her, wrapping his arms so tightly around her shoulders that she was enveloped.

It was too late then, to say anything sensible.

He pushed gently, encouraging her backwards until she brushed up against the broken wall, his lips still fixed to hers. Anchored now, he unwrapped his arms, moving his hands to her waist and holding her there, finishing the kiss slowly.

Ellie could not help but lean into him. She nuzzled against the sandpaper skin of his jaw and let herself rest there against him. It seemed magical, for a moment, as though the world had dropped away, suspending them in space.

Fifteen

The books had been piled into cardboard boxes and crates from the grocer's, and taken to one of the empty almshouses to be stored. A carpenter had removed the shelving. Panels of bricks had been knocked from the wooden frame with a modest wrecking ball.

Gadiel swept debris into sacks and barrows, wheeling it through the slosh of a muddy alleyway and dumping it out of sight on a slope that banked down to the river and the chemical works. In no time at all, the library became skeletal, the flesh stripped from its weathered bones.

No one in Marlford had actually moved a building before, but it was common knowledge that the feat could be achieved in a day, with organization. So, now it came to it, there was little fuss. The village was placid, ordinary: shoppers stepped round the muddy puddles; boys rolled stones under the boards and into the pit; a bus pulled up beyond the bank, its engine idling.

A lorry manoeuvred awkwardly in front of the Assembly Rooms and reversed down Victoria Street. Men began to gather in anticipation, sloppy in their work clothes, and soon there were more children, older women in pairs, the vicar flanked by parish councillors, someone with an ostentatious camera. The 3rd Marlford Boy Scout Pack and the Barton Infantry Volunteer Brigade formed an uneven cordon. The lorry dropped its tailgate with a clank and the delivery of logs clattered down, splashing onto the muddy road in front of the fishmonger's.

The operation went smoothly for an hour or more. They hoisted the rollers and packed them close, creating a track that ran from the front of the library across the boarded crater to the far pavement. The logs sat snugly in the layer of damp mud that coated the cobbles. Braithwaite Barton offered stoic encouragement.

Gadiel took up a position alongside one of the ropes. In front of him were two infantrymen, attentive, and to either side there were two more lines of volunteers, talking companionably. The ropes lay slack.

A Boy Scout handed out cotton gloves, beige and floral, too small for broad hands. Then a policeman gave a signal, ceremoniously, holding his handkerchief above his head and dropping it into the briny sludge, and they began to heave, digging their heels into the ridges between the cobbles, bending their knees, leaning back and resisting the burn of the rope on their skin.

After a few minutes there was a shout. Gadiel looked across and saw the men on one of the other ropes standing up, relaxing their hold. He, too, released his grip. Those around him were coughing and massaging sore hands. The spectators still waited, optimistic.

It was impossible to tell what was happening to the building. At the front, two or three men were on their hands and knees examining the footings; after a few minutes, they went to the far corner, repeating the investigation. Someone stepped forward with a copy of the plans and held it up, a blueprint of possibility. Discussions went on.

Another Boy Scout emerged with plastic cups of orange squash. The ropes lay dormant in the mud.

Half a dozen volunteers began digging around the perimeter of the library, their spades clanking against stones and rough support timbers. After ten minutes, the chug of an unsteady engine heralded the arrival of a small, red tractor, an earth shovel attached to the front, bouncing. It came from the cricket ground at the far end of the village, manoeuvred around the nymph and approached warily over the cobbles, like a small boat negotiating a rocky inlet in a spring tide. Several children ran to greet it. The men with spades straightened, leaning heavily on the handles.

The crowd parted just enough to allow the tractor to pass. The groundsman who drove it touched the peak of his cap in thanks, lowering the shovel when he reached the library.

For several minutes there was the pleasing growl of the engine as the tractor moved backwards and forwards; the hopeful scrape of the shovel extension; a spray of brine, sand and mud anointing the spectators.

The tractor worked diligently but slowly. The lines of men along the ropes disintegrated, children lost interest. The afternoon peeled away. Behind the works' chimney, the clouds were stained with colour and the chill of evening began to coagulate around the cracks and fissures, clinging to the damp mud that was slung across the street. The clatter of machinery seemed too loud for the escaping day.

With the ground loosened finally, they tried to pull one more time. The tractor made its way to the back of the building, where it could lever and push. The ropes were aligned again; the men set themselves with care. Gadiel resumed his place, feeling the tug of effort already stiffening in his shoulders. Those who had remained to watch pushed forwards.

The library moved, timbers creaked, groaning in complaint; the tractor engine could be heard whining with effort – but there was definite movement. Nothing perceptible: no jolt or collapse, nothing more than a slight change of tension on the ropes, but enough to be encouraging. A tremble of delight animated the spectators, sending children cartwheeling. Gadiel, in unison with the men ahead of him, took a small step backwards and continued to pull. At the front, a rhythm was called out with anxious enthusiasm, choreographing each heave. They took another step back, no more than six inches – but progress, nonetheless. A shout from someone on the left rope forewarned of too much force on that side as the corner of the building slid onto the rollers, gathering pace, tilting the frame. On the right rope they attempted to redress the balance, putting extra weight into their efforts; more men fitted into the lines to help, one of them pushing in front of Gadiel. They tried again, pulling until their eyes bulged.

By dusk the tractor had run out of fuel. Its wheels had worn trenches, which quickly filled with water, stranding it: it would have to be towed away. The groundsman kicked disconsolately at its tyres, sending stones and mud skittering into the ruts.

The library had been pulled only slightly out of place, its frontage balanced askew on the logs, its rear dragging in the mud and seeming to have sunk even more. Like a crooked tooth, it jutted awkwardly, poking from the neat row of buildings on Victoria Street with defiance.

Gadiel stepped away from the worst of the mud and rubble, finding a quiet place below the bank. He leaned against a wall, weary and aching, staring at their achievement.

'Why is it stuck out like that?'

He started at Dan's question.

'What? What are you doing here? I thought you were at the squat.'

'I just came to see.'

'Now that it's all finished for the day, is that it? When you wouldn't have to help?'

'No way, man – I've been busy.' Dan sent a quick, narrow glance towards his friend and then looked away to the library. The last daylight teased webs of shadows through the empty structure.

Gadiel lit a cigarette.

'I met Ellie,' Dan said.

'Did you?'

'I told her what we were doing. At the squat.'

Gadiel shifted; Dan's view of his face was obscured.

'She gets to you, doesn't she, because she's so different?'

'No, it's not that. It's nothing like that,' Dan protested. 'Man, you're... you're wrong. I just explained about our aims and principles. We talked about stuff.'

'I thought she was everything you hated – the old hierarchies and all that.' Gadiel still did not look at his

169

friend. Instead, he studied the stub of ash at the end of his cigarette.

'No way – she's pretty cool.'

Gadiel blew smoke slowly.

'We had a bit of a walk,' Dan said.

Gadiel shuffled the stiffness from his limbs and came back to resettle against the wall. He did not reply.

'We went for a prowl, man, in the long grass.' Dan made the words wink, sly between them, his boast hanging in the short silence. 'I think I seduced her.'

Gadiel was very still.

'One over for the forces of change, man.'

Gadiel threw down the end of the cigarette. 'But she's not here now?'

'What, Ellie? No. She went home. I told her I'd see her later.'

'Yeah, and what about the squat?' With a sudden lunge, Gadiel grabbed at Dan's arm, pulling him round. 'Weren't you supposed to be looking after the squat? Isn't that what you said? Isn't that what you said was the most important thing? Well, isn't it, Dan? And instead, you've been… I thought we weren't supposed to allow her to "infiltrate". Isn't that the rule?' He laughed bitterly. 'You want to be part of it, don't you? Marlford and Ellie and all the history – you can't admit it, but it really turns you on. The more you snipe at it, the more you love it.'

'Ow! Let go!' Dan pulled free. He stepped away, glaring at a point on Gadiel's chest as if the fact of their physical difference was located there. 'All right – calm down. Man, it's not like it's some big love affair. We only had a bit of a smooch.'

Gadiel spoke very carefully. 'You shouldn't do that. She's not like that. She won't understand. She'll think you're serious.'

Dan shrugged. 'It doesn't matter. She's cool.'

'Yes, it does matter. She's not like the girls you usually go with.'

Gadiel thought of Ellie under the towering oaks in the woods, something inexpressibly solemn and old tangled with her youth, an irretrievable sadness that allowed her to hold her own against the ancient stateliness of the trees. He sighed. 'So, what are you going to do?'

'What do you mean?'

'About Ellie? What are you going to do? I thought you told her you'd see her later.'

'I had to say something, man. She wanted it all agreed. She wanted a... a "tryst" she called it.' Dan laughed. 'Perhaps she thinks I'm going to marry her.'

Gadiel's voice seemed to come from somewhere new, ricocheting bluntly from the stones behind him. 'So – are you?'

'What? Am I going to marry her? Man, don't be—'

'No. Are you going to see her later? She'll have believed you. She'll be waiting for you.'

Gadiel watched Dan's thoughts settle, seeing some kind of resolution solidifying in the contours of his friend's face. 'I'm going for a walk.' He was suddenly exhausted. 'Or a drink. I need to buy some ciggies.'

'I'll wait for you,' Dan said.

'No. Thanks. No need. You ought to get back. There should be someone at the squat. Isn't that right? Besides, there's Ellie.' Gadiel pulled at his damp sleeves. 'You promised Ellie.'

He took a step towards the abandoned skeleton of the library but then changed his mind, picking his way across the crumbling cobbles and settled grime at the top end of the street and dropping towards the nymph. He was aware of Dan for a while, walking down the pavement on the other side, returning to the manor. They remained in step, their paths parallel until Gadiel broke the symmetry, pausing at the greengrocer's to study something in the uneasy reflections of the lit window. Afterwards, when his friend had gone, he retraced his steps, settling himself finally on the bench at Braithwaite Barton's feet and watching the night clamp down over the village, the lights from the works thrusting into the dark on unfamiliar trajectories.

Sixteen

Ellie was at the side entrance to the stable yard, the door hanging loose from its hinges behind her, gaping. In front of her she saw Dan, standing with his van, one hand flat against its side, as though he were patting the rump of a large horse.

'I didn't know where you'd be,' she said. Bats emerged from the broken roof and skimmed close to her head; a barn owl chittered. 'I didn't know where to look for you. I thought... well, you'd promised we were having a walk again, but I couldn't come to your side of the house and I just – I saw you going past, when I was looking from the window. So I came down.'

He seemed to be assessing her, deciding something. He ground his finger against the vehicle's rainbow flank. If there had been flesh there, he would have left a hard, black bruise.

'I'm supposed to be manning the squat. Occupation is key, a continual presence.'

'Weren't you going to come?'

He drew his hand along the glossy bodywork. The space between them seemed to be darkening quickly, pulling Ellie away into the shadows as the night sank into the enclosure of the yard. He felt something unexpected might happen if he let his touch fall from the van and went to her.

'If we stayed on here for twelve years, we'd acquire rights to ownership.' This was a fact, incontrovertible. It settled his queasiness. He threw a glance back towards the manor.

'Are you staying that long?' Ellie felt her heart begin to throb, as though she had been running. 'That's a very long time. Twelve years.'

'It's a legal requirement, man, a minimum occupation. A continuous occupation.'

'You'd be... well, we'd both be – we'd be... you'd know Marlford as well as I do.' She crossed to the wall, closer to where Dan was standing. 'I can't imagine it.'

She perched on the top of the mounting steps that climbed alongside the stable door and stretched out her legs.

He had not meant her to like the idea. 'It wouldn't have to be me that stayed for twelve years, not all the time. That's not how it works, man. It would be out of my hands – once the others arrive and the squat gets known... it would get a life of its own. It would roll over from generation to generation, each one sustaining the principles we're setting out now.'

'But if you wanted to stay—'

'Yeah, man, of course.' He laughed sharply. 'If I wanted to, I could stay. But why would I want to?' He smiled into the murky distance beyond the arch, appearing to consider the prospect of such a future. 'But, man, it would be politically powerful, an established squat like

174

that, so deep-rooted – a living tradition of freedom and democracy.'

He pushed his hair from his face. There was a moment of absolute stillness. Then he broke back to the present, brisk now, purposeful. He moved over to her and flashed a kiss at her cheek; a tease, perhaps, a slight token.

Ellie felt a shiver, tantalizing, like cold water on hot skin. He had sealed it then, his promise to remain at Marlford.

'I didn't know, earlier,' she said. 'When we were walking together – I didn't know... I'm not very used to romance. I was worrying all afternoon, in case I'd misread the situation.'

He sat down beside her, pushing up close so that there was room for them both on the narrow step. He slung an arm around her shoulders to balance himself.

'What is there to misread?'

In the fading light, it seemed as though the yard walls were leaning in.

'I'm sorry,' she replied. 'You have to understand – I've never had a lover before. Not an accepted lover. I've thought about it often, of course. Very often – I've imagined what it would be like – but that's not the same at all. I can see that now.'

'Is that what I am then? An accepted lover?' Dan frowned at the quaint phrase.

'Well, aren't you?'

Her certainty was beguiling. Dan pulled his arm tight, bringing her closer. He kissed her again and then again, harder, squeezing his hand against her breast. He felt her flinch.

'Come on. We can't stay out here. Come in the van with me.' He eased her from the step, fumbling in his pocket for the key. His breath came hot against her neck.

She could not quite see his face. 'Oh, but – wait…'

His hair obscured his features; he was busy with the lock. She heard the creak of the hinges on the van door and, for a moment, she glanced behind them, thinking she heard another noise – the men perhaps, creeping through the shadows.

'Dan. Wait.' She was anxious now. 'I can't. If anyone found out…'

He held out his hand from the doorway and swung her up into the van. 'It'll be fun,' he said. 'That's all. We'll have some fun.'

'No. I can't risk it.' She pulled her hand from his and turned away.

He was close to her, pressed up against her. 'Come on – Ellie!'

'I don't know. I think I might just go back. To the house.' She looked hard into the dark corners of the yard, but there was no one else there, she was sure of that now. Oscar Quersley would be on patrol at this hour; the men would be at the hutments, perhaps even asleep – it could not have been them she had heard. There was just the two of them, and he was looping his arms across her shoulders and settling his chin against her.

'Don't let me down, man. It'll be old patterns repeating,' he complained lightly. 'You know the kind of thing – the false promises of the upper classes, the potential for change unfulfilled.'

He held her tighter. He was laughing. But when she

looked at him, he was surprised by the solemnity of her expression.

The barn owl screeched, forlorn. Dan started at the noise and then drew close to her again. 'Ellie?' She seemed wedged in the doorway.

The frogs gulped their strange accompaniment.

Her smile came slowly. '*And yonder all before us lie deserts of vast eternity.* Isn't that it?' She leaned into him.

He had no idea what she was talking about. 'Ellie – it's no big deal. Just a bit of fun, man. Trust me.'

She raised her lips to be kissed again, taking his hair in her fingers. She was surprised by the grip of the curls.

She heard the door click shut quietly behind them, the smallest of sounds, but one she remembered.

Seventeen

Oscar Quersley took the shotguns to Marlford at the end of the morning, when the chores at the farm were finished. He found Ernest kneeling in an overgrown flower border at the front of the manor, half-hidden behind a gushing purple buddleia, squinting at an upstairs window.

Ernest signalled to Oscar to duck down alongside him. 'I've been speaking to the men, Quersley. There's been a development. They tell me the squatters have taken the girl hostage.'

'Ellie?'

'They're right – she's not in her room, she's not anywhere in the house. Hasn't been seen since some time yesterday.'

Ernest had a new energy; an elasticity. He seemed to have cast off his age. 'It's decided at least – we've got to go in – they leave us no choice. You'd better get those bloody guns loaded. I'm not having my daughter in danger. Not that.'

Oscar remained standing, despite Ernest's invitation.

'I'm sure she's busy somewhere, that's all,' he replied, coolly, looking away to the mere. The water lay shiny and still, as though covered by a brittle film of unseasonal ice. 'She may have simply – gone off, to reflect, perhaps.'

'That's rubbish. Utter poppycock. She's not busy anywhere – she wouldn't just go off. Never. All this time she's stayed, Quersley. Why would she go off now? But I've done a full recce. The men are right – she's gone. Those blighters have nabbed her.'

The edge of anxiety in Ernest's voice made Oscar begin to doubt himself. He propped the guns side by side against the wall and edged closer.

'She can't have gone.' He tried to make it sound certain. 'It's not possible.'

'Of course it's bloody possible, man. For goodness' sake, pull yourself together and pay attention. The girl's gone – vanished. Not a sign of her. They've stolen the initiative, Quersley – we've got to get a move on. We've got to get her back.' Butterflies skittered round his head. He flapped a hand at them distractedly. 'They told me this would happen. They warned against intruders. The men knew, all along – they saw it all. All I have to do is this one thing. All I have to do is protect Marlford – we all know that. And now, Ellie...'

Oscar saw Ernest's drawn, anxious face; he saw that Ernest believed completely that Ellie had been taken. There was an odd sensation in his stomach, like the plop of a flat pebble into deep water.

'How long, then?' He found that his throat was suddenly dry; the words came stiffly. 'How long has she been missing?'

'At a guess, over night. At least. The men weren't clear. I can't say exactly.'

'What do you mean, you can't say?' Oscar's panic overtook him all of a sudden. 'Why didn't you come straight away, when you knew? Why didn't you come and fetch me?' He did not give Ernest time to answer any of the questions. 'How can you fail to know how long she's been gone? If you'd simply acted promptly, if you'd come for me, we could have—'

'Pull yourself together, Quersley – you're here now. Soon enough.' Ernest spoke loudly over Oscar's garbled interrogation, but his voice wavered. 'I didn't know myself. The men came this morning, first thing – gave me a start, I can tell you, creeping through the house like bloody cat burglars. They said they had news. Information. They said Ellie was with the squatters.'

'But what if we're too late?' Oscar moaned quietly.

'Oh, damn it, man. We couldn't have done anything before we were sure she was gone – and, last night, you had the frog patrol to see to. Can't do everything at once.' Ernest sat back on his haunches and stared up again at the line of deep, stone sills poking out above their heads, but there was nothing there except the clouded sky cracking above.

'She must be up there – in their den. Bloody squatters.'

Oscar shivered. 'She's a sensible girl – she might just come back. She might... I don't think Ellie would—'

'She's not gone of her own accord, Quersley – haven't you been listening, man? She can't come back. She's been taken. A hostage. A bargaining chip. They're sneaky buggers, Quersley. Sneaky buggers.' Ernest drove his hands into the flowerbed, his fingers grazing against stones and roots, chafing on the sharp edges of broken roof tiles; his skin tore, a nail split. He pushed further in until he was up to his wrists.

'I can't believe they'd hurt her,' Oscar said, weakly.

Ernest threw back his head, a plea of some kind to the ageing Marlford stone that rose above him.

'Look – bring those guns inside. Let's get our act together. I've not been through everything to get mired in this kind of bloody game.' He spoke to Quersley without looking at him. 'They're making us look like fools.'

The men found Ernest in the dining room, carefully building a tower of cream crackers. The bottom of the tower was stuck directly onto the battered wood of the old table, each biscuit cemented neatly to the one above with meat paste scraped from a series of small jars lined up in front of him.

He began constructing another storey.

'Ah, gentlemen. You join me when I'm breakfasting.'

His *robe de chambre* hung looser than ever from his shoulders, billowing around his chair. He waved his knife at the expanse of empty table, drawing their attention to its bareness, or perhaps inviting them to take a seat. Tiny drops of meat paste spun off the blade, catching the light; his robe, barely tied, gaped open to reveal the sallow skin over his ribcage and an unexpectedly thick clump of wiry white hair.

'There're just these damn soggy crackers – and the Shipmans.' He leaned towards them, conspiratorial. 'Tastes a bit odd, actually – I think it might be off.'

'It's almost midday,' Ata pointed out.

Ernest looked surprised. 'Is it? Already? Good Lord! I do seem to have fallen behind. Got an early enough start, but without Ellie... Is that it? Has the morning gone?' His face sunk suddenly, as though its bones had been pulled away. 'I thought you'd have been back here sooner.'

It was a regret, not an accusation. He took a final cream cracker, layered it adeptly with paste, set it on top of the tower and sat back dolefully to admire the work. 'Can't bear to think that they've taken her. Got her hostage up there in that damned squat.' He flicked his knife at the ceiling, spattering paste again; shivering, he pulled his robe closed. 'What would they want with her?' He groaned. 'Dear God, I'm not having Ellie... I'm not having my daughter... I need her back.'

His voice came tightly, too breathy, as though Ellie had punched him in the stomach before running away.

The men encircled him. Hindy took the meat paste jar from Ernest's grasp and fitted the lid back with a quiet snap; Ata, too, reached forwards and eased the knife from his hand, placing it with care alongside the tower of crackers.

'Are you ready, Mr Barton?' he asked. 'Are you ready to liberate Marlford?'

Ernest did not stand up. His reply was subdued. 'I've got Quersley in the study, casting his eye over the arsenal.'

'That's very good.' Ata was encouraging.

'I've got all sorts ready. All sorts.'

'Excellent. Then we're prepared.' Hindy gestured towards the door. 'We knew you would rise to the challenge, Mr Barton.'

'You can take your pick – whatever you fancy…' Ernest's voice still had a dullness to it, an unaccustomed lethargy. 'Ata, you were always handy with the rifle, I remember.' He was rocking now, slowly, in his chair. 'We'll have at them, won't we? Right at them – right at the heart of them.'

The men did not respond. Ernest continued to rock, gazing out of the long windows, rolling shreds of meatpaste absently in his fingers.

His change of mood surprised them all: he stood suddenly, pushing back his chair with desperate energy, rattling the table. 'They'll wish they never saw Marlford. Taking my supper, damn them – sitting at my table – and then… and then… the scoundrels – with Ellie. Come on, let's be at them. Let's get the guns and be at them.'

The men took a step back.

Hindy was stolidly matter of fact. 'Mr Barton, we appreciate your invitation, but I'm afraid we're not able to join you on this occasion. We've talked about it, of course, and we've decided that enforcement is best left to you, as master here.'

'We feel the defence of Marlford is best in your hands,' Ata added.

Ernest did not understand. He frowned, tugging his robe across his chest. 'But you always chip in. Always. And look at it this way—'

Luden did not let him speak. 'We're quite decided.'

'But don't you see – Ellie… my daughter…'

Hindy smiled. 'Mr Barton, we've provided you with information. We feel we've fulfilled our special role. It's not really our job to rid Marlford of the squatters. That's for you to do.'

'Just shoot them and have done,' Luden urged.

Ernest stared at them.

'But I don't see why you won't join me. For goodness' sake, what's happened to you? You used to be… yes, you used to be proper men.'

'You're very kind.' Ata smiled.

'We used to do all this kind of thing together. A crack squad. A task force. Don't you remember?'

All three faces regarded him blankly.

'We're comrades. We're comrades in arms. That's how it all began.' Ernest closed his eyes for a moment, remembering. 'Hindy – I've seen you fell a deer at a hundred yards, man.'

Hindy gave no indication that he recalled the achievement.

'And I've got the shotguns from the farm. There's enough for all of us – you can pick your weapons yourself. There's the rifle – damn it, there's a bloody cricket bat if you want to cudgel the blighters to death.'

They did not reply. Luden simply shook his head very slowly, as if the movement pained him.

'Well, I tell you – I will not be held to ransom.' Ernest slammed his fist on the table. Paste and broken cracker spat into the air. The men did not move. 'I will not let them get away with this. If you won't join me; if you won't… damn it, I don't know what game you're playing this time, but we can't afford to mess around.' Ernest howled, 'Do what you bloody well like. I'm rescuing Ellie.' And he strode from the room, his robe floating, flashing scarlet.

In the hallway he paused, expecting them to come after him, to call, at least, to bring him back. But there was hardly a sound from the dining room, merely the slightest rustle of clothing.

Ernest grunted, then he tried to whistle, a jig of some kind, but the notes were desolate and shrill and he let them fade. For a long while afterwards, he felt the grip of the abandoned tune squeezing at his heart, making his blood run slow.

'Quersley!' He drew himself up and strode on towards his study. 'Quersley! Load the damn shotguns. Might as well shoot the whole blasted lot of them.' His words were newly savage, echoing.

Eighteen

Gadiel jerked open the door and swung up into the van. Ellie yelped, yanking the sleeping bag up around her shoulders and pulling it tight under her chin, exposing Dan the more: uncovering his torso and leaving his legs bare, a scrap of brown nylon across his thighs and groin.

Dan stretched out, flexing his feet.

'Are you still part of the squat, or what?' Gadiel spoke only to Dan. 'Dan?'

Ellie saw the way Gadiel looked around, taking in the disorder already cramping them into the van: flung clothes pressing in around them, a narrow pathway from the door to the makeshift bed.

She noticed that he avoided the slightest of glances in her direction.

Dan picked up his spectacles from the floor and settled them slowly on his nose; he followed Gadiel's gaze, too. 'Yeah, man, but you see – we're rather marooned.'

'Marooned.' Gadiel repeated the word flatly.

'She is all states, all princes, I – nothing else is.' Dan tugged at the sleeping bag.

'What?'

'It's poetry, man. Ellie taught me. It's about love.'

'John Donne,' Ellie explained.

Gadiel ignored her. 'I didn't know you were in love,' he said to Dan.

Dan reached across to sling an arm around Ellie. 'We're in bed.' He offered it as absolute proof. 'Together.'

Gadiel was forced, finally, to look at them both, to look at Ellie. She blushed, tightening her grip on the sticky nylon.

'Well, I thought you wanted to run a squat, to experiment with a new society, or whatever it is your manifesto is. But if you're holed up here with your' – Gadiel glared – '*poetry*, well, that's different.' He threw his head back, despairing. 'Oh, come on. What were you thinking?'

Ellie could not tell if the question was for her. 'It's only temporary,' she replied. 'We're not staying in the van for—'

Gadiel kicked at a shoe. It skidded into the air and hit the side of the van with a clank, silencing her.

Ellie wished he would go away. She knew that much, the hope faintly nagging, as though it might later be important, but it was the feeblest of desires: everything inside her had been doused, the spark of her thoughts entirely quenched, leaving only the incontrovertible weight of her flesh, which seemed overwhelming.

She let the sleeping bag drop towards her shoulders and lay pushed up against Dan, leaning across and kissing him gently on his upper arm, sinking back, tasting him on her breath, the van seeming the complete world, Marlford fading.

Dan inclined his head towards Ellie and winked at Gadiel. 'The sexual revolution,' he said, quietly.

Gadiel reddened, his features tight. He opened his mouth to speak but no words emerged, only a faint, low moan. He threw a final, vicious glance at Dan and stormed out of the van.

Dan sat up so quickly that Ellie fell away from him. He seemed to be listening hard, trying to hear Gadiel in the yard, perhaps waiting for his friend to shout to him.

Ellie opened her eyes sleepily.

'He's fed up with me, man.' Dan found his T-shirt by the side of the mattress and slipped it hurriedly over his head. 'I was only... he needn't rush off like that.' He leaned across and tugged the cover from Ellie with a flourish, the peremptory movement of someone snatching away a tablecloth to leave the tea set undisturbed.

Ellie squealed, clasping her arms over her breasts and slamming her knees up to her stomach.

'Come on, get your clothes on.' Dan stood to pull on his trousers. 'You'd better get dressed in case someone comes. I can't leave you here like this.'

'But where are you going?' Ellie fumbled for her clothes in the mess of sleeping bag and grubby linen. She felt hurried and clumsy, too much aware of her nakedness; she bent away, surprised by the stinging heat in her cheeks, as though someone was slapping her face. She tried to get her dress over her head. When she finally pushed her arms through and pulled it down, all she saw of Dan was a raised hand as he hurried outside. The door slid closed behind him with a hollow smack.

*

Gadiel had not left the yard. He was under the arch, his attention still fixed on the van. He did not seem surprised to see Dan coming towards him, his clothes awry and his feet bare.

'It's not fair, Dan. It's not fair what you're doing.'

Dan stood on a pebble and yelped, hopping theatrically for a pace or two and then picking his way more gingerly across the cobbles, his eyes fixed to the ground in an effort to avoid more obstacles.

'I told you yesterday,' Gadiel went on, 'but you didn't listen. And I never thought you'd go this far.'

The large, flat flagstones beneath the arch were softened with moss, which grew damp and thick near the walls. Dan found a comfortable place to stand and settled his feet, breathing out contentedly as though relaxing after the most strenuous of tasks. Then he looked up and grinned. 'I went all the way,' he said.

Gadiel shook his head. 'You're so pleased with yourself, aren't you?'

'I am pleased, man. It was cool. It was a great night.'

'And is that all that matters? Is that it, Dan?'

Dan wriggled his toes in the nest of moss. 'Look, man, be cool. I get it – you want me back on duty at the squat. It's cool.'

Gadiel examined his friend's face, his gaze steady, but Dan's breeziness was unshakeable. He sighed. 'I just think we should decide if we're going on with the squat, or if we're just… messing about.'

Dan nodded cheerfully. 'Yeah, I'll come back with you. You're right, man – you're right to keep your eye on the bigger picture. We've got to be steadfast warriors in the battle for change.' He glanced down at his feet. 'What about my shoes?'

'You can go back for them,' Gadiel answered. 'And check that Ellie's OK.'

Dan wrinkled his nose in the direction of the van. 'I don't know, man...' His face brightened again. 'Why don't you carry me, Gadiel? You can give me a piggy-back back to the squat, can't you?' He leaned forwards so that he could see the manor, judging the distance across the weedy gravel. 'It'll be a cinch, man.' He leapt onto Gadiel's back, clamping his legs around his friend's waist. Gadiel puffed at the sudden weight and stumbled. 'Oh, come on, Dan. Get down. This is ridiculous.'

He flipped his shoulders sharply in an attempt to dislodge Dan's hold, but it had no effect. Dan just giggled, jabbing his heels into Gadiel's thighs in an attempt to spur him forwards, flapping his elbows like a jockey. Gadiel resisted, planting his legs apart to balance himself and then, gradually and purposefully, backing up towards the curved wall of the arch.

Dan complained: 'Stop it. What are you doing, man? You're trapping me.' He slapped at Gadiel's face but Gadiel kept pushing back, using the strength in his legs, leaning with all his weight so that even when they were tight against the wall he could continue to press, crushing Dan against the bricks.

Dan's protests took on an edge of panic. 'Gadiel... stop it, man. Come on – it hurts.'

Gadiel did not seem to hear.

In a frantic effort to halt the struggle, Dan pulled at his ears, twisting them hard; when this had no effect, he leaned forwards and bit Gadiel's shoulder.

Gadiel pulled away suddenly, silently, and Dan slipped from his mount. They faced each other, both of them rubbing their wounds, accusatory, and then, without a word, Dan stomped away towards the squat, bringing his bare feet down defiantly on the gravel, exposing the pain of his progress for his friend to witness.

Gadiel waited until Dan was no longer in sight and then returned to the van. He knocked gently.

'Ellie?' There was a pause. 'Ellie? Are you all right? Can I come in?' He heard something – it might have been a reply – and he opened the door quietly.

Ellie was straightening her dress, paying attention to the creases, a twist in the narrow belt, the unsteady slope of the neckline. She did not look at him.

'I just thought... Dan's gone back to the squat,' he said. He made his way further into the van, his eyes on the floor, and bent down to pick up Dan's shoes, hooking the broken backs over his fingers. 'He – he forgot these.' He held them out to where Ellie was perched on the bed, uneasy, looking at her knees, her hair falling about her face.

'You should be careful,' Gadiel went on, his words undemonstrative.

'I'm quite all right,' she replied. 'Thank you.'

'No, but, I don't think you understand. Dan's not... we've been friends for ages. But, well, with girls—'

He let the warning ferment.

Ellie raised her head, looping her hair behind her ears and glancing at him finally. 'I'm not sure it's any concern of yours. But, anyway, as it happens, it's as Dan told you – we're in love.'

'But love for you and love for him – that might mean different things.' She was so pale and dishevelled, so forlorn. He stepped towards her. 'Look, Ellie—'

'Don't be silly. Love is love.'

They faced each other, the stagnant air of the van holding them close, Dan's shoes gaping between them.

'Really, I'm quite all right. I'm fine.' But some of Ellie's certainty was already gone.

'Please, Ellie, please. Just think about what you're doing. Just be careful, that's all. You don't know what it's like. You don't know how you might be hurt.'

Ellie pulled her legs towards her, clutching them uncomfortably around the knees. Her face seemed fleshy, loose; Gadiel wondered if it was just the unaccustomed cascade of her hair distorting her features.

'You'd be surprised what I know,' she retorted. 'The world's great literature deals with just this kind of thing. I'm quite prepared. I've been prepared for ever.'

He sighed. He had done his best. 'It's different, when it happens to you,' he said, quietly. 'That's all. You might find it's different. Not the way you'd thought it would be.'

She smiled at him. 'Saucy pedantic wretch, go chide late schoolboys and sour 'prentices.'

But he did not recognize the quotation, and he had no reply for it.

'I've got to go,' he said.

When Ellie finally emerged – stepping down cautiously from the van as though from a very great height – it was several minutes before she began to remember how it had all come about. In the warmth of the day, an unperturbed quiet hung over the estate, the sun high above the stable roofs, the summer light unusually calm and soft. Swallows twisted in greeting as they skimmed her head, and the lean of the old walls offered a welcome of some kind. It was tranquil and settled, indifferent, as though what she had done was in the order of things. But still, it did not seem quite right. She felt oddly dislocated from it all; she could not tread with any certainty. And she was distracted by the clumsiness of her body, which seemed to drag like an unseasonal coat, stifling.

She took a step or two away from the van under the dilatory gaze of the stable clock. The hands jerked round, making an effort, but it did not feel like Marlford.

Ellie gazed up at the washed blue of the sky and found that she was weeping.

Nineteen

When Ernest saw Dan's colourful figure kaleidoscoped through the small panes of the front window, he hurried across the cavernous hallway, his footsteps pounding against the old stone, the rifle clutched to his chest. He unlocked the central door on the disused side of the manor and kicked it open, pushing into a small room – a butler's pantry of sorts – stacked with letter openers and shoe horns, walking sticks, croquet mallets and riding crops: relics of lives lived out. Ernest brushed straight through, taking another door, which led from the back of the cupboard directly into the cluster of abandoned rooms, one opening into another, the manor rolling out before him.

Surprise was important in an attack of this kind, surprise and cunning, speed of thought. So Ernest galloped, ignoring the flush of pains. He found the old panelled stairway that climbed to the bedroom corridor and squeaked his way up on the creaking boards; the noise took him aback – a sudden drench of nostalgia. He paused briefly at the top, gasping, leaning into the corner so that he was hidden.

He peeked round so that he could see along the corridor, looking past a bust towards the blocked arch at the far end. There was nothing – the mess, of course, the squalid evidence of the squat – but no sign of life.

He fired the rifle.

The noise was astounding. The bullet sank into the wall somewhere at the far end near the breeze-block stuffing of the arch-making such a satisfying thud that he fired again almost immediately, the first recoil of the gun still humming in his shoulder. He heard someone shriek. The blood rushed, thundering, into his head; his arms and legs trembled; he could not contain the flood of excitement.

He jigged, fleet-footed, on the spot, the rifle flapping. 'Squatters? Are you there?' Dust and plaster fell, drifting lightly. 'Do you hear me? Squatters?' He reloaded smoothly and settled the rifle more firmly in his grasp. 'I know she's here. I know you've got her. Consider this fair warning. Give her safe passage and get out of my house. Get out of Marlford.' He aimed the gun towards one of the haphazard piles of old furnishings, lining up the sights on the obscene poke of an upended chair leg. 'Or I'll shoot you,' he finished, with a flourish. And he fired off another bullet.

Dan crouched in the doorway to the gold bedroom, staring down the corridor, open-mouthed and pale. Gadiel was kneeling on the bed. They were both very still for a moment, listening.

'He's mad,' hissed Dan. 'He's going to kill us.'

Gadiel had returned only a few minutes before the

attack; he still had Dan's shoes clasped in his hand and a look of contempt in his eyes. He did not reply.

'Oh, come on, Gadiel – you can't be grouchy, man. We're in this together. Haven't you noticed? There's a mad man shooting at us.'

Ernest shouted again. 'Do you hear me? I know you're bloody well there.'

'Gadiel! We've got to do something.'

Dan crawled backwards, moving quickly. He reached up to the bed and pulled at Gadiel's arm.

Gadiel shook him off. 'Keep still. Just sit it out. He's blustering.' His whisper was angry, unforgiving. He pulled further away.

'But we should say something. We should try and talk him round. That's what happens, isn't it, in this kind of situation?' Dan pushed at the bridge of his spectacles while he thought of a solution. 'Effective lines of communication, I bet that's the thing, man – the priority.'

Gadiel shrugged.

'We'll offer a negotiation,' Dan hissed. 'We'll tell him that either he lets us come through and talk to him about this, rationally, in a proper spirit of debate – or... or we'll call the police.'

'How do we call the police?'

'Oh, come on, Gadiel – at least try and help.'

'I'm just wondering how we call the police, that's all. I'm just wondering how we bargain with the man with the gun.'

Ernest called again. 'Gentlemen, I have given you more than fair warning. Release my daughter immediately, do you hear? It's the lowest trick. Taking a female hostage – it's low down, despicable...'

'What's he talking about? He's *got* to be mad.' Dan shook his head at Gadiel, his eyes wide.

Gadiel slid from the bed and went across to the window. 'He must think she's here.' He looked out as he spoke, his words directed towards the still mere. 'He must think we've snatched her or lured her or—' He turned to face his friend. 'He'll have missed her when she didn't come home, and he won't know about the van. He won't know you're... in love.'

Dan winced but before he could reply Ernest called out again: 'And I should inform you, gentlemen, that I have several boxes of ammunition, a man posted at the rear and reinforcements arriving very shortly to take up weapons against you.'

Dan started at the renewed threat, dropped to his knees again, and crawled quickly towards the protection of the bed. 'He's bluffing. Don't say anything.'

'What would I say?' Gadiel wiped the window and leaned forwards, his forehead against the glass. 'You're the one who's done that to Ellie. You're the one who should talk to him.'

Ernest began again. 'Hand the girl over.' He hammered on the door nearest to him. 'Get. Out. Of. Marlford.' He punctuated his words with the thump of his fist. 'Get out now. Give up and go on your way. I've got you penned in like Christmas geese and there's no escape.'

Gadiel stepped away from the window. He took a deep breath. 'We don't have Ellie,' he called out. 'Mr Barton, she's not here. We can't help you, I'm afraid. We don't have her.'

But Ernest did not hear the words, or could not take in their meaning. There was a growl from his end of the corridor, and then the blast of the rifle again, reverberating through the fabric of the building, making Marlford tremble.

From his position at the back door, Oscar heard the shots, feeling the ricochet of their echo around the enclosed courtyard. He clicked the cartridges into the shotgun, his finger already on the trigger.

Ernest came into full view at the far end of the corridor. He stepped forward and stopped just past the bust, his feet planted, his rifle perfectly parallel to the floor. He was red in the face, but his voice was measured. There could be no doubting his absolute delight in the success of the manoeuvre.

'Squatters?'

Gadiel poked his head around the doorframe. Dan groaned quietly.

'There you are.' Ernest glared at Gadiel's exposed face. He aimed the rifle at the open doorway and lifted his chin.

Gadiel ducked back into cover. Ernest took several long strides along the corridor until he was barely a couple of feet away from them. His shoes squeaked on the floorboards, a slight, soft creak of leather that seemed suddenly terrifying.

'You – there – in the doorway.'

There was no answer.

'Boy!'

Gadiel leaned out just enough to be able to see Ellie's father. 'Mr Barton – it's me… Gadiel. Look, about Ellie—'

Ernest swung sideways to re-adjust his aim. He paused and jiggled the rifle, perhaps playfully. 'What have we here?' He strung the question out, as though it were the most perplexing of problems.

'Mr Barton—'

Ernest did not care about the answer; he knew they would not understand. 'What we have here,' he offered, patiently, 'is what is known as a pincer movement. You have been outflanked. Quersley is downstairs, armed to the teeth, cutting off your exit. You have nowhere to run behind and I – as you can see – am in front of you, also very much armed and very much ready.' He shook his head at their pitiful tactical awareness. 'There are no alternative exits; this corridor is your only potential escape route. If I may say, it's a poor choice of base camp – you're rather hemmed in; it's a death trap. You really should never have got yourselves into this situation. Now, you see, I'm going to shoot you.'

He lifted the rifle sight to his eye and his order rang out as though it had to be heard above a chaotic skirmish, the noise of close engagement, dying men: 'Fire!'

It was a scramble, shouting and pushing, confusion. Gadiel dashed from the room and hurled himself at Ernest, falling against him with such force that they both slapped back against the wall, letting out simultaneous grunts. Ernest managed to keep hold of the rifle but it slumped to his side; winded, he could not do anything but struggle for breath.

Dan darted from cover and rushed out into the corridor, his arms flailing and his eyes wide. He barged past the struggling men, the piles of furniture and the teetering bust, which was nodding vigorous encouragement; he heard nothing but the pounding of his fear, like the uneven heartbeat of the weary manor.

Feeling himself sinking under the weight of his younger, stronger assailant, Ernest grabbed between Gadiel's legs, squeezing ruthlessly. Gadiel yelped, the surprise of the attack making his voice come hard and high. He pushed and Ernest fell heavily, crashing onto the floor with a stifled puff, ending up half sitting against the wall, his legs splayed, the rifle finally dropping from his grasp.

For a moment, Gadiel was nauseous, reeling, but he stumbled forwards, floundering along the corridor. Behind him, Ernest was already rising to his feet, he knew that; he breathed hard, clearing his head and gathering his strength. As he finally careered down the stairs, he heard the explosion of a long, furious battle cry.

'Quersley! Quersley, man, can you hear me? Move out – move out! Head them off.'

And then another rifle shot, screeching through the thin air.

Twenty

Dan paused at the bottom of the stairs, not knowing where to go, bewildered. There was a moment of quiet. He stared into the greedy shadows of the disused wing but there was no sign of Ernest, not the slightest shudder of noise. The building looked exactly as it had always done, its inalienable composure settling around him, calming the panicked rhythm of his breathing. The battle with Ernest, the bursts of gunfire, seemed suddenly distant, or even imagined.

But, in an instant, Gadiel spewed from the stairway, flapping his arms in hurried warning. 'Quick, Dan – he's coming. He's coming after us. Run!'

Immediately, there was a clatter on the stairs. It scattered them.

Dan set off after Gadiel but took a wrong turn, and found himself alone in the stale enclosure of an old dining room. He pushed through a heavy door into an intestinal succession of small rooms, each seeming smaller than the last; all bare except for odd strips of faded wallpaper. It felt like a conjuring trick with boxes. He paused, confused, ran on, turned back but thought he heard a noise and turned again, going on. He let the manor swallow him.

Gadiel slowed, dragging his hands along the wall to guide himself in the dim light. He did not want to run. He wanted to talk to Ernest; he wanted to explain about Ellie. She was not in danger, after all, or at least not the kind of danger that Ernest imagined. She did not need this extravagant rescue. He fingered a scratch on his face and felt the rise of bruises already on his arms and shins.

Oscar heard the squeak of one of the rusty casements opening. He gripped his shotgun and looked up, trying to find the place from which the noise had come but seeing only the syncopated rhythm of frames, blocked windows, imperfect stonework.

There was a whistle, shrill and brief.

'Quersley,' Ernest hissed. 'Come on, man, quick. I think I've got one of them. I need you to come through so we can flush him out.'

Oscar found the head poked from a ground-floor window. He tried to hurry over but he was stiff from the strain of perfect readiness. He swayed, hobbling finally towards Ernest's pale face.

'Ellie isn't here, then?'

'Quersley, are you listening?'

Oscar tried to concentrate. 'Yes, yes, of course. But if I leave the back door unguarded…'

'Stop whittering, man – a bird in the hand, Quersley, a bird in the hand.' Ernest flung his head sharply in the direction of the interior, an invitation. 'Come on, come through. We've got him. Let's make it count.' Ernest's head pounded from the struggle, his left arm throbbed and he felt a dull ache across his ribs and chest. The pain was extraordinary, exhilarating; it tugged sharply in his brain, re-igniting old desires and spurring him on.

Gadiel heard voices. They seemed to grumble around him, indistinct and subterranean, the old manor regurgitating the past. He paused, listening, straining to hear through the cloying half-light. He thought he caught something of Ernest's low, urgent tone, a brittle confidence, but the sound dissipated too quickly; he could not work out from where it had come.

He was completely lost. He seemed to have found his way into an unvisited wing of Marlford: nothing was familiar, and there was no sign of Dan. The smallest of landmarks had been eroded, leaving only identical rooms and corridors, yards and yards of dark, indistinguishable oak panels and flagstoned floors. The house seemed intent on holding him.

He heard footsteps then, sharp and suddenly close. He started and, almost immediately – sooner than seemed possible – he caught sight of Ernest emerging purposefully through a doorway, his rifle held ready, his hunter's eyes peering through the shadows.

Gadiel chose a door to his right and pushed quickly through it into a large, plain room. Light sank through a small, square window high in the far wall, reluctantly illuminating a flight of broad wooden stairs in one corner. They went nowhere, rising only as far as the ceiling, where they were cut off by a neat cornice, a later intervention. There was nothing else, no exit; just the unmistakeable slide of Ernest's footsteps, like a long sigh, and the thump of Gadiel's fear, loud now in his head, apparently filling the room.

Behind the staircase there was a dark recess, a forgotten nook. It would have to do as a place to hide. He took a deep breath, tasting dust, then he ducked and slid into the gap, pushing himself back into the angle between the walls, the stairs climbing above his head. Cobwebs were sticky in his hair and across his face; something crunched under his feet, droppings or bones. There was a smell like putrid cardboard.

Ernest was perplexed by the boy's disappearance. He had caught a glimpse of him as he closed in – a blur of uneasy colour – but he had lost sight of him for just a moment and in that time Gadiel had vanished. The rooms seemed empty, the passage quiet. He flicked his hand to signal to Oscar coming up behind.

'The bugger's here somewhere,' he hissed. 'Flush him out. I'll go forward.' And he hurried on, his rifle raised, grinning with delight at the way things were turning out.

Two rooms opened up from where Oscar was standing: the poky one on his left contained a small, wooden trestle and a bucket; the room to his right had an odd staircase in it. He was about to go on in pursuit of Ernest when he realized how such a bizarre architectural remnant might act as a hiding place.

He stepped into the room as quietly as he could, holding the shotgun ready, easing himself level with the staircase, then edging forwards. The slightest suggestion of mauve cotton stained the unmoving shadows. Oscar smiled, satisfied, as though he had solved a complicated equation of some kind. 'I can see you.'

Gadiel pushed back as far as he could, scraping the skin of his shoulder against the gritty stone behind him. He was surprised by the voice; he did not recognize it. He had expected Ernest, but this was someone he did not know and could not judge. His fear was suddenly sharp, slicing cold into his guts.

'You'd better come out,' Oscar said.

Gadiel found he was fixed, trembling.

'You can't get away. There's no means of escape,' Oscar pointed out. 'And if you flee, I'll shoot you.'

Gadiel shifted heavily. He tried to push back yet further against the wall; he spoke through the shadows, his voice fragile. 'No – wait. I'm not... I haven't really done anything. I can explain.'

Oscar thrust the gun towards the gap under the stairs. 'You should come out.' He did not like talking into a void in this way, as though the conversation might be imaginary. 'Come out. Surrender yourself to my custody and I'll not be forced to shoot you. That would suit us both. Mr Barton can deal with you in due course – not leniently, I'm sure, but then you don't deserve leniency. What you've done here at Marlford is despicable. But I'll take you to him and you can plead your case directly.'

'Can't you just let me go?'

'Let you go? Of course I can't let you go.' Oscar huffed. 'Just come out and accompany me quietly. Look, I have to get on; I have to chase the other one down.'

Gadiel crept from his hiding place. 'You can't just shoot us.' He had his hands in front of him, raised in surrender.

'I have my orders.'

'But, really, think about it. What have we done? You're being unfair.'

Oscar flinched at the accusation. His voice stiffened. 'Just come with me.'

'I don't want to go anywhere with you. I don't trust you.'

Oscar pointed the shotgun at him for the first time. 'I can shoot you.' He was matter of fact.

Gadiel backed into the stairs, instinctively pulling his arms across his body for protection, stubbing his heels against the bottom step with a thud. The desperation was hard in Oscar's eyes. This was something other than Barton's flailing distress, something more terrible.

Gadiel steadied himself. 'Wait! Don't shoot — really — just wait.' He tried to see his opponent clearly in the unsettled light. Oscar's face had an odd sallowness to it, his lips bulged unnaturally, his hands were rigid on the gun. 'You see, I think you've got it wrong about Ellie. It's not the way you think. And even the squat — I mean, we're not doing any harm. Not really.' Gadiel realized he was speaking too quickly. He gulped a breath. 'Look, you're standing there with the gun, trying to scare me. I see that. But I won't run off, I promise. Let's just talk things through.'

He took a step forwards. Oscar let out some kind of noise, a strangled scream, and slung the gun anxiously towards him. Gadiel raised his hands again quickly and felt his heart bump. They examined each other's fear.

'Stay where you are.' Oscar strained to keep his voice steady. 'I want this business accomplished cleanly.' He made his words come crisp and properly, by an act of will that drained the remains of any colour from his face. 'Since you've taken Miss Barton hostage—'

'What? No – no way!'

Oscar blinked, confused. He took a moment to reply. 'You don't have her?'

'Of course we don't have her. What do you think we are?' Gadiel tossed an angry gesture towards the shotgun and stalked away across the room. With the extra distance between them, in the indefinite light, Oscar's anxieties seemed less clearly etched on his face, soft-edged and deceptive.

'I was told she'd been taken. I was told you had her held captive,' Oscar persisted.

Gadiel shook his head. 'Why on earth would we do that? We like Ellie. I like Ellie. You can come with me and search the squat if you like, but she's not there – there's just a pile of dirty underwear and some stale bread.'

'But she's not at home. Mr Barton is certain she's nowhere to be found.'

Gadiel sighed quietly. He felt his fear leak away, dissipating into the gloom of the house. 'Look, perhaps she just went away somewhere. Of her own accord,' he suggested, as gently as he could. 'Perhaps she wanted to try something different.'

He was taken aback for a moment by the expression on Oscar's face.

'Look – really, don't worry. Don't worry about Ellie,' Gadiel said. 'Why don't you put your gun down? Hold it away from me, right away from me, and I'll try to help you. I promise.'

Oscar still clung to his weapon. 'I'm not falling for that. What you're proposing. It's a trick, a confidence trick. Nothing more. I see that. You can't trick me, boy.'

'No – I'm not trying to trick you. I'm trying to help you. Come on – if you're worried about Ellie—'

'Miss Barton is none of your business.' Oscar turned on him so fiercely that Gadiel jumped back. 'She's gone. Don't you see that? Don't you understand what that means? If she's gone... if she's thrown herself upon the world in all its viciousness...'

'She's only in the van,' Gadiel said, wearily. 'Parked in the yard. She's fine. Or she was when I saw her.'

Oscar stared. 'In the van? What on earth is she doing in the van?'

'She was with Dan.'

The shotgun was already dipping away, as though its weight was too much.

'What do you mean?'

'What do you think I mean?' Gadiel felt a riptide of sudden anger, at Oscar Quersley with his ridiculous gun; at Dan, at the whole grubby seduction – it seemed to tug him from his feet. 'What do you think? Do I have to spell it out for you? Come on, I've told you – she was with Dan. *With* him.'

Oscar slumped; the gun finally fell to the floor. Gadiel saw that he understood.

'But I agreed to help him,' Oscar was saying. 'It was a mutual bargain, honourably sealed. There are ties that cannot be broken, old loyalties... you wouldn't understand. I can't go back on my word.'

Gadiel was surprised by the unstudied passion of the words. He found he could not answer them.

He looked at Oscar, unsure for a moment, then he kicked hard at the shotgun so that it slid over the floor, away from both of them, and fled. He had a sense of Oscar crouching behind him, his head in his hands.

Twenty-One

Thunder rumbled in the distance, the land flattened under heavy anvils of cloud. From farming habit, Oscar studied the sky for a moment, but its patterns meant nothing to him in his state, and the action was simply some kind of duty fulfilled. He hurried on towards the stable yard, tidying his appearance as he went, brushing down his jacket, pulling his sleeves into shape, fastening his buttons, rubbing his shoes in clumps of clean grass – all awkwardly achieved because of his insistent grip on the shotgun.

In the slanting greenish light of the on-coming storm, the van's elaborate paintwork shone, the gaudy rainbow making the air shimmer in the tight square of the yard. Oscar blinked at the display.

'Ellie.'

He called quietly at first, as though he still could not believe that she might be there, but then he caught a glimpse of her, sitting on the mounting steps, her hair tumbling about her shoulders.

'Ellie.'

This time he spat her name. She jumped up and hurried towards the van, but as she pulled herself up through the door the hem of her dress caught beneath her, snagging in the door mechanism and pulling her down. She struggled quickly to work it free, tearing at it, in the end, in the hope of slipping inside, pulling the door closed and blocking Oscar out. But time seemed to clog around her, slowing everything; she could not work swiftly even in her panic. He was upon her.

He placed a firm hand on the handle of the van door, preventing her from closing it. 'I'm pleased to have found you. Here – in our midst, after all. I believed you might have taken off somewhere; for a while I was rather anxious.'

Thunder broke close to them; Ellie flinched and moved away from him, her skirt stretching out from where it was held so that it gave the impression that she had grown a wide, bright tail.

'I want to talk to you, Ellie.'

'Why have you got the shotgun? Was it you that I heard? I thought I heard shots.'

'Are you here with that boy, the squatter? The Marxist?'

'Mr Quersley, I heard shots.' She looked hard at him.

He was forced to reply. 'I believe there were several shots, yes.'

From her position on the door-ledge of the van she was slightly above him; it appeared to her that this should help her divine the truth of things.

'What were you doing? What happened?'

'I was assisting your father. It's my duty to assist your father.'

212

'Oh, my goodness, what have you done?' She sank into a crouch, dropping her face into her hands. 'Tell me you haven't been shooting them – the squatters. Please tell me, Mr Quersley, that you've not followed Papa's crazy scheme, when you know he's just...' She looked up.

There was too much to answer all at once.

'I haven't shot anyone,' he replied.

'But you fired at them? That's what I heard?'

'It's your father... he has a rifle.'

'But don't you see? How can you just...? I thought you'd see, of all people – I thought you'd be sensible. You can't shoot them.'

'You thought I would—'

'—know better, Mr Quersley,' she finished for him, wearily. She sank back to rest on her heels. 'Yes – I thought you'd be better.'

He offered her a slight bow. He looked thin and worn, a stick man with a heavy gun. 'Thank you.'

'But it's not a compliment, is it? Because you've been shooting at them, at my friends, as though it's a sport of some kind... as though they don't matter.'

'But if you thought that of me, at least... if you had a good opinion of me...'

'Oh, for goodness' sake.' With an angry tug, she yanked her skirt free of the mechanism and tried to stand, wanting to flounce from him and leave him there so that he would know he was ridiculous.

But he reached up and put a hand hard on her leg. 'And, bearing in mind that in assisting your father in this manner I have, indeed, maintained my side of a mutual agreement, a bargain, if you like; one in which you are implicated…'

'You're hurting me.'

Her words distracted him. He became aware of the softness of her flesh in his hand, the down of the hairs on her leg prickling lightly, like baby-bird feathers. He made himself speak with purpose. 'Ellie, I agreed to help your father rid the place of squatters in return for your hand in marriage.'

'Mr Quersley, stop it. You're hurting me.' But she could not manage to pull away, and then she realized what he had said.

She stared at him.

'Don't be ridiculous, Mr Quersley. That's nonsense.' But even as she protested, she was disturbed by the intensity of his gaze. 'Surely you don't think—'

'It was agreed upon in good faith, Ellie. I shook hands with Mr Barton upon the matter and therefore consider it binding, on both sides. It's for that reason that I agreed to bear arms for him.'

She groaned. '"Bear arms for him?" What are you talking about?'

He let go of her leg and held up his hand instead, its palm flat to her, concluding the debate. The gesture was balanced, unwavering, allowing the sense of where they were to settle upon them, so that she would know herself again, feel the binding embrace of the Marlford stone and smell the ancient lives in the crushed air; hear the inescapable crank of the stable clock pushing everything into the past. There was another rumble of thunder, further away, the storm blowing over harmlessly. He dropped his arm slowly and spoke calmly. 'I've come to claim you, Ellie.'

He could never have imagined it.

She laughed.

She looked at him from her perch on the ludicrous vehicle and she broke into a real laugh, unrestrained, her eyes disbelieving.

He floundered, grappling for something to say. 'Ellie, you're mistaken if you believe that some kind of dalliance with another man might—'

'I've not been dallying.'

He could not bear her laughter. 'This is not a matter for mirth.'

'Sorry, yes – I know it's not.' Her laugh petered out; gradually her smile faded. 'It's just the way you're so... so sure of it all.'

'I'm sure of what is right. The deal was made, Ellie. I'm at liberty to claim you.'

'But it's complete nonsense. You must see that?'

'It was an agreement, Ellie.'

'Well, I don't care. I won't have it. I won't go along with it.'

He stared at her. 'Of course you will. It's settled. There's no reason for you to object.' He looked away for a moment, along the colourful flank of the painted van. When he spoke again, his voice was soft, a plea. 'Step down, Ellie. Step down here and we'll discuss it sensibly.'

'This place. It's horrible. I hate it.' She folded her arms, pressing them against her stomach as if the pain of everything was located right there, deep within, unshiftable. 'I hate it all – Papa and you and... all of it. Don't you see what it's done to us?'

He did not answer, shaking himself hard instead, like a wet dog, as though he could fling off his doubts. 'Look, Ellie, you're overwrought. Overstimulated. That's all. The squatters have been filling your head with unfounded theories, with foolishness, and you've taken it to heart. I don't know what's been going on here, with the van – I can't believe what he told me, I can't believe that, but – you're young. You have little experience of things. I can see that—'

'They have not been filling my head with anything.' Ellie's interruption was fierce. 'If anyone's been filling my head it's you, with all those lessons at the library, teaching me all those old texts as though they were somehow… relevant. As though we might go on living like that.'

'But, Ellie, you wanted that, you wanted to read that – you requested those texts yourself.'

'Because I didn't know anything else.'

'No. That's not true. Because you liked it. We both liked it – don't you remember the excitement of the Dante, Ellie?'

Ellie laughed again, but briefly, too harshly. 'While we have been reading medieval Italian, Mr Quersley, the rest of the world has been setting a man to walk on the moon.'

'But, Ellie, does that really matter? Does it? To us? What difference does it make to us? Oh, Ellie, dear Ellie, you're very naïve.'

'Of course I'm naïve. What else could I be?'

'Ellie—'

'The point is, Mr Quersley, I realize – now – that I've listened too long to you, and to the men, shut up here with your fables and nothing else, as if Marlford's the whole world. It has been, to me; you've made sure of that, haven't you? It's been my whole world and is that a good thing, Mr Quersley? Do you think that's a good thing?' She shook her head wildly in reply to her own questions. 'It's as if I'd been sunk with those poor babies, isn't it, cast down into the depths of the mere, submersed and forgotten and—'

'Ellie, calm yourself. You're being ridiculous. I won't have it.' He held out a hand to her, offering to help her down. 'Come with me now – come inside the house and we'll discuss these matters rationally; we'll discuss the terms of the agreement with your father.'

She put her hands behind her back, where he could not reach them. 'There's no agreement, Mr Quersley. There's no agreement I could possibly recognize.'

'I expect you to marry me, Ellie.'

He would have pulled her down perhaps, and forced her to come with him, settling it for her there and then. She thought she saw him begin to lunge at her. But there was a cry from the archway, and they both turned to see Dan running towards them, shouting.

Immediately, Oscar stepped back and lifted the shotgun. 'Stay back. Stay away.'

'What are you doing? Leave her alone.' Dan slowed, wary. He put his arms up in a gesture of surrender but still came forward.

'I said stop.'

'Come on, man. You wouldn't fire at me. Let's just talk.' He threw a glance at Ellie. 'Are you all right? I was coming back to the van. I thought I could hide out here. I didn't... I'm sorry—'

She nodded.

Oscar saw the look they shared in that instant and felt Dan intruding still, coming closer, steadily, without fear. He thought of Ellie behind him, watching him.

He fired the shotgun.

The blast filled the stable yard, sinking into the damp stone, held there, repeating. Ellie screamed.

The impact of the shot made Dan stumble backwards; he gripped his right shoulder, his eyes wide, unbelieving.

Oscar levelled the gun again.

Ellie screamed a second time and leapt from the van, catching Oscar by the arm in the same movement, pulling him off balance, the gun skewing at an angle.

It was not a struggle. He yielded to her immediately, becoming limp in her grasp, as though exhausted or sick, toppling towards her; the gun fell at his feet.

Ellie tried to wriggle from beneath Oscar's weight; the smell of his clothes and hair, spiked through with the musk of gunpowder, disgusted her. She looked desperately towards Dan, who had his back to them, bent over. 'Are you all right?' She dared the question. He was not dead at least, not yet; there might be a way to save him.

He did not answer.

'Dan? Dan, are you all right? Say something.'

She pushed at Oscar, trying to free herself. He groaned. 'Oh, for heaven's sake, Mr Quersley – stand up.' She dug her nails into him where she could. 'Get out of my way.' She shoved him again and ran to where Dan was now crouching, bending alongside him.

'He shot me,' he said to her, raising his head.

'Yes, yes, I know.'

'At that range… he could've killed me.'

'Is that it? Is that where he shot you? In the shoulder?'
Ellie bent closer to look. There was blood seeping from the
wound, reddening Dan's hand where he was pressing at the
pain. The relief of such a small calamity made her dizzy;
she had to steady herself on the wet ground. 'You'll be all
right then, won't you? If he hasn't... shot you properly.'

'What do you mean "properly"? How was he supposed
to shoot me?'

It was a joy that he could be so irritable. She smiled.

'I just meant – well, he didn't kill you. It looks fine.
Can you walk?'

'I suppose so.'

'You won't collapse or anything?'

He shook his head. Ellie looped her arm around
his waist.

'Lean on me. We'll go back to the house together. Then
if we need help... a doctor—'

'But your father... he's charging through the house. He
came up to the squat, man, and... and Gadiel – I haven't
seen him. We lost each other somewhere. He might be
trapped in the house, hurt...'

She could not think about this just now.

'Just lean on me – come, gently. We'll be fine. Don't
worry about Papa.'

They eased into a slow walk and hobbled through
the archway, the sound of their slurred footsteps fading
quickly in the damp air.

They had forgotten Oscar Quersley. He was slumped
against the side of the van, shivering, his head slung away
uncomfortably so that the string of vomit dangling from his

tight mouth might fall aside from his body. The shotgun lay where he had dropped it. He felt the jab of Ellie's nails still here and there, hot prickles on his skin like ant bites, or the stab of fresh hay stalks. He called out to her to help him, to come to him at least, but she was no longer there.

Twenty-Two

Ellie installed Dan in her father's high-backed chair, pulling it round to catch the shreds of late light slinking through the dining-room window. Everything was still faintly purplish from the storm, bruised.

Dan winced at the effort of settling himself.

'Let me see.' She tried to prise his hand from the wound but she could not quite concentrate. She could not remember how long she had been gone from the manor; it seemed important to know. It must have been no time, surely, a day perhaps, a night. It could hardly have been longer. But as she bent over to tend to Dan's shoulder, she felt that everything about the house had changed. It was as though her act of leaving had been too great a thing: she had the impression that the manor was completely empty, nothing more than a shell, the scuttling patter of human occupation ended. It distracted her; she prodded too hard.

He pulled away with an injured snarl. 'Can't you just send someone for an ambulance?'

She hesitated. 'Maybe it's not that bad.'

'Not that bad? I've been shot, for God's sake.' He

was trembling now, exhausted, cold and bewildered, intimidated by the confident decay of the dining room. He dropped his hand, sucking in his breath sharply with the pain of even such slight movement.

Ellie bent close to his shoulder. Very gently, she attempted to lift the fabric of his T-shirt, but it was sticky with blood, sunken into the wound. She could not bring herself to pull. 'I'll go and find my scissors. And we've some bandages somewhere, I'm sure. Wait here.'

'Ellie – if you… can you go and find Gadiel? Find out if he's all right. I haven't seen him… Can you go and look for him?'

'Just wait here,' she said again.

She found no evidence that Gadiel had returned upstairs. Nor was there any sign of him elsewhere, no sound or commotion, no trail of blood; the back kitchen was empty.

But her father was in his study.

'Oh, Papa – I didn't know…' She had fetched scissors already from her room and a yellowing roll of bandage from the bathroom; it had been a last-minute idea to collect some brandy from her father's sideboard.

'I lost them, Ellie. Both of them, damn it.' He slammed his hand on the table, making it rattle. 'Good God, in the old days I would have had them in a trice; a good, solid pincer movement like that, known territory, two fellows with good weapons.' He looked away at the wall, seeing the maps of old battle campaigns in the peeling wallpaper. Age pounced upon him in an instant, distorting his features, buckling him. He sat down hard in the nearest chair. 'I should have had them, Ellie. They were easy pickings.'

'I'm sorry, Papa.'

222

Her sympathy stirred him. He noticed how drawn her face was, how large and dark her eyes. He leaned forwards. 'They treated you well? You're all right, my dear?'

Ellie clutched the bandage. 'I'm fine, Papa.' She found she wanted to cry. 'But there's something… I need to get on.'

Ernest stood up and came towards her. He put a hand on her shoulder. She seemed tiny in his grasp.

'The buggers had the decency to release you at least. When I heard they had you held hostage… well, my God—'

'Papa? What are you saying?' She pulled from him. 'Who had me held hostage?'

'The damned squatters.'

'But that's ridiculous. For goodness' sake, why would they do that?'

He was uneasy in front on her. The arm that had dropped from her shoulder hung loose and awkward.

'Don't be cross, Ellie.'

'But you're being absurd. And I don't have time for this just now. Where on earth did you get the idea I'd been taken hostage? That's horrible – to think that they'd do such a thing.'

'But the men told me, Ellie. They were sure you'd been taken. They'd seen you.'

'The men? Oh, Papa, they're just meddling. Can't you see that?'

There was a long quiet. They stood apart. Ellie clicked the blades of the scissors together once or twice, a tiny clink. It seemed for a while as though they might be lost in their own thoughts for ever.

In the end it was Ellie who spoke: 'Is that why you came with the guns, Papa? Did you come to rescue me?'

He flinched at the gentleness of her questions. He had

never heard her speak to him in that way before.

He sniffed. 'Of course I came to rescue you, my dear.' His voice did not come as firmly as he had hoped. 'I wasn't going to leave you, was I? Who'd have known what they might have done.'

'But, Papa, I was fine.'

'No, Ellie – you weren't in your room. We did a recce. You weren't at Marlford.'

She dipped her head. Her sorrow felt very old and worn. 'Papa, I was in the van, that's all,' she said.

He frowned. 'What do you mean, you were in the van?'

'There's a van... in the stable yard. It belongs to the squatters, to Dan – it's broken.' But she could not tell him. He would not understand. She sighed; her next words came clipped. 'Look, Papa, just wait here. Sit down and wait. I'll come back and see you.'

He accepted the command, edging backwards, reaching out to feel for the chair arms and sinking down onto the seat. But he was still troubled. 'Ellie – you're all right?'

'Yes, Papa.'

He persisted, unconvinced. 'But you seem – different. I don't know, Ellie... are you sure they didn't hurt you?'

'Papa, I've told you. They didn't take me hostage. There was nothing like that.'

He smiled at her, but he shook his head, too, not quite believing her version of events.

'But you know I would have rescued you, if you'd needed me to.'

She resisted the temptation of the idea and flattened her tone. 'Yes, Papa. I'm sure you would. But I didn't need you.' She pulled at a frayed edge of the bandage. 'Now I really have to go. It's very important. You'll just have to wait.'

Twenty-Three

Oscar staggered forwards. He could not be sure now that it was not he that had been shot; he put his hand to his side, searching for the unequivocal wet pain of a wound. His thoughts tiptoed away from him in all directions. He had a sense of them abandoning him; when he tried to pin one of them down it dissolved, leaving nothing but a nagging discomfort.

'Are you all right there?' Gadiel paused in the back doorway and scanned the yard. 'You seem in a bad way.'

Oscar did not look at the intruder. 'It's nothing.'

'You haven't been shot, have you? I heard a gun going off again.' Gadiel started towards the van. 'Are you on your own?'

'It seems that way.'

Gadiel ignored Oscar's blistered tone. 'It's just — I've come back for Ellie... I thought... I was hoping she was OK.'

'You came for her, too?'

'I couldn't leave her.' He stopped, keeping his distance, the space between them inviolable. 'Did you shoot them?'

Oscar hauled himself sideways to face him. 'Only him.'

'Dan? Is he all right, though?' Gadiel could not believe his own calmness, as though none of it mattered.

'I presume not. On a good day, I can shoot a rabbit at fifty yards.'

'Where's he gone? If he's hurt—'

'Why did you come for her? If you thought I'd be here, with a gun?'

'I didn't know you were here. I didn't know that – I just came… to the van. In case Ellie…'

'That's very heroic.'

'She might have needed me.'

'Why you?'

Gadiel could not answer this. She would not have needed him, it was true; there was nothing he could do for her, nothing she would accept from him.

'Look, young man, she went back to the house with the Marxist.' Oscar felt a new swell of nausea and swallowed hard. 'He might require some help. They both might. Perhaps you should go after them.'

Gadiel looked down, seeing the uneven sag of the stones under his feet. He did not move.

Oscar watched him for a moment and then straightened, as if fortified. 'I see. Well, if you're not going after them, I think I will.' He offered Gadiel his stiff bow. 'There's still a great deal to be resolved. And I should find Mr Barton.' He picked up the shotgun and began to walk away.

'Leave the gun.'

Oscar paused, surprised at Gadiel's authority.

'I don't think so. It belongs to me,' he said.

'Leave it here. I'm not letting you go after them with the gun.'

'You think I'll shoot them?'

Gadiel reached out a hand to take the weapon. 'You should leave the gun here.'

The stable clock chimed an impossible hour.

'I won't hurt her.' Oscar wanted this finished; he imagined Ellie with the wounded squatter. 'I'll take the shotgun to the farm. But I have to go – I have to speak to her.'

Gadiel stood firm, larger than Oscar, more certain.

'Just leave it. Drop it there – I can't trust you. Leave it.'

Oscar recognized Gadiel's determination, and his sorrow. He let the shotgun fall to the ground and stepped away. Gadiel made no effort to collect the weapon and for a moment they both hesitated, not quite sure how to escape the clutch of the old walls. Then, with a sudden movement, Oscar broke free and went quickly towards the house, keeping his face averted as he slipped under the arch.

Gadiel remained still. He stared at the cobbles around the gun, feeling himself empty into the cracks and joints, spilling away. He could not think where to go or what he might do. He did not have the energy for anything. He wished he had never come there and never seen Ellie. He realized that the rest of his life would be foolish and blunt and precarious without her.

He shook his head at the shotgun and wondered, vaguely, without interest, how he would ever leave that spot in the stable yard.

Twenty-Four

When Ellie heard the door slam, she had only cut the sleeve of Dan's T-shirt; she had not begun to clean away the blood or examine the ragged patch of shoulder torn by the shot. She did not bother to look up but quickened her fingers, trying to work more rapidly. Dan attempted to shift in his chair but she held tight to him in her efforts to continue. Perhaps, this way, the interruption might never happen.

'Ellie?'

Ernest sounded perplexed. He rounded the table to a point where he could see Dan clearly and squinted at the boy bleeding in the shabby dining room, a specimen in a bell jar.

'Oh. It's you. Did I wing you?'

'Mr Quersley shot him,' Ellie said.

'Did he? Good fellow… jolly good.' But he sounded lost. 'It's nothing that, man – a graze. I've seen worse at fairground target practice.'

Ellie lifted her hand from the wound but did not retreat. 'It needs cleaning,' she insisted.

Dan spoke to neither of them in particular. 'I still want an ambulance.'

'Just wait, I'll—' Ellie gave a little shriek. They followed her stare to the door.

'Good evening, everyone,' said Oscar Quersley in response, offering them the slightest of bows.

He had returned to the farm, changed quickly and combed his hair. He appeared at the doorway now in his very best suit, his eyes hollow, ringed with dark, his mouth tight. He stood unnaturally still and spoke slowly, as though breathing was a strain.

'I've come for Ellie. I've come to settle our agreement, Mr Barton.' He gestured loosely at Dan's wounded shoulder. 'You see?'

Ernest nodded, his movements slow now, too, as if in response, or as if time was unwinding, stranding them both. 'Yes, I see you clipped him. Good work.' His tone was flat, exhausted. 'Better if you'd finished him, of course, but nonetheless – a decent effort. Good man.'

'It's enough though, isn't it?'

'Wait – Mr Quersley…' Ellie began.

Oscar ignored her.

'We simply need to agree the finer details,' he went on. He kept his eyes on Ernest. 'We need to clarify the matter, so that we know where we stand. So there's no mistake.' Finally he turned to her. 'And I wanted to say something to you, too – I wanted to tell you, Ellie…'

'Look, what's going on?' Slumped in his chair, Dan was below the line of their gaze. 'What's all this about? Come on, I need help. I've been shot.'

They ignored his exasperation, each of them looking steadily at the other, knowing how long this moment had been coming.

'Go on,' Ellie prompted, quietly. 'Go on, Mr Quersley.'

'It's not just an agreement, Ellie, or some kind of deal with your father. You know that, don't you? You know that all these years… all this time, I've been living in the hope that one day, you and I might… that I might have the chance to ask you this question. I want you to marry me, Ellie. It's the right thing, for both of us, for everyone, for Marlford.'

Dan groaned, with pain perhaps, or disgust.

'Shut up,' Oscar hissed at him. 'What right do you have? It's nothing to do with you. If you think a few days, a few hours, makes any difference to the way things are —' He collected himself, pushing aside the thought of the sordid van. 'Ellie, you know this is the right thing.'

Ellie was very still for a moment.

'How on earth can I agree to marry you?' she asked at last. 'You've shot Dan.'

'But that was nothing. Look at him. He'll be fine.'

'Mr Quersley, you shot him because he was in your way.'

'I shot him because he's a squatter. I gave my word to your father—'

'You shot him because I was with him. Because I wanted to be with him.' She felt the prick of tears but swallowed them down. 'So how can I marry you, Mr Quersley? Why would I marry you?'

'It's your duty, Ellie.'

'I don't agree.' She waited, perhaps expecting her father to intervene. But Ernest said nothing.

'Ellie – you're making a scene.' Oscar was wringing his hands so hard that the squeak was audible. 'In front of a stranger.'

Finally Ernest spoke, but uncertainly. 'He has a point, Ellie. This kind of thing… you know.'

Ellie placed her hand on Dan's uninjured shoulder. 'It's because of Dan that I know what I want to say to you. It's good that he's here. Besides, he and I are – tell them, Dan… tell Mr Quersley why I can't marry him.' She moved round in front of Dan and crouched.

But he looked at something on the far wall: a scruffy picture frame or a tear in the paper. His voice was expressionless and tired. 'I don't understand. I have no idea what's going on, man. What do you want me to say, Ellie – that you can't marry him because we've been having it off in the van? Is that it? Oh, for God's sake – I've been shot. Hasn't anyone noticed… I've been fucking shot.'

He tried to pull himself from the chair but gave up, squawking with pain, clutching the wound on his shoulder. He threw his head back and closed his eyes, shutting out the sight of the veins of damp patterning the ceiling. 'Just let me go. Get me an ambulance, or put me in your horse and carriage or whatever it is you've got here – just let me go.'

'But, Dan—' She could not believe it. This was his moment – he could explain. He could begin, if he liked, with the structures, the hierarchies, the crumbling aristocracy, the new world. The squat. Although none of that would matter. She placed her hand very gently on his knee. 'We'll go and fetch help, if you want – for the wound. I promise. But you need to tell them about me, about us.' She was gentle, as though prompting a child. 'They'll listen now – they have to. Make this little room an everywhere.'

Oscar snorted at the poetic quote.

'Come on, Dan.' She was suddenly impatient. She recognized an encroaching fear, not yet quite tangible. 'I'm sorry you're hurt; I'm really sorry. But it'll only take a moment, that's all. It'll set everything straight, you see, once they understand.'

She looked up at her father. 'Just give him a little time,' she pleaded. 'He'll be all right. Just give him a minute and he'll explain it to you, Papa. You'll understand. You'll see.'

Dan opened his eyes; he lowered his head and looked at her. He took a deep breath and finally heaved himself from the chair, clinging to his injured shoulder as though it might detach. His face was drawn, old.

'I'm going, man. I'm sick of the lot of you. Of this whole stupid place.' He took a few steps, then seemed surprised by the distance still to be covered, the dimensions of the dining room deceptive.

'Dan – no! Wait.'

Ellie hurried to him but he brushed her away, lurching on towards the door, his face furrowed as he concentrated on holding his shoulder still, stifling the pain. He ignored Ernest and Oscar, the way they scrutinized him, as if he were a novelty, an inexplicable intruder from another world. He did not cry.

At the door he paused.

'Do what you like. All of you. The squat is officially ended – kaput. I'm fed up of it all, man, of everyone – I've got nothing to say.'

Ernest spoke gently, understanding the defeat. 'Good man. Quite right – quite the right decision. Take your friend and leave Marlford and we'll pretend it never happened.'

'Perhaps it didn't.' Dan snorted. 'Perhaps it's some crazy dream.' But he winced again in pain, real and inescapable.

Ellie felt as though she were floating, drifting away, cut loose from the threads that had bound her to things. She had little sense of Oscar Quersley or her father, only of Dan being swallowed into the gut of the manor, dissolving into the liquid shadows of the entrance hall.

'Wait – Dan, please. Wait.' She tried to hurry, but her limbs were loose, unruly, and by the time she caught up with him it felt as though she had run a long way. She was breathless, already exhausted.

'Ellie, I'm going to find Gadiel and I'm going to get help for this shoulder and then I'll arrange for the van to be picked up and we'll be out of your way.' It was a shopping list of intentions, blandly delivered. He did not look at her. 'I think you'd better do whatever you like; whatever you think best,' he said, flatly.

The evening was falling fast; he was not quite tangible in the speckled gloom.

'You're just going to leave?' Ellie stared at him.

'Yeah. I think so.'

'But that's a horrible thing to do. It's not gentlemanly.'

'Sorry. But you have to be clear, man – I never promised you anything.' He smiled. 'I never promised to be gentlemanly. You can't say I did, Ellie. I've not misled you.'

234

He winced at a new pain. His voice hardened. 'If anything, it's Gadiel and me who've been let down. It's not at all what I thought it'd be like, man, not when we started, when we set up the squat. We've not had the opportunity to make our point. We've not got the message across – it doesn't look like the others are coming. It's – it's confusing, Ellie.'

'Confusing?' It seemed the slightest of objections.

'Yeah. It should have been perfect – politically and socially – an endless spiral of decadence, man, of usurped power – you know?' He stopped, frowning, surprised by the clink of his words, brittle somehow against the unforgiving stones, the solid doors and dense histories. 'But, I don't know – it doesn't quite seem… with you…' Perhaps it was simply the shock of the wound, unsettling him. He felt the pain in his shoulder again, a twinge, and gestured towards it. 'You see, you see – I've been shot…' It was incontrovertible.

'But that wasn't me. I just like being with you, Dan. I thought… I presumed – it's old fashioned, I know, but—'

'I don't love you, Ellie, if that's what you're after.' He had to say that; he had to be clear. 'Man, there's nothing like that going on.'

She guessed this might be true – she imagined it was the way he saw it – but still she did not believe him.

'Wait – I didn't mean… it's new, I know. We don't know each other, really.' She could not help blushing at the fleeting thought of his nakedness above her, inviting her. 'But I don't want you to storm out of here… I don't want you to leave me here, Dan.'

She looked at him hopefully. It would take only the slightest softening on his part to bring her to him but he hesitated, pressing his hand harder against the wound to stimulate the pain, to distract him, because she was, at that moment, everything he wanted: her neat face, the scrape of her hair, the outmoded silhouette of her simple plumpness, was the promise of a truly radical future.

'You're here, at Marlford,' he said. Perhaps it explained everything.

'Yes, but I could come with you. If you're travelling…'

'Ellie – look.' He laughed disconsolately. 'We've just been trying out the van. That's all, really. When I'm not at university, well… I don't live far from here – if you go on past the salt works, another eight or ten miles or so… well, that's where I live, man, in a little village, with my mum. I can see the works' chimney from my bedroom window if it's a nice day. Look, I didn't know about the manor or you or anything but, still—'

'But that doesn't matter, does it? It doesn't matter where you've come from, not really.' She could not, just then, piece together the deception.

'It didn't seem to matter, not at first. When we broke down and ended up here – it seemed like fate. You know, man, like it was meant to be. I thought it was my chance to make a mark.' He looked away, engrossed for a moment in the memory, already nostalgic. 'I thought we could change things.'

She held out her hands. 'You can change me, Dan.' It was perhaps a joke, lightly made, cheerless. She already knew it was not enough; she was already disappointed in him.

She stepped back.

The movement jolted him from his daydream. 'Ellie, it's just bad luck, man. You're always going to be implicated in the kind of institutions… the sort of people and places, the world view, that I'm committed to defeating. It's not your fault. But I can't get tangled up in it… I can't. I told you, it's confusing.'

She saw regret already gathering in the close lines around his eyes, partly concealed by the rim of his spectacles but precisely etched, so that the furrows would deepen as he aged and come to define his face.

She mistook it for something else, annoyance or distaste, the soreness of his wound.

'Never mind.' She was brisk again. 'It doesn't matter.'

'Man, I'm sorry.'

'You're not at all the person I thought you were, Dan.'

There was no malice; it was simply a statement of fact.

It was the last moment when he could have changed things, but it hardly existed, skittering past without trace. He fiddled with the cloth of his T-shirt, the blood drying dark, and then he left.

Oscar came for her. He stood for a while, watching, thinking she might crumble but she was still and quiet, her feet firmly planted across a deep joint in the flagstones, her sadness a strength.

'I made a mistake.' She raised her eyes.

He beckoned. 'Come inside. We'll talk to your father.'

'Yes, in a moment. If you could wait, just a moment, Mr Quersley – if you have the time.'

'Yes, of course – I'll wait.'

Ernest rose for his daughter's arrival, pulling a chair for her from the corner of the room, its tapestried seating sprouting threads. Oscar had opened a window and was standing in the cool, damp air, gazing out into the dark shrubbery.

'I'm sorry.' Ellie sat down. 'I wanted to think about things.'

'They have gone, though, haven't they?' Ernest shivered, glaring at the open window.

'The squatters? Yes, Papa – I believe they've gone.'

'Damn good riddance.'

'Indeed. A relief,' Oscar agreed. 'And so our bluster has been spent and we come – at last – to me. And to our arrangement. Our agreement.'

'I'm not going to marry you, Mr Quersley.' It was as though she could put it aside, a minor inconvenience.

Ellie looked at her father. 'You should never have set guns on them, Papa.'

'He was grazed, that's all. It's a rite of passage, one's first wounding; he'll be all the better for it.' But Ernest's ebullience was ragged. He scratched at his head.

'Don't do it again, Papa.' She was in charge now; she felt that. 'Don't ever do it again. It will only cause trouble.'

'Well, in the long run, perhaps you're right, Ellie. Yes, quite right, I'm sure. As you say.'

Oscar pulled at the hem of his jacket as though to brace himself. 'Ellie, I've waited some time to talk to you. I don't think we need to concern ourselves with the squat again, or those persons. Not just now.'

She found she could look at him quite steadily, almost as though she did not know him. She was tired of him; he was ridiculous. Smaller too, she thought. More wizened.

'Look,' she began, 'Mr Quersley—'

But her majesty infuriated him. 'No, Ellie. No, Ellie.

Don't talk to me like that. You have a duty now that we all recognize. I simply want to make arrangements.'

There was the slightest of noises, like the distant baying of a lone hound, eerie in the dark.

Ernest started. 'The frogs. Quersley, was that the frogs?'

Oscar ignored the question. He came closer to Ellie, until he was standing directly in front of her chair, almost touching her, but he spoke to Ernest.

'I'm not leaving here until my claim is recognized.'

'Really, Quersley – I know we said that we—'

'We shook hands, Barton.'

'Indeed. But think about it, man. Would I really give away my daughter for some kind of wager? For God's sake!' He stepped towards Ellie, but Oscar blocked his path and he came to a hesitant stop at the side of her chair. 'I never meant to go through with it, Ellie. No sensible man would ever have fallen for it.'

'You're reneging?' Oscar was sharp.

'There's nothing to renege on, Quersley.' Ernest spun round to face Oscar. 'Consider it null and void. That sort of thing – it's just not on. What kind of man do you think I am?'

'I do not consider it null and void. I shot the boy, Mr Barton and the agreement was sound. You know that.'

Ellie wanted to stand up but Quersley had her trapped there, blockaded by the exact weave of his tweed and the hurried rise and fall of his breathing. She wriggled in her seat. The stuffing sighed.

'Ellie, I was just – gambling,' Ernest said. 'That's all. I know, I shouldn't have. But you can't doubt me, Ellie – you must know how much I love you?'

She could not see the expression on her father's face.

'Let me talk.' She spoke to neither of them in particular, facing out through the gap between them. 'I think I probably have the right to say something about this.'

'Actually, I'm not sure you do,' Oscar replied. 'We know your wishes, Ellie. You've made them perfectly plain. But, frankly, that's not the matter for discussion. It's all decided – long decided.' He paused and stuffed his hands in his pockets, an attempt at insouciance. 'And, as I've been trying to make clear, it's simply a case of agreeing practical arrangements.'

The frogs called again, the sound clearer now, more desolate.

'Quersley, close the damned window.'

Oscar did not move.

Hemmed in, her frustration uncontainable, Ellie scrambled onto the seat of the chair. She bobbed gently on the old padding, giving the fleeting impression that this was all some kind of frivolous game, but she was taller than both her father and her suitor now, and her face was absolutely calm, all doubts gone.

'There's no reason why I should marry you, Mr Quersley. I tried to tell you… At the van, I tried to explain, but you wouldn't listen.' She did not mind the quiet, or the way they looked at her. 'This agreement you think you've made with Papa – it's nothing. I don't understand it; I don't understand how you could do such a thing. Surely you knew that Papa would never be bound by it? Surely you knew that I would never respect something like that? Not even before… not even then.' She smiled at him. 'You've been foolish, Mr Quersley.'

He flinched. 'No, Ellie – I've not been foolish. You are surely aware that even had this agreement not been entered into… well, you know, of course, that the men and I have worked for considerable time towards this outcome. It is not foolishness.' He took a deep breath. 'You've had your head addled by that squatter and you're forgetting yourself. Don't you remember? What your father has done?'

'Ellie? You don't really believe I meant to barter you?' Ernest shook his head energetically. 'The man's talking poppycock. Worse than that – if he thinks I would let him anywhere near you—'

But Oscar refused to give up. 'Ellie, you can't stay with him – you won't be able to trust him. And if you were to leave, what would you do beyond Marlford? There's a very good reason for you to marry me, Ellie: it's the only option you have.'

From where she was standing, she could see the hair thinning on the top of Oscar's head, his scalp stretching as he talked. Its indecent pallor disgusted her.

'I'm not sure that's true any longer, Mr Quersley.'

'Ellie, be sensible. All these years we've been preparing for this. Nothing has changed.'

'I think it has. Surely it has.'

'What, Ellie?' His face split into a haggard grin. 'Prove it to me. What? It seems to me that you're still here, alone, with your father. You're not free of any of it, of me or Marlford, or the memory of the girls or—'

'That's not true. It can't be true. Not now.' She scrambled away from him over the arm of the chair and thumped down near her father. 'Don't say that. Leave me alone.'

Ernest caught her by the wrist. 'What does he mean, "the girls"? What does he mean, Ellie? What has he told you?'

She was impatient. She did not notice the catch in her father's voice, his urgency.

'What, Papa?' She pulled free from his grip.

There was a brief pause, nothing more than a natural hiatus of speech, but it seemed – in that instant – to draw the silence of the manor upon them. The moment stretched: it had colour to it, midnight blue, and the texture of fine satin running across their skin, barely felt.

Oscar and Ellie both looked at Ernest.

'What do you know, Ellie, about the girls?' he asked very quietly, afraid to tear through with his words.

'Mr Barton—' Oscar came forward.

But Ernest put up a hand sharply. 'I'm speaking to Ellie.' He narrowed his eyes. 'And, actually, I think I'd prefer it if you left now. There must be work at the farm.'

As if prompted, the frogs began their song again, revelling in the damp evening air. 'And there're the damned frogs, Quersley. The frogs. For goodness' sake.' He closed his eyes, pained by the incessant croak. 'Ellie? What has he told you?'

She gathered herself. 'Mr Quersley simply gave me the facts of my family history. I asked him to – I didn't want to ask you. But I felt I needed to know.'

'He shouldn't have breathed a word.' Ernest glared at Quersley. 'You were sworn to secrecy, man.'

'No, Papa – that's not fair. I asked him.' Ellie spoke with quiet firmness, somewhere between anger and grief, like the mixing of watercolours before the tint comes clear.

'I relied on him, Papa. I had to. I asked him and he told me. He can't be blamed for that.'

Oscar was slipping away.

With an unexpected dart, Ernest grabbed him and pulled him by the flap of his jacket, hauling him back from the doorway. 'Don't you dare, man. Don't you sneak off like a coward. Stand here and tell me what you've said to her.'

Oscar tried to summon some dignity, shaking himself, disgruntled, his jacket still bunched in Ernest's fist. 'There were things I believed she should know.' He was too pompous.

'You betrayed Elizabeth? You poisoned Ellie against her own mother?'

'No!' Oscar screamed, despairing.

'Papa – don't say that.'

'Well, I'm sorry, Ellie, but he's a worm, a bloody slug.'

The noise of the frogs swelled, the distance to the mere disappearing in the murmur of their song; it was as if they surrounded the manor now, besieging it.

'He's only ever been respectful to my mother's memory,' Ellie said. 'He's only ever remembered her and brought her to me. When you would have me forget her, ignore her, as though she'd never been here – it's Mr Quersley who's given me my mother all these years.'

Ellie was weeping now, finally. She slapped at her cheeks, angry with the tears. 'I couldn't have lived here without her, Papa. I needed her.'

Ernest yanked again at Quersley's jacket. 'Tell her.'

'I suggest you leave matters as they stand,' Oscar replied. 'What harm is there in it?'

'What harm is there? Quersley, it's corrupt – a corrupt memory – some kind of fable that you've spun for her. I don't know what you've been up to, Quersley, but there's harm in that – all kinds of harm. Tell her.'

Oscar looked at Ellie. Her face was pale and hard, but across her mouth there was a flicker of misgiving, the fleeting cirrus of tangled thoughts.

'I'm sorry, Ellie.'

She did not understand.

Ernest shook him. 'What good is that, man? Some weedy apology and a long face? We need more than that.'

'Papa, really – it's fine. I don't want this now. I just want to go to my room.'

The sound of the frogs crescendoed once again through the open window. Ernest let go of Oscar's jacket and pulled his head away from the noise, as though he could escape it. 'Ellie,' he moaned. 'The frogs.'

'Yes, Papa. I'm sorry. I'm sure Mr Quersley—'

'No – don't you see? Don't you see? I can't bear the frogs.'

'I know that, Papa. But it's a humid evening – I'm not sure there's much we can do. I'm sure Mr Quersley will resume his patrol.'

There was just the song, the strangely musical gulp.

Ernest looked at her wildly and pulled at his hair, his own tears now shining back at hers. 'Because it's those beautiful girls – don't you see, Ellie? My daughters. My beautiful daughters. All the time, I hear it, reminding me. Crying to me from the mere as though I could just... if I was just quicker, if I was just braver, I could save them. If I was just a better man, I could reach down and I could save them.'

All his bluster was stripped away. He was a skinny old man crushed by the unconscionable burden of the past, bent over, leaning on the chair for support, his face drawn, his tears squeezing from him. His loneliness was absolute.

Ellie walked slowly across the room and closed the window, pushing at it to make sure that it was tightly sealed. She stood still for a moment, as though examining something puzzling in the shrubbery, wrapping lengths of hair around her fingers and coiling them into a loose knot at the nape of her neck.

When she finally turned, she saw that Oscar had slumped into a chair, his head in his hands, while her father was at the sideboard, clinking his tumbler against the disappointing emptiness of the decanter.

'It's good that you – that there are regrets, Papa,' she said. 'That's something at least.'

She had moved apart from him long ago, when Oscar Quersley had first told her the secret; she had simply stepped away, as though walking into an adjacent room, bricking up the exit behind her. She could not come back to him now. She did not know how.

'It's right that you're sorry.' She glanced at Oscar. 'Perhaps you'll see to the frogs, Mr Quersley.'

He did not raise his head or answer.

It was Ernest who spoke, his question coming slowly. 'What have you done, Quersley?'

'I needed to know, Papa. That's all.' Ellie was too tired for her father's drama. 'Mr Quersley explained about my mother; he told me how you – how you took the baby girls and drowned them all.'

It sounded quite ordinary, the way she said it, as though it could be put aside.

Ernest groaned. He held his empty glass towards her, as if he were simply bemoaning the lack of whisky. 'Do you believe that, Ellie? Do you think that of me?' He winced, and went on, answering his own questions. 'I know what you think I am. I know now – but I had no idea. Quersley, how could you? For God's sake – she's lived with me all these years… my own daughter believes I'm some kind of…' The word would not come out.

Ellie frowned. 'What are you talking about, Papa?'

'What am I talking about? About the girls. I'm talking about the girls, Ellie.'

She could not bring herself to look at him. He seemed to be in such wrung pain that it made her doubt herself.

'Oh, Ellie, of course it wasn't me.'

He reached for her again. She shrank back.

'But you gave the order, didn't you, Papa? Didn't you give the order to have them killed?' She could not have been wrong about this, not for such a terribly long time. 'I don't understand. Mr Quersley's father took the babies to the mere in a wheelbarrow and drowned them. That did happen? At the mere? They are dead, aren't they?'

'Yes, Ellie,' Ernest replied. 'They are dead.'

'Then that at least is true.'

'Yes, that at least is true.'

Oscar coughed lightly, clearing his throat. He spoke quietly, through the clutch of his hands. 'It wasn't your father that had the girls disposed of, Ellie. I might have misled you.'

'Misled me?' Ellie looked at them both, but could not

grasp the meaning of their expressions. 'That's not possible. Not with something like this. What do you mean? Mr Quersley – what do you mean?'

More than anything, she was aware of her own heaviness, like thick folds of dead skin draping to the floor. For a moment she closed her eyes and let her head loll, but she could not slough it off. She found she had to be there with them, the weight unshakeable.

'Please. I don't understand. You have to explain... Papa? I've always thought you... Mr Quersley always insisted it was at your instigation. You decided, in consultation with the men, that the girls were a nuisance and best disposed of. Isn't that true? If that's not true – who then? Who killed the babies?'

Oscar raised his face slightly. 'Well, my father did. You know that.' He paused. 'He performed the act, followed the orders. But it was Elizabeth, Lady Wilshere – it was your mother – who requested that it be done.'

Ellie wanted to laugh at such absurdity. 'My mother? No. That can't be right. Why are you saying that? There's no reason why she'd... Mr Quersley, you've always been unequivocal – and why on earth would she do that? She wouldn't do that.'

She knew, for sure. She had seen her mother's poise and grace, imagined it and honed it.

Oscar shrugged. 'It may be true, I grant you, that I've sometimes suggested your father was more – more intimately involved in your sisters' deaths but—'

'No, not "suggested", Mr Quersley. It's been quite clear. You've always been quite clear, quite certain.' This was the worst yet: nothing as it had seemed, everything an

247

illusion, stranding her. 'I don't understand. Papa? I don't understand.'

Ernest sighed. 'It's caddish to bring it all up, Ellie. It's best left. That's why I never said anything. Whatever she was, she has a right to rest in peace.'

'What are you suggesting?' Ellie's voice was hard and high. 'Papa, you're not going along with Mr Quersley's story, are you? Not now? Surely you'll own up to it, won't you? You'll admit what you did? You won't let Mr Quersley say these things about my mother?'

'I'm sorry, my dear.'

'What do you mean, sorry? No, Papa – you have to be clear... do you mean you're sorry for what you did? Is that it? You're sorry for killing the babies – yes, I can see that... I've always thought you might be sorry. If you'd just say it – so I'm clear.'

'Ellie, I can't say it. I can't say it because it's not my fault. Not all of it. Not this. Ellie, I'm sorry because Quersley's right in what he says. Your mother didn't take to the girls. She didn't want them.'

'But that can't be right.'

'She was from another age, Ellie. A throwback of some kind. That's all I've ever been able to say. When she married me – well, you know, I'm just a Barton. She got the house she wanted and the estate, but she had certain... expectations. She felt her lineage very strongly. Very strongly, indeed. I didn't suit her sense of things. I was never very good at being what she wanted.' He smiled at her, loosely. 'Even now – after all these years... you see yourself – I'm not very good at all this.'

Ellie took a deep breath but it did not clear her head.

'Even so, even if that were true… Papa, that doesn't explain why she'd kill her daughters.'

'Your mother was most concerned that her line should not die out,' Oscar said. 'She was of excellent stock. Impeccable.'

'Yes, I know that,' Ellie snapped, keeping her eyes fixed on her father. 'The coat of arms and everything. I know that.'

'And she wanted sons,' Ernest added, simply. 'She felt daughters were – unnecessary. I never bred her the right kind of heir.'

Through the closed window, the sound of the frogs could still be heard, but muted now, desultory.

Ellie listened to the casual to-and-fro of the call for a long while; neither her father nor Oscar disturbed her.

'I don't think that can be right,' she said in the end, her voice quiet and steady. 'I don't think my mother would do such a thing, just because they were girls. She wouldn't do such a thing.'

Ernest came towards her and offered his hand to his daughter. 'You were willing to think it of me.'

'And so when I was born – another girl—?'

'She rather despised you, I'm afraid. Despite your loveliness.' His fingers trembled in the air between them. 'She would never have loved you, Ellie. Not like I've done. She would never have treasured you.'

'She would have killed me, too?'

'No, no!' Oscar broke in, shaking his head wildly. 'We can't be sure of that. There was no time… she was too poorly.'

'Shut up.' Ellie rounded on him, furious. 'Don't talk to me. Don't ever talk to me again. You've lied to me, over

249

and over – the worst possible deception. I can't – I can't think of it just now, not all of it, but don't speak to me. Never speak to me.'

Oscar reached towards her. 'Ellie – please… it was just…' His objections were stifled by the murmurs in the old manor as the night settled.

She smiled. *'The whole house is built in the air and must soon come to the ground.'*

'Baltasar Gracián, yes, the Jesuit. You see, Ellie? You see what I've taught you?'

'You've taught me nothing. You've done nothing to help me. I would never have married you, Mr Quersley. Never.'

He saw in her face that this was true.

'But they promised.' His words faltered. 'The men… all this time. I thought this was how they wanted it – they promised – this was the future for Marlford.' He seemed disorientated suddenly, his eyes darting from point to point in the room, bewildered. 'All these years, they asked me to wait – Ellie, they never let me tell you how I love you.'

Her eyes flickered briefly with pity, nothing more.

'They've played me, haven't they, all this time? They've duped me?' His questions quivered, his voice small. He knew that she was lost to him. He sank back.

Ellie took the hand her father offered, gently, as though it were very fragile, old paper or crumbling clay.

He closed his fingers over hers. 'How could you have ever thought that of me, Ellie? You'd never have thought it, would you, if I'd been better at living here. If I'd done better here, at Marlford; if I'd been more—' He could not say any more; he felt his suppurating wound torn fresh apart, wrenched open, a long-held pain suddenly so brutally sore that he was left gasping for breath.

But Ellie was hardly listening to him. She let his hand fall. 'I'd never imagined things that way, that's all. I'd never imagined my mother to be like that. I'm not sure where it all came from – my way of thinking about things. I mean, it was what they told me, of course, but not just that... It was something else, as though it was all just meant to be a certain way.' She looked at Ernest, puzzled, as though he might not be quite real, just a trick of the dying light. 'I'm sorry. I don't understand anything,' she said. 'I have to go.'

She reached for the door; it felt as though the house pitched around her.

Contained within their own miseries, neither her father nor Oscar Quersley attempted to stop her; they hardly glanced at her as she left.

Twenty-Five

The men stood in a line, their faces flattened with the surprise of finding the study so changed: the walnut table was pushed to one side, with the chairs stacked beside it; the bookshelves dismantled; the cocktail glasses put away.

They looked from one alteration to the next in silence.

'We were unsure how it would end,' Hindy said, finally.

Ernest remained seated; his gaze was steady. 'You let me down, gentlemen. Abandoned me.'

There was the slightest of pauses, enough for Ernest to know that they were surprised by his strength. He stood up. 'It's been rather an evening – quite a day, all in all. But they've scarpered, anyway. The squatters.'

Luden nodded, slowly. 'About time.' But his gnarled face twitched.

'Indeed. Exactly.' Hindy, too, seemed to be struggling to find his usual tone. 'We knew events would take their course. We just called by to be certain.' He frowned at his colleagues, who looked back at him in blank dismay.

'We'll go back to the hutments, Mr Barton, and come again tomorrow for faro.'

They perhaps expected him to reply, but he said nothing.

Ata smiled, feebly. 'We just wanted to wish you goodnight, Mr Barton.'

Ernest was very still. 'One of them was hurt.'

'Unfortunate, but unavoidable.' Hindy found something of his usual aplomb. 'Nothing of any concern, I'm sure.' He scanned the room again, as if trying to fix in his mind the changes that Ernest had made. 'We're delighted you accomplished your task, Mr Barton. We're delighted that things will return to normal.'

Ernest smiled at them. 'Ah, but that's the thing, you see. I'm not sure things will return to normal, gentlemen. I'm not sure it's that simple.'

He saw them flinch, a ripple of concern that pulsed down the line of old bodies.

'What? We don't understand.' Hindy could not quite conceal the brusqueness of panic. 'Why not?'

'The intruders have left.' Luden snapped. 'You've assured us of that.'

Ernest smiled more widely. 'Yes, I have assured you of that, and you can take my word.' He paused. 'But, gentlemen, even so, I do believe everything might change.'

'Mr Barton, you shouldn't say such things.' Ata's distress made him slide his words, his accent coming strong.

Ernest ignored him. 'It's about time. About damn time, wouldn't you say?' He gave them the slightest of seconds to answer, huffing a laugh. 'It seems that Ellie—'

'That girl!' spat Luden. 'We need to be rid of that girl.'

'Don't start that. Don't you dare.' Ernest glared.

'You've been telling her all sorts, I know that. Feeding misinformation – that's what we used to call it – having her on. But the game is up, gentlemen. We're on to you. She's seen that rogue Quersley for the conniving, underhand scoundrel that he is, and she's seen through your stories. She's decided she'll have none of them. None of them. Not a word of the lies you've been telling.' He paused and looked hard at them. 'Which leaves us with a question – which of course you will have foreseen. And the question is – what shall we do?' He spoke with sudden clarity.

His anger was so contained, such a real threat, that the men stepped backwards together, pushing up against the doorframe.

'Do?' Hindy echoed.

'Yes, indeed. *Do*. About you. About our situation here.' He took a breath and went on more cheerfully. 'You see, my boys, I seem to be getting the hang of things, too. After all this bloody time.' He snorted. 'I'm getting to understand Marlford, that's the thing.'

The men exchanged quick glances. 'We shouldn't leave you then,' Hindy said. 'The affair with the intruders seems to have unsettled you. We should stay.'

'Very kind, gentlemen, but absolutely no need. No need at all. I'm in fine form. I don't need you.'

'You're sulking,' Luden hissed. 'Because we wouldn't fire guns.'

'No. I don't think I am. I just don't think I need you. I'm all right here.' Ernest stepped forwards. It was unclear what would happen next; the men watched him warily, ready to defend themselves, but he simply reached out and offered to shake hands.

Luden was perhaps too stiff in the joints to respond. It was only very slowly that he raised his hand in reply and placed it limply in Ernest's.

'Good fellow.' Ernest closed his grip, rattling the old man with the force of his shake. He smiled steadily, delightedly, and passed along the line, finally slapping Hindy on the shoulder.

Hindy puffed and wobbled; for a moment it seemed as though the three of them might tumble, like dominoes.

'I rather think it's time to take charge of things, don't you?' Ernest finished by asking.

'Charge of things here?' Hindy managed to reply weakly.

'Good God, man, what does it matter to you? What business is it of yours?' Ernest's bluster gave way to a laugh. 'My word, she was quite right... Ellie was quite right about your damn meddling. And I won't have any more of it. Now' – he flapped his hands at them, dismissing them lightly – 'scoot off, the lot of you, to bed. Haggard old stumpies – you look like you need your beauty sleep.'

His playfulness was unanswerable. He walked away from them, across the study, so that they found there was no choice but to do as he commanded.

Ernest heard their shuffle, the puffs and grunts of exertion as they crammed through the door, none of them allowing the others to pass in front. He shook his head at their absurdity and, when the sound of their footsteps had receded, he found it was an enormous relief.

He eased into his chair again, stiffly, an old man. He was not quite sure yet what would come of the long evening, but he suspected already that it might free him.

Twenty-Six

Ellie stared into the black corners of her room. She shivered, chilled through. Her mind seemed quite empty, devoid of even the most insubstantial of thoughts, her feelings vanished and her knowledge snatched from her, irretrievable. She could not summon a single verse: not a line of philosophy in any language, not the shortest of epigraphs. She could not place herself anywhere but here, sitting on her bed in the absolute dark, her candle burnt out, nothing in the house made to hold or comfort her; her grief nothing more than the faintest of whispers, a moment of confusion in the duplication of steady years.

She seemed to be left with nothing.

She pulled herself stiffly from the bed and tried to relight her candle, but her hand was shaking too violently and the wick was exhausted, so she simply accepted the dark, feeling her way out onto the landing, the faint slap of her bare feet provoking only meagre echoes.

As she made her way down the stairs, her presence did not seem to register at all: it was too slight a thing. It was only when she switched on the light in the billiard room that she made any impression on the slumbering house.

Ellie picked up her cue and chalked it. She began to play a game, easing the reds towards a pocket. But nothing was quite right: the click of the balls was impatient and teasing, the cue felt heavy in her hands; her action was clumsy. The brilliance of the light over the table seemed too harsh, the rest of the room too dark and damp, and there was an odd swelling lodged behind her breastbone, building, shifting, distracting her, as though she had swallowed a storm cloud. She racked up a score easily enough, but she could not see the point of it.

She stabbed at the white ball but the cue's tip skidded sideways with the force of the thrust, plunging through the tattered baize and ripping a long tear up to the top cushion. Ellie stared at the damage, the disconcerting smoothness of the dark slate beneath, like new skin, and, without warning, the cloud burst inside her, years of anguish unconsoled.

She began to pull at the cloth, tugging apart the tear yet further, sliding her nails into the baize, scratching through the threads, clawing down to the grey stone. She yanked at the cushions, tearing the pockets from their fixings, and then, again, back to the baize, gouging at it over and over until she was in a dull, green haze, tiny threads floating about her, a dust of old fabric filling the air like a fine rain.

In this sudden shower she was fully alive.

Drifting up to the hot, bare light, the dry tinder of the shredded baize, still stiff with traces of old glue, caught fire quickly, sparking flames that ignited the messy electrics. The blaze appeared suddenly at switches, crackling in the walls in a way that Ellie would have thought impossible. There was smoke stuffing the room within a moment, thick and acrid; noises suddenly all over, like a wind howling within the house. Even as the flames around her stuttered, perhaps dying away, burning themselves out, she knew that they had lit a touch paper to a much larger conflagration.

Marlford was on fire.

Twenty-Seven

When Dan was released from hospital, three days after he was shot, Gadiel went to meet him at the bus stop at the far edge of the village, beyond the cricket ground. He seemed quite well. Nonetheless, they walked unhurriedly, at an invalid's pace.

'It looks all right.' Gadiel gestured at the bulge of dressing under Dan's T-shirt.

'Yeah, man. It's cool.' Dan was melancholy.

It was odd, how little they had to say. They did not seem to know each other. Dan's journey to the hospital had already been enough to separate him from Marlford; his return had a temporary air, a concession.

'I did some exploring, while you were laid up,' Gadiel said, eventually. 'I went down to the works, camped out a couple of nights, by the side of the salt lakes there.'

'Flashes,' Dan corrected him. 'They're called flashes.'

They walked on, the lines of cottages stretching out to meet them and gather them in, the hedges and trees, the open cricket field giving way suddenly to the firm enclosure of the grid of streets.

They paused at the nymph and lolled against the fountain ledge.

'I wanted to head off,' Gadiel continued. 'I wanted to think about things.'

The water plinked steadily behind them; ahead, Victoria Street was barred, cordoned off with heavy barriers. The village seemed deserted, as though Braithwaite Barton's experiment was over and time had moved on, abandoning the elegant buildings, the sculpted stonework, the tended flowerbeds and identical window boxes; abandoning the heaving pit of wet rubble and the skewed library, leaving it all as testament to something not quite decided.

Dan puffed thoughtfully at his cigarette. 'I don't know what I'm going to do about getting my van.'

A coil of yellowish smoke wound across from the works, hardly carried by the still air. They could hear the clank and groan of a heavy vehicle edging round the bend at the top of Victoria Street, piled with equipment: girders and pulleys, bulky chains. They watched while the load was delivered and stacked by the benches at Braithwaite Barton's feet. Then the lorry reversed and disappeared, the rumble of it fading.

'It'll be all right,' Gadiel said. 'We can talk to Ellie about it.'

Dan shook his head energetically. 'That place is vicious. We've escaped once. I'm not going through it all again, man.'

'But don't you feel sad for her? We've just left her there, on her own. I was thinking about it while you were in hospital, and I reckon – well, she must have liked you, to go with you in the van like that. She must have thought—'

'She was messing about.' Dan stabbed a foot at the stone fountain. 'Just hanging out. That's all. Expressing herself… experimenting.'

'You don't mean that. You know that's not true.'

'After I was shot, she told me she never wanted to see me again. She chucked me out of the house, man. She's one of them, through and through – unreconstructed. There's nothing we can do with her.'

Dan remembered it that way now, having thought it over. He dropped his finished cigarette-end, a stubby finger. It pointed at him, accusatorily; he kicked it away. 'That was it… you know. One of those things.'

'I think we should go back.' Gadiel was firm. 'I think we should go back and see her. We can't just leave her, we can't just run away.'

'I am not going back there.'

'Oh, come on, they're not going to shoot you again, Dan. It was just a confusion, that's all. It got out of hand.'

'No way, man.'

'But you want your van back, don't you? You're not going to just leave it there to rot?'

Dan glared at him. 'I'm working on a strategy for it.'

'But you don't need a strategy. You just need to go and talk to them. It's no big deal. We can go and face up to things.'

'What do you mean, "face up to things"? We haven't done anything to face up to.'

Gadiel splashed his hand through the water pooling at the nymph's feet. 'Let's just go back, Dan. One more time. You need to get your van, I want to… I want to talk to Ellie. We can show them that you're all right now, that it doesn't matter about being shot. It'll resolve things.'

Dan huffed. 'I think it matters. I don't like being shot.' But he recognized Gadiel's determination. 'Look, if it wasn't for the van, you know – if they didn't have my van, I wouldn't set foot there again.' He thought of something else. 'And I'm not getting into debate with Ellie. We're done with all that, man. I'm not getting into it all again.'

'I'll talk to Ellie,' said Gadiel.

Dan shuffled up against the rim of the fountain, leaning back to take the weight from his injured shoulder; Gadiel took a step or two away across the cobbles.

'I'm going to stay on and help,' he announced, finally.

Dan sniffed. 'What on earth for?'

'They still need manpower, for the library. And generally, for the repairs.'

Dan looked with him at the skinned library, loosely held by the rubble at its base, forlorn and out of place, an eyesore.

'They'd be better off knocking it down and starting again.' The building seemed to flounder, to shift and creak, even as they were gazing at it. 'I don't see the point. In any of it.' He rubbed thoughtfully at his bandages. 'But I suppose, if you like. We could get the van fixed and bring it down and find a good place to park. I suppose a couple more weeks won't make much difference.'

Gadiel spoke with quiet steadiness. 'I didn't think we'd both stay. I didn't think you'd want to. I thought it would just be me.'

Dan pushed himself up, awkwardly. 'Oh, come on, man. You want to come in the van, don't you?'

Gadiel smiled. 'I think I'll just stay. On my own. And do something useful.'

'But, man, we were going to travel together. That was the plan. It was going to be cool.'

'I know. But things have changed, Dan.'

Dan pushed at his spectacles, leaving his hand across his face for a long moment, obscuring his eyes. 'Yeah, well, things are changing everywhere, aren't they? That's the point, man. All over the place. This was just a setback. An anomaly. Whatever we'd done here – well, time's up on places like Marlford, and pretty soon it'll all be different. The squat – it could have been something. Given a chance. It's a setback, that's all.'

'I'm not travelling with you. I'll come and sort out about the van. I'll help you get it back. But after that—'

'You're going to split on me, man, aren't you?'

Gadiel offered him a sad smile. 'I don't think I can look out for you any more,' he said.

The manor looked much as it had always done, the stonework resolutely intact, undiminished and unconcerned. But there was a car, parked in the smear of shadow beneath a beech tree, and it drew them across the front of the house.

They stood looking at it, stupidly: a small black car, unremarkable.

'I'm not going in. Not if mad old Barton's there,' Dan said.

'He doesn't have a car. It won't be him.'

'But it'll be someone visiting him, won't it?'

'Hello.' A voice sounded close behind them. 'Can I help you?'

They knew it was not Ernest bearing down on them, but they started nonetheless; Dan gasped, clutching defensively at his injured shoulder.

'Sorry.' The man fiddled in his pocket for keys. 'Didn't mean to frighten you. Spooky old place, though, isn't it? It gets you like that.' He smiled amiably and then lowered his voice, as if giving away a great secret. 'Gives me the willies.'

'We were looking for Ellie,' Gadiel explained. 'We know Ellie.'

The man shook his head. 'Can't help you. The family's gone off somewhere. Someone at the office might know, if I ask – but I haven't got any information myself, I'm afraid. I think the fire was the last straw for them.'

'The fire?' Gadiel pushed his hair hard behind his ears. 'Has there been a fire? Has anyone been hurt?'

'No one was hurt. It was just a case of faulty electrics. It started with a light in the billiard room. The girl…'

'Ellie,' prompted Gadiel.

'That's the one. She was playing a game, apparently.' He shook his head and raised his eyebrows to signal Ellie's certain madness. 'At four o'clock in the morning, mind you. All by herself. Loopy or what?'

He caught sight of Gadiel's expression. 'No offence. Just an observation. She got the house evacuated, that sort of thing. It could have been a whole lot worse if they'd all been asleep in bed. A whole lot worse.'

Dan stared at the façade. In the clear afternoon light it looked cleaner than before. 'It doesn't look like there was a fire.'

The man came alongside and looked with him at the lurching cadence of stone and glass. 'It's gutted inside, more or less. This wing.'

'But you know we've got our stuff in there, man. We've got things, upstairs, in the house. I mean, do you think it would be all right if we went to get them? Would it be safe?'

The man grimaced. 'I don't think I can let you go in.'

'But we had a squat – upstairs. We've got belongings there, man. Clothes and the radio and some books,' Dan continued.

'A squat? In there?' The man whistled, shaking his head. 'What on earth for?'

'We were making a statement. We were challenging obsolete structures and anachronistic opinions.'

'Were you?' The man shrugged, giving them a quizzical, sidelong look. 'Well, sorry – you can't go back. It's dangerous. The staircases are gone; the ceilings are down – there're whacking great holes in the floor. I've done the assessment and, frankly, the place is a wreck.'

'But what should we do? We had rights there. We were squatters.'

'If it were me,' the man said, 'I'd cut my losses. These things happen. Old places like this – they're death traps.'

Gadiel scanned the front of the manor once more. 'But there's no one in there? He's not there – Mr Barton?'

'Nope.' The man shook his head. 'Just me. And I'm off now. I've got another appointment.'

'And Ellie – you don't know where she's gone?' Gadiel asked, too quietly, knowing the answer.

The man did not seem to notice the question. 'Even before the fire, the place must have been crumbling. There's damp, dry rot, woodworm. All kinds of leaks. That's without the dodgy electrics. That's what happens these days. No one can afford to keep these houses up.'

He made a looping descent with his thumbs. 'And so they come down. Crash, bang.' He clapped. 'Wallop.' He waved a hand across the expanse of estate. 'Look at it all. It's a mess. A waste. Good land going to waste. There's even some weird old codgers camped out down there – God, they've been there for years, apparently. We're getting rid of them.' He looked at his watch. 'Look, I'm sorry, like I said, I have to go. If I were you, I'd keep out of the way.'

He turned the key in the car door and stamped his feet gently against the ground to shed loose dirt from his shoes. 'Don't go in. You'll get hurt.'

He raised a quick hand, a brief farewell.

The car pulled away, taking the sweep of the drive slowly. Dan and Gadiel watched until it had disappeared into the stippled shadows of the lime walk.

'Do we dare it then? Do we go in?' Dan asked.

Gadiel was ahead of him already, making for the portico. He looked back over his shoulder but said nothing. Dan ran a step or two to make up the ground between them; they went on together.

The front door to the manor was open, or perhaps it was no longer there at all. As soon as they stepped up onto the portico, they were struck by the cold air, the pungent smell of smoke and charred wood, the vacancy where the grandeur of the old hallway had been. It brought them to a halt.

Gadiel went forward carefully. He placed one hand on the doorframe, an anchor, and leaned forwards as far as he could.

'Well?' Dan pushed up behind him. 'What is there?'

Gadiel pulled back, moving quickly away from the manor, stepping down onto the churned gravel.

'Gadiel? Are we going in? What's it look like in there?'

'It's gone,' Gadiel replied. 'Gutted. And it's like—'

'Like what?'

Gadiel smiled uncertainly; he shook his head. 'It's weird, that's all.'

'What is, man? What's weird?'

'Well, it's like you can still hear the fire. It's like you can hear it rushing through the house and the roar of it and the crackle of the flames. I thought I heard the crack of glass – with the heat.'

'But that's impossible, man. It isn't on fire. It must have been put out days ago.'

'Yes, I know. And it's freezing in there. You feel the cold coming out. But even so…'

Dan laughed. He pushed his spectacles up with a jab of his finger, glanced at Gadiel and stepped up to the threshold, poking his head through the doorway.

Gadiel stayed where he was, scuffing the gravel with his boot. He saw Dan flinch and draw back, a moment later making a hurried retreat.

'Well?'

'Let's just get the van. We'll leave the squat. It must have gone.'

'Did you hear it, though? Did you hear the fire?'

Dan refused to answer. He put his hand on the wound in his shoulder, still sore.

'This place plays tricks,' was all he said.

Dan stared at the space in front of the abandoned stables.

'My van. It can't have gone. It didn't work, man. It was kaput – broken down. It can't have gone.'

But the yard was empty, and there was no one to ask.

They went down the track to Home Farm, but the house there, too, was deserted, the pigs rushing at them noisily across the yard. Gadiel climbed a tree, sliding into a nook from where he could see into the windows and hallooing, cupping his hands, shouting out as loudly as he could, but there were just the animal noises coming back at him, restive.

Dan leaned his forehead against the top bar of a gate. 'I can't believe it. Insidious, that's what it is. This whole thing, man – insidious. We should never have come.'

'Well, we didn't come on purpose, did we? It was just luck.' Gadiel slid easily onto the ground and put a hand on Dan's back. 'Don't worry, we'll look for it. We'll look all over.'

But it felt hopeless even as they began. For an hour or so they trailed around, peering into fields and following faint tracks. Even though it was obvious that no one could push a van through the dense woodland that circled the mere, they tramped through the undergrowth anyway.

Finally, Dan stood at the water's edge, watching the thin waves slap against a tree root. 'What if it's down in there?' He leaned over as far as he could, as though to catch a glimpse of submerged bodywork shimmering below the surface, but he saw only his writhing reflection.

'I think we have to accept it's gone, Dan.'

'But it can't have. It can't have just vanished, man. I don't believe it.'

In the end, the men told them what had happened. They were seated on folding chairs in a line on the scrappy roadway in front of the hutments, waiting; as the squatters approached, they rose, steadying themselves.

Hindy stepped forwards. 'We had wondered if you might return at some point,' he said.

Dan frowned at a coil of barbed wire that curled into the mud, trying to make sense of its viciousness. 'My van's gone.'

'And we heard about the fire,' Gadiel added, more kindly. 'We're very sorry.'

'There was no tragedy.' Luden was brisk. 'Not in the end. There was no need to come.'

The men exchanged glances, condemning such extravagant behaviour.

'No – we didn't come for that. We came to collect our things,' Dan explained.

'Look,' said Gadiel. 'We don't want to bother you. But do you know where they've gone, Mr Barton and Ellie? Did they tell you?'

'And about my van?' Dan prompted. 'We're looking for my van. It was in the yard, man, but it's disappeared.'

Hindy seemed troubled. He cleared his throat. 'Mr Quersley took the vehicle, I understand.'

'What? The librarian? How?' Dan stared.

The men all nodded solemnly, confirming Hindy's story.

'We were unable to prevent him.' Ata was apologetic. 'We didn't even know about it until it was too late, I'm afraid.'

'And he was hell bent,' added Luden.

'But how…? It was broken. He couldn't have taken it. Not without equipment.' Dan looked from one to the other of them. 'I don't understand.'

'He spent some time on repairs, I believe,' said Hindy.

'But he had no right to do that. It's my van.'

'Yes, indeed.'

Ata looked at Hindy, and then took up the explanation more fully. 'It seems he acquired a manual of some sort and worked hard to make the vehicle ready. He simply drove off. He never mentioned a word to Mr Barton, nor even to us, after everything. It was the evening of the fire, around midnight – or possibly later. We couldn't be sure of the exact time. We were having rather a lengthy hand of cards and we heard the engine whilst we were playing.'

'The thing was spluttering,' Luden pointed out. 'It's not the finest example of motor engineering.'

'We were going to investigate. But at that hour…' Ata allowed the idea to drift away.

'Do you think he's coming back?' Gadiel asked. 'There're animals still at the farm and it doesn't look… He won't have gone for good, will he?'

Ata looked at Hindy, who replied with great care.

'My own opinion is that he will be gone for some time.'

Dan was sharp. 'But this is theft, man. In anybody's book. It's a crime. I'm going to inform the police. I need to get on; we both need to get on. We need to find the van. We can't just let him drive off in my van.' He stormed off towards a clotted mound of broken stone and rusting wire and kicked at the debris.

Luden sat down heavily, as though things were concluded. 'Well.' It was a dismissal of sorts.

'Yes, we'll be going. I'm sorry,' Gadiel said. 'But just… can you tell me where I might find Ellie? I'm – we're rather concerned about her. She didn't go with him, did she? With Mr Quersley and the van?'

The men fixed flat expressions on him.

'I'm afraid we can't tell you,' Hindy replied.

'Oh, come on – you must know something.'

'We know rather less than you might think. We were not party to Mr Barton's plans. Nor Miss Barton's. Not in any way.'

'Is Mr Barton coming back? Do you know that, at least?'

'Mr Barton was lost here at Marlford.' Luden leaned back in his chair. He spoke gravely, as though delivering a legal judgement. 'His attempts to be a fitting incumbent were – as you saw for yourselves – ridiculous. Why would he come back?'

Dan circled around, coming towards them again to hear the end of the discussion. 'But you're still here,' he pointed out. 'Why would you stay on here if no one's coming back?'

'We keep an eye on things,' Hindy said.

'We fill a gap,' Ata added. 'A void, if you like.'

'A gap in what?' Dan glanced involuntarily back towards the manor, as though it might be some kind of architectural service the men performed.

Hindy, too, looked away towards the house. 'In people's minds, I suppose.'

Dan snorted. 'But if they evict you, then you'll have to go. The man we met at the house was damn certain they would evict you. You see? You should have supported us, man. You should have joined the squat. Then you couldn't have been evicted.'

'We'll ignore any attempt to evict us,' Hindy responded, evenly. 'I imagine we're quite secure here. We'll continue as we've always done.'

Dan shook his head at them. 'I'd like to see you – just the three of you – trying to hold out against bailiffs and enforcers, and what-have-you. I've seen this kind of thing before. It takes skill, you know – political nous. To play the game the right way. But if we'd only got going here, if people had come and joined us—'

'That was never a possibility,' Luden said.

'Yeah, but don't you see? You stand no chance. You're defeated, man.'

The men looked at him, puzzled, as though he were asking them to solve a complicated sum.

'You can't stay here. You'll be chucked out – sent to an old folks' home or something.' Dan wondered if they had grown deaf in his absence: they showed no signs of understanding. 'I mean, what have you been trying to do, man? What have you been holding out for?'

He gave them time to answer, but they just looked at him, uncomprehending. They were shaking, it was true, each of them trembling, but it may have been the cool breeze from the mere chilling them through, or their age catching up with them.

'Marlford's finished. It's done for,' he said, slowly. 'It's succumbing to the inevitable forces of change.'

Ata smiled, at Dan first and then in turn, carefully, at each of them. Hindy and Luden took up the smile and stretched it between them.

Gadiel sighed. 'Look, we're sorry, about everything, but you really don't know about the Bartons? You can't tell us where they are?'

'We know nothing.' Hindy's smile was still fixed.

'Nothing? Not the slightest clue?'

'Nothing.'

Gadiel frowned at them, baffled, knowing that they would not help him. He had the odd impression that he was talking to mannequins, outdated, dumped in a tangled strip of wasteland, lined up on chairs as a joke: they seemed suddenly to have shed their flesh, taking on the sickly, disturbing sheen of old plastic. He turned his back on them.

As he and Dan returned to the village, Gadiel took one last look – he could not resist – but what he saw was uncertain, the cluster of dilapidated hutments meaningless, the rotting debris a confusion, the men still unmoving; none of it really worth his attention.

Twenty-Eight

One of the diggers dropped its load, adding to the clamour around the library, trussed now in wires and chains, boarded up and braced, veiled with plastic sheeting, unrecognizable. Victoria Street had been churned into a filthy track of black mud, most of the buildings wore complicated strata of grime; the Hepworth Barton Bank had acquired solid bespoke shutters. New walkways promised novel ways of negotiating the streets, suggesting different vistas, disrupting old routines. Most of the shops had found ways of serving customers from side doors or back windows, from borrowed premises and disused garages. At the newsagents, a stone's throw from the nymph, they were selling postcards of modern Marlford, views of buildings slumped by subsidence, of the gaping pit in the middle of the village, of Braithwaite Barton gazing serenely over his dismembered legacy. The disintegration had brought an element of fame.

The almshouses at the edge of the village remained untouched by the worst of the upheaval. Ellie paused on the path that cut across their prim garden frontage, watching a bee burrow into a spike of delphinium. Its buzz grew shrill for a moment, and then it emerged dusted in pollen, taking flight clumsily. When it had disappeared into the summer light around the nymph, she turned away, seeing nothing else. She could imagine, if she wanted to, that the village was as it had always been.

She walked behind the row of cottages, crossing a narrow yard. There was a row of back doors, each painted an identical bottle green and fixed with a brass handle. Ellie went to the middle door, which was ajar. As she pushed it further open, she called, stepping inside and calling again, emptying the contents of her shopping basket onto the small kitchen table.

Finally, Ernest shouted back to her from the sitting room. 'There's someone coming. Ellie — there's someone coming. Up the path. To the front. To the door.'

A moment later, she heard the rapid knock. She paused, wiping her hands on her skirt.

The knock sounded again, more resolutely.

'Ellie!'

'Yes, Papa. I hear it.'

'It's a man. In overalls. A workman of some kind.'

'Leave it, Papa. It's nothing, I'm sure.' She could not imagine who it might be. 'Something about the library, perhaps. But I don't want to bother with it. Not now.'

'Don't be a fool. We can't leave it. He's seen me. He can see me through the window.'

Ellie sighed. 'Very well. But you know we agreed we wouldn't allow visitors here, Papa. We promised ourselves that.'

Her father did not reply.

Ellie went through to the front, leaving the back door standing wide open, a breeze blowing through, an escape of some kind.

Gadiel was too tall for the scowl of the thatched porch. He had to stoop. Despite this, he stood quite still on the step, smiling with uncomplicated delight.

'I saw you. I've seen you once or twice before, just for a moment, coming and going in the village, but I never worked out where you were living. Then I saw you, just now, and I guessed you were living here, in one of these cottages. You are living here, aren't you?'

'Yes. With Papa.'

'Yes, I saw him, at the window. That's how I worked out which door to knock on. That's how I was sure.'

Behind and alongside her, the narrow hall was stuffed with library books, neatly stacked, crammed close and high, piled against the walls almost to the ceiling, leaving the slightest of passages, like the cut of a steep ravine.

She saw Gadiel's surprise. 'They're everywhere.' She shook her head; it was still a wonder. 'The house is full of them. They stored them here when they began work on the library. The cottage was empty then. But, after the fire – well, it was the only place we could find and we agreed that if they let us stay here, we'd make room for ourselves, and I'd do some work on the books at the same time, so they'd be ready to go back.'

'Isn't it cramped, though?'

'Yes, I suppose. A little.'

Gadiel stepped back, away from the porch. 'Well.'

He straightened to his full height. 'The library should be moved today.'

'Yes, I know. I read about it in the newspaper.'

'I'm working with one of the engineering firms.' He gestured at his overalls as explanation. 'Just for a while. As experience.'

'I imagine there's a great deal to learn.'

'Yeah.' He stuffed his hands in his pockets.

'A great many technical skills.'

He glanced at her. 'You're not interested in that kind of thing, are you? You don't think it matters.'

'Oh, yes, I do. Of course I do. I didn't mean to suggest… It's just not something I understand, that's all.' Ellie pushed at one of the piles of books, dropping her gaze.

'No,' Gadiel said. 'I suppose not.'

'But it's valuable, of course, I'm sure it is.'

'I like it.' He crossed his arms over his chest. The action seemed too deliberate, the ensuing silence too long.

Ellie rubbed her hands on her skirt again. 'Can you spare a moment? Would you like to come in and see Papa?'

'Oh, wait – no. No thanks.' Gadiel grimaced exaggeratedly, in mock horror, and it drew her eyes back to his face. She recognized the sparkle about him, lodged under his skin. 'Poor old Dan's still telling stories about his gunshot wound. I don't fancy another scuffle like that.'

'It'll be fine, really – Papa's much better here.'

'Even so. I don't suppose he'd be too pleased to see a squatter again.'

'He won't mind, I'm sure. He doesn't even seem to think of Marlford any more. He's much quieter, without things to bother him, without the worry of the place and the frogs at the mere...' She stopped and smiled, an invitation. 'You'd be very welcome.'

'Well. Thanks... that's kind.' Gadiel saw something new in the lines around her mouth; he tried to work out what it might be. It was hardly anything – the slightest flutter of expression – but it disconcerted him. He felt as though he had been away a long time. 'I could step in briefly, if you like. I'm allowed a break from work – twenty minutes or so.'

'Good. That would be nice.'

He followed her through the alley of books. The almshouse was compact: there were just two small rooms opening from the hallway, the kitchen, at the back, and the sitting room to one side. Ernest was in an armchair by the window of the sitting room, surrounded on all sides by piles of books, uneven in height, pushed into elaborate patterns, like the eroding columns of a limestone pavement.

He rose, offering a hand to Gadiel. 'Ah – yes. I saw you coming.' His voice was too big for the tiny almshouse, too great a challenge to its respectability.

'How do you do, Mr Barton. I'm Gadiel Hampton. I was – I was one of the squatters. At Marlford.'

'Were you?' Ernest peered at him as though looking for a landmark lost in fog. 'Not the blighter that Quersley shot?'

'No, sir.'

'No. I thought not.' But he did not sound sure. 'You're the one who knocked me down, then?'

'Yes – I'm sorry about that. It was just a panic... but I'm sorry about the whole squat thing, really. It wasn't really what we thought... we shouldn't have—'

'Bloody mess. Best forgotten.' Ernest shook off the memory and glanced at Ellie. 'Not that good things didn't come of it, in the end.' He reached for his daughter and gripped her hand as she stepped towards him. Regret seeped through the bags of his old skin. It was very calm for a moment, their reconciliation revisited.

Then Ernest started, as though he had been pricked, slung a nod at Gadiel and pushed past him. 'I'm going to watch them shift that thing,' he said, smiling at Ellie. 'I'll go the back way and fetch my hat and coat from the kitchen.'

'If you wait, Papa, I'll come with you.'

But Ernest had sidled through the labyrinth. 'Don't need an escort,' he called cheerfully, from the hallway.

They heard him dressing to go out and then the pull of the back door.

Ellie looked towards the noise. 'You've no idea how cruel a trick was played on us,' she said, quietly.

Gadiel was not sure whether he was supposed to answer. 'A trick?'

'A kind of trick. Mr Quersley led me to believe – well, he turned me against my father. He poisoned my ideas.'

Gadiel could not measure her tone. 'Really? You didn't seem very close, you and your father.'

She smiled at him, ruefully. 'No. That's because of what Mr Quersley told me, because of things in the past. I regret it now. And now that it's just Papa and I—'

'I wish you'd drop that whole "Papa" thing.' Gadiel was suddenly nettled. 'It sounds stupid. Like you're some Victorian half-wit.'

Ellie frowned. 'What should I call him then?'

'I don't know.' He tugged at the pocket of his overalls. 'I just think – it makes you seem old-fashioned.'

'I am old-fashioned. Look at me.' She opened her arms to show him the extent of her dress, plain, beige cotton.

'But, Ellie—'

'Oh!' Her moan seemed involuntary; she looked surprised for a moment that such a wretched sound had been drawn from her, but then went on in a low, urgent tone. 'I've been so unfair to him. All my life I've been so wrong.'

'No – Ellie, stop, I'm sure that's not true. Whatever this Mr Quersley did, whatever he said to you—'

'But I believed it. Exactly as it was told to me. I failed my father; I failed to imagine how it might have been different. I did a terrible thing – arrogant and stupid. If I'd only talked to him. But I was so frightened that I'd be weak, that he'd make me love him, when I didn't want to, when he didn't deserve it…'

Gadiel wanted to comfort her but he felt awkward there, with the books closing in on all sides and her distress so tangible.

'I'm sure it'll be all right,' he reassured her feebly.

She did not seem to hear. 'It'll take us so long now to know each other. And we don't have all that much time, do we? A few years, perhaps, that's all – everything else is lost. Everything that could have been is lost, and we can't even begin to know what it might have been like.'

Gadiel realized for the first time that he was intruding: another man had come before him, captivating her.

'I'm sorry,' he said.

'I'm learning to be his daughter, you see, so that we're not on our own again, with everything uncertain and no one knowing what to believe. Nothing else matters, does it, other than that – nobody cares about the Bartons or the past or anything. I know that now.' She blinked, still puzzled by the revelation, vapid and unsatisfactory, unwanted.

'Ellie, I wouldn't have come after you if you hadn't wanted to be found.'

She looked up at him, perplexed, as though she had just discovered him there among the mounds of old books and rotting papers. 'Oh, no – I'm pleased you came.' But she sounded rueful, distracted. 'I didn't know the squatters had stayed in the village. I presumed you'd gone, straight away.'

'Look, I should probably go back to work.'

'Are you both here? Is Dan here?'

She gave nothing away with the question. He could not tell what answer she wanted.

'No. He's out of hospital – he's fine. But it's only me here now. He's gone off.'

She heard the fragility of his regret. 'I'm sorry – if you've fallen out. I'm sorry that you're on your own.'

'Oh, no, it's fine. It was me who... I met one of the engineers in the pub and got talking. They suggested that I helped with the library and it seemed too good an opportunity to miss, so I decided to hang around. When that's done, well, I'll go on to another project, if they'll have me.'

Ellie took a sharp intake of breath, as though she had been stung. 'But what about your studies?'

'I think I'll let them go.' He smiled sheepishly. 'I've told you – it's not really my thing. The summer's made me clear on that, at least.'

'No… really? You've decided that… since coming here?' The flutter in her voice suggested a greater tragedy. 'But that's terrible, that your visit to Marlford has made you abandon your learning.'

The mantelpiece clock – a cheap round face in an arched plastic case – chimed the half-hour neatly.

Gadiel examined the hands sadly, avoiding her disappointment. 'Look, I'd better go. I'm glad you're all right, though. We heard about the fire. We went to the house.'

'I'm fine.'

'They wouldn't tell me where you'd gone.'

'I'm not sure it was a great secret. It was just confused, at first, trying to find somewhere.'

'There was a man there, at the house; an official bloke.'

'Yes. Marlford's being demolished.'

The words came impassively, but in Ellie's glance something trembled, a tiny movement, like the ripple of a gnat against a blue sky.

He stepped towards her. 'Oh, Ellie – no. I'm sorry.'

'Oh, it's fine. Really.' She pulled away. 'The land can be used for other things. They want to – build. Again.' She could not concentrate; could not think about Marlford. She felt she was breathing too quickly. 'But it doesn't matter. We couldn't have gone on there, anyway. This way we'll have money to live on; when it comes through, we'll perhaps find somewhere else to go – somewhere less cramped.'

He filled the room, the breadth of his shoulders seeming to stretch from wall to wall. She leaned against the books. 'Will you tell me, about the library?' Her question was too abrupt. 'I'd be interested to hear how the arrangements have been made.'

'Another time.' He was suddenly annoyed. They were back where they had started. 'I'd better get back now before they start winching.'

'Yes, all right.'

'And I won't be able to come again. I'll be moving on. I'll have to get lodgings and everything.'

She nodded, and just her movement softened his anger.

'Look, Ellie – I just wanted to say… to ask…' He did not know, now, what it was that he could ask. He felt the crush of the books around him, the heavy scent of discarded paper; he looked away from them, out of the window. There were glimpses of activity at the end of the street, construction vehicles gathering, the lines of the houses blotted by equipment. Noises reached them, grating.

'I should go after Papa,' Ellie said.

'He'll be all right, won't he?'

'But I want to see, anyway; I want to see the library moved. It should be quite an occasion.' She went to the window and leaned against the glass to look towards the nymph. She felt the soothing coolness against her cheek and pulled away.

'I stayed because of you.' Gadiel spoke quietly.

'I don't understand.'

'Yes, you do, Ellie. If you think about it. If you let yourself.'

She laughed briefly, tightly, tapping one of the books at her side. 'Have you read *The Elmridge Chronicles*? It's here somewhere.' She scanned the room quickly, the merest suggestion of a search. 'Well, anyway – I don't suppose you have. It's not a well-known book. It's not a classic or anything; it's long out of print. We might be the only library that still keeps a copy. And the plot is silly really, not very credible. But the point is… well, you see, the point is…'

But she could not think what the point was. It was slipping from her.

'I don't want to bother you, Ellie. If I'm stepping out of line… if you're not interested…'

'No, but you see, in the book, there's an incident in the narrative… there's a girl… Oh, I can't remember. I had it in my head, and it's gone.'

It was his fault, gazing at her in that way, filling the room as if nothing else existed. She looked despairingly at the evidence of learning wedged against the walls.

'Just tell me, Ellie.' He was encouraged by the tears she did not seem to have noticed. 'You can explain about the book later. For now, just tell me how you feel. That'll be enough; that'll be fine.'

It was such a singular request. It was too much; it sapped her strength.

'Just look at me, Ellie.'

She raised her eyes to his.

'I couldn't leave Papa,' she said. 'Not now.'

'No, I know. That's fine. I'm not asking that. I only want us to spend some time together, that's all. I want to get to know you.'

'I don't know.'

'Why not? Don't you like me?'

'Yes,' she answered, steadily. 'I do like you. Very much. But it's not as easy as that.'

'It could be.'

'No, Gadiel, I've been telling you – my father isn't the man I thought he was; he's a good man. An honourable man, who loves me. And I'm not the person I thought I was. I'm not some kind of accidental life, just clinging on, like I thought I was, at Marlford, by chance. I'm his daughter. He wants me, as his daughter.' She looked at him gently, knowing she could not explain so that he would ever understand. 'I'm sorry. Everything is confused. I have to work it all out.'

She felt the tears now and pushed them softly from her cheeks, looking at the gloss of damp on her finger.

'And I do like you.' She smiled, but without looking at him. 'And if I've been hard on you, or unfriendly…'

'You shouldn't wait for Dan.'

'No, no. I know. I'm not. I'm not waiting. I know that was just… that was nothing. I was foolish, that was all.' But tears again came, nonetheless, flowing more quickly at the memory.

'I'm not crying about him – really, it's not that. But when Mr Quersley left too… I've been lost, that's all – there's just so much…'

Gadiel was kind. 'We heard about the farmer. He took Dan's van.'

'I know.' She dropped her head, and picked at something under her nails. 'I don't know what to do,' she said, finally. 'If my father had done wicked things, like I thought he had – if he'd been a bad man, like the men made out… well, then, I suppose I could have started again. But now, without all that – I don't know who to be.'

'Just be Ellie.'

'But I don't know how. I don't think I'm like you. I can't just begin from here. There's too much from before.'

She looked at him, understanding the gentle way he leaned towards her and the sincerity in his eyes. She felt submerged, all of a sudden, as if caught by a riptide, clinging fast to something – a rock or a post. She felt she had been holding on for a long time – for ever perhaps – forcing herself to keep her grip, concentrating above all else on not giving in and being swept away; until her hands were numb, her skin rubbed away, her arms stiff with pain.

She felt the irresistible urge to let go.

'What would we do?' she asked him.

'I don't know.' She saw the hope in his face. 'We can decide that as we go along, I suppose. We could have a walk, or go for coffee. Have a day out somewhere.'

She sighed. If this was a book, an old tale, one of her favourites from the past, this was how it would end. All the stories she had spun in her head over all those years, they came to this, a resolution, romance achieved. It should have been enough.

She sighed again, more slowly, gathering her courage. 'Thank you,' she said. 'That sounds nice. It really does… But I think Papa needs me.'

Gadiel examined the cover of one of the books to his side, running his finger loosely over the binding. 'Not all the time, surely? Not every moment of every day? It might just be an hour or so, at first, if that's what you want. We don't need to do very much.'

'You don't understand.'

'Ellie – please. Whatever it was that went on, whatever this Mr Quersley told you, you can't let it ruin the rest of your life. You can't feel guilty the whole time. Your father wouldn't want that. He'd want you to be happy.'

'But that's the thing,' she replied. 'I am happy. For the first time, really.'

'But stuck on your own here' – he swept an arm around – 'in this funny little hole full of books?'

She shrugged. 'I'll be busy.'

'But I waited for you, all this time.'

'I'm sorry,' she replied. 'I am sorry. But, really, it's not been much time, has it? You've only been in Marlford a few weeks. It just seems longer. But it's been nothing, a blink – that's the astounding thing. And it's not my fault. I never asked you to wait. I never gave you encouragement.'

'But you did. I could always tell. I could always tell how you felt.'

She laughed. 'Then you're cleverer than I am.'

She felt the tide ebbing. It tugged at her still, but gently, allowing her to rest in its buoyancy. She held on now with little effort, the familiar pull in her arms a relief, of sorts.

'Ellie, just think about it, that's all I ask.' His voice was tightening. 'I can't see you waste yourself here, hiding yourself away.'

'I won't hide. When the library is moved, I'll have a great deal to do. Especially in Mr Quersley's absence. I imagine it will take a great deal of my time for a while.'

'But after that, Ellie? What will you do after that?'

His question sparked only a momentary jolt of alarm, barely visible. 'I suppose I'll have to wait and see.'

He came towards her slowly, until he was very close. 'And that's it?'

She smiled at him without reserve, her eyes bright

now, stepping back so that she could look directly into his kind face.

'I think that's all I can do,' she said.

Later, Ellie walked back to Victoria Street, to the groan of timbers and metal under strain, the creak of engines. She was forced to remain behind the barriers, watching from a distance with the rest of the villagers, but, through the crowd, she could see the corpse of the library rise above its familiar level, levitating above the grime. Progress was fractional and laboured. Several times there was a shout, and the winch was halted; for long periods there was no activity, the long, low platform lying bare, insinuating failure. When a plump man in tweeds came out of the door of the Assembly Rooms and paused on the steps, he attracted a great deal of attention but, after a minute or two, he simply walked away. There was a brief murmur of disapproval.

For a while, the work switched to the far end of the village, below the nymph, where preparations were being made for the library's eventual arrival. Two men walked slowly across the cleared land with their eyes fixed to the even ground, moving deliberately, a few yards apart but in parallel, as though they might be searching for something. When they reached the boundary of the site they came together, satisfied, apparently having found nothing.

Ellie saw Gadiel perched on the back of a pick-up truck with one or two other young men, part of a small convoy. She kept her eyes on him for as long as she could, but her view was obstructed by the crowd; she caught sight of him only in fractured moments: the bounce of his head as they hit a bump in the road, his hand clutching at the tailgate, the dark sheen of his overalls. Only once or twice did his face become visible, thoughtful and preoccupied.

She saw her father, too, standing on the other side of the street, cut off from her by a cordon. She waved at him, and he doffed his hat in reply.

Standing behind the barrier, hemmed in, it did not seem possible that the ground could be shifting beneath them, the village inexorably vanishing. Ellie wondered at the stillness she felt.

The crane pulled away; the winching chains released, swinging free, and a lorry reversed, workmen ducking behind. Perched awkwardly on its platform, the emaciated library was outlandish now, a weird attraction; the spectators edged forwards to watch it being manoeuvred over the cobbles and to admire the novel view that opened up through the gap where the building had once stood: a curve of river, trees beyond; the chemical works from a different perspective, the permanence of the village loosened.

The lorry made careful progress down the street, travelling slowly past the bank and the greengrocer's, negotiating the cracks and bumps and fissures. The driver leaned one arm nonchalantly from the cab window. Behind, the village settled back, re-imagined. From his post in front of the Assembly Rooms, Braithwaite Barton could not even see the library in its new position; it had escaped his gaze entirely.

With steady persistence, Ellie made her way through the gathered spectators until she was at the edge of the crowd. She paused and then turned down the row of cottages that dropped away from the nymph, following the pavement as it dipped towards the scrubland and the chemical works. She walked briskly, with confidence, barely hearing the sounds rattling behind her, hardly thinking about the library or what might become of it. It did not seem to matter very much.

It would be there for her, that was all, in its new place.

She walked for a long time, returning, in the end, to the mere. The water lay flat and unremarkable: mallards bobbed, their heads tucked away; seeds and water boatmen plucked the faintest of creases, disguising the depths below. Through the trees, in glimpses, the mansion was visible, but Ellie kept her eyes on the water. A frog croaked; the noise faded quickly. It was just one frog unexpectedly disturbed, calling out, unanswered, but it was confusing, nonetheless, and disorientating.

Ellie stood and waited, hoping that it would call again, but it remained quiet now, and she could not be sure that she had heard it at all. In the insistent silence, she was left with the sense of time ebbing and flowing around her with the pull of the slight waves, the sound even of her own breathing doubtful, insubstantial. She found she was left with the uncertainty of life, unimaginable.

Note on the Author

Jacqueline Yallop read English at Oxford and did her PhD in nineteenth-century literature at the University of Sheffield. She has worked as the curator of the Ruskin Collection in Sheffield and is the author of the non-fiction work *Magpies, Squirrels and Thieves* and the novels *Kissing Alice* and *Obedience*. She currently divides her time between France and Wales.

Origins of Marlford

By Jacqueline Yallop

The first kernel of a story that became *Marlford* was something told to me by a friend some time ago: she told me how, when she was a student in the 1960s, she lived in a kind of commune at a large farm in the country. The farmer who occupied the main house – a wealthy, gentleman farmer – hated the noise the frogs made when they sang on warm nights, and employed a man to patrol the lake to silence them. I have no idea how he did this; she didn't say. Nor do I know how successful the tactic was. But I immediately loved the quirkiness of her story and wanted to make something of it. I have noisy frogs in my own garden and knew the sound intimately, the mournfulness and the comedy.

And so *Marlford* began with the frogs at the mere.

But there were other ideas, too. At the same time as I was working on the novel, for example, I was also researching a book about Victorian villages: I was walking around all kinds of places built by philanthropists for their workers, everything from tiny abandoned hamlets to well-known examples like Saltaire and Port Sunlight. I was intrigued by the motives of the founders, and the role of these odd remnants in a changing world: I wanted Ellie to be part of this.

Many of the ideas for *Marlford* were not the product of formal research, however, but came from memories of the places in which I grew up: the salt-mining areas of central Cheshire and the subsidence that undermines them. I'd seen photos of lop-sided houses, crumbling shops and sunken pubs; I'd heard stories of fields and animals simply disappearing; I knew that the public buildings in my home town were designed to be hoisted onto rollers and simply moved if the ground gave way – these were moments that intrigued and delighted me and which helped create the crumbling world in which the Bartons find themselves stranded.

There's a country estate, too, not far distant from the town. The house fell into ruin and was pulled down, as so many country houses were, in the 1960s: all that remains are the occasional flight of stone steps, leading nowhere; the outline of the mansion marked out in the turf; and a long sweep of mere. It's a place with a tangled history: it was used as a barracks and a school; it hosted a prisoner of war camp in its grounds, where the men lived in hutments which, until recently, still existed. Some of these men remained long after the war was finished; when I used to take the bus to school they could still be seen camping at road junctions in derelict caravans.

Which all means, I suppose, that in many ways *Marlford* is a true story, or at least that its inspirations emerged from true stories. These places existed, and still exist; some of these events happened. All I've done is bring them together and re-imagine them into something new.